About the Author

Stephen Don is an award-winning screenwriter from Co. Down. Before becoming a writer, Stephen travelled widely and lived abroad for a number of years. He has been an actor, a teacher, an office dogsbody, a gravedigger, a barman, and a nursing assistant. All things must pass is Stephen's first novel.

To Allan
from Stephen Don

To the memory of:

Denis Doyle
(1938-2020)

Sean K Donovan
(1998-2020)

Dedication

To Denis, mentor and bard. To Nick, prince among men.

And to Heather, whose forbearance and support kept me on track.

Stephen Don

all things must pass

AUSTIN MACAULEY PUBLISHERS™

LONDON · CAMBRIDGE · NEW YORK · SHARJAH

A CIP catalogue record for this title is available from the British Library.

ISBN 9781398407329 (Paperback)
ISBN 9781398415683 (Hardback)
ISBN 9781398415690 (ePub e-book)

www.austinmacauley.com

First Published 2021
Austin Macauley Publishers Ltd
1 Canada Square
Canary Wharf
London
E14 5AA
+44 (0) 207 038 8212
+44 (0) 203 515 0352

Acknowledgements

I would like to thank Austin Macauley Publishers for their act of faith in accepting my novel for publication.

Chapter I
Noboguchi

i remember when i first saw it and where i was stalking along by the river in chelsea following this kid and thinking all the time what i could do him if i got him alone like tie him up for starters and take a dump on him clamp his mouth open somehow with rope even if it was narrow as a letterbox and piss in it ive done that plenty of times pissed on a pooch once silly fucking thing didnt move just kept yapping and yapping until id finished i was laffing that much i almost got my dick caught in the flap of the letterbox that wouldve fucking hurt i know that then i wouldve cut off one of his ears or maybe the tip of his nose but it all ended in a fucking daytime wank of frustration cos the little cunt disappeared into a house and i was getting pissed off with the river and all the cunts who trail along it so i fucked off to the kings road feeling like a cunt myself and thats when i saw it see there are any number of anteek shops down that way and most of the stuff you wouldnt believe the prices they fucking charge i get so narked off looking in the windows at all that shit i really wanna take a switchblade out and go to town on it like zorro you know leaving my mark as a warning not to peddle that overpriced crap in their windows and thats when i saw it 3:26pm precisely by the clock over the window it was so beautiful i just stopped dead in my tracks and stared i even forgot to breathe for half a minute i can honestly say i dont think ive ever seen anything as beautiful in my life the sheath was of a deep red deeper towards the handle and paling along the length of the sheath to the pale rosecoloured tip the handle was black beaded with studs of gold and some sort of smooth material silk most likely and it hung from a gold cord made up of threads all wound together it was so fucking lovely i wanted to grab a brick and smash the window and run off with the sword before anyone could nab me ive owned machetes and flickknives butchersblades and fuckloads of hunting knives but they were toys compared to this japanese sword i mean i hadnt even seen it out of its sheath yet but i could imagine it cos of all the japanese films id seen those fuckers didnt mess about one flick of the blade and some cunt was lying cleaved in two awesome it seemed id been staring in the window for at least twenty minutes but when i looked up at the clock it said 3:28 as i pushed open the door a bell tinkled over my head the thing was an anteek itself made of brass and with a little bell on an arm extended like a fishing rod and it was still vibrating and tinkling when i heard this voice say has something taken sirs fancy i saw sir looking in at the window now what could it be that has taken the fancy of sir i found the man who spoke behind a long wooden counter a head thats all i could make out an old fart with smoothed down hair old style glasses held together with sellotape and a beard around his chin more white than anything else he stood up to give me a better look at him and i cant remember when ive seen a dafter looking twat he had a bowtie you couldnt pay me enough to wear not to mention a sort of dirty mustard cardigan and check trousers he was getting on my tits and i hadnt been in his shop more than a minute and he wouldnt stop talking cos the next thing he says now would it be presumptuous of me sir to suggest that sir is interested in the japanese sword i nodded slowly like ive seen them do a hundred times in the japanese films just one nod down then up again fucking says it all they dont mess about the japanese economy of effort is everything why say anything when a nod will do or a flick of the hand very good sir and before i knew anything else this man stepped out from the back of the shop like hed stepped out of one of the walls i hadnt seen him coming and it gave me a bad feeling in the gut cos a warrior should always be prepared and never taken unawares you let that happen and youre the one who ends up tied up in the chair with some other fucker pissing in your mouth and taking a dump on you mr wilkins will show you the noboguchi is sir a collector a connoisseur perchance wilkins had gone past me at this point and was already taking hold of the sword and lifting it out of the window then he was backing into the shop and i thought he was gonna turn round and hand me the sword which wouldve been a stupid fucking mistake on his part cos i fancied lopping off his head with one beautiful masterstroke and then going after the cunt with the bowtie always take out your strongest opponent first and wilkins was that for a kick off he was about half the age of the old fucker behind the counter and he looked like he could handle himself yeah with him out of the way i could have my fun with the bowtie id definitely take a dump on him and tie his bowtie to the end of his little cock his pants would be down around his ankles and id bend his legs backwards so his arsehole was pointing up into the air and then id take something long and thin like the end of a feather duster and shaft him with it so the feathers were all spreading out from his button like a strange flower itd be a fucking work of art but he didnt hand me the sword course he didnt he handed it to bowtie who handed it back to wilkins with these words perhaps you would care to demonstrate the fine workmanship of the noboguchi to our connoisseur mr wilkins it was his turn now wilkins turn to nod once to the bowtie and i knew then for a certainty that hed watched all them films id watched like the one about the two women a mother and her daughter who play tricks on these warriors and lure them to their deaths so they can steal their armour and weapons and sell them to get food youd better stand back sir to give mr wilkins some room and to preserve your good self from any harm i tried to smile at this like i was in on the joke but i dont suppose it come across as a smile i dont do smiling a teacher once told me i had a smirk an insolent smirk i fixed him for that just like i wanted to fix bowtie and wilkins but especially bowtie cos he was having a right old laff at me i could tell i could feel it in my guts and they never ever lie wilkins stepped one pace back from the counter and then made a turn through a right angle and took three large paces away from me he drew the sword from its sheath it seemed to go on and on for ever the blade and i couldnt breathe until the very tip of it had been removed from the sheath it was so beautiful such a fine killing blade that i swear i wanted to burst into song or sob my heart out but i wasnt gonna make a cunt of myself in front of these cunts and there you have it sir a rare noboguchi samurai sword of finest tempered steel probably made by the master himself can you supply the dates the place of manufacture is certain and that would have been in the masters forge in kawasaki some time between 1770 and 1795 yasunari noboguchi dating from circa 1730 to circa 1805 but sir knew all of this did he not there was something strange about the way bowtie said the last words but sir knew all of this that made me turn to him cos to tell the truth i hadnt been listening to him witter on like an old fart id been watching wilkins go through a routine that was nothing less than a martial arts display all wrist movement and thrusting with right leg forward and all the while the blade swinging through the air like an arc of silver like a silver scarf almost liquid at one moment and then a solid arc the next i was mesmerised drugged in a fucking trance i hadnt had so much fun since i was a kid at the circus watching the tightrope artist and praying hed fall off and break his stupid neck but what bowtie said next was well below the belt and totally uncalled for get out before i get the police onto you youre no more a connoisseur than im mahatma gandhi there is no yasunari noboguchi i made that up as a little test which you have so demonstrably failed to pass whatever your intention was in coming into my shop you can forget about it i was dumbstruck i looked from one to the other from bowtie to sword and i saw that wilkins was very grim about the mouth and lightly jogging the handle of the sword up and down in the palm of his hand i knew the look he had in his eye id seen it so many times before when some cunt is set to strike and pulls out a blade and tries to stitch you so i started to back off towards the door and not a moment too soon cos the fucking nutter raises the sword high over his head and lunges at me i swear i got out of that place with my life in my hands and i could hear the pair of cunts laffing at me as i flew out of the shop and sprinted for the kings road the pair of bollocks id soiled my fucking underpants on account of them i could feel this squidgy patch around the crack of my arse and i was in half a mind to slip my underpants off in some alleyway and run back to the shop they wouldnt be expecting me so i could burst in and rub bowties superior twat of a face in my shit before wilkins could get to me any money theyd already replaced the sword in the window and it was the thought of it the image of it like a beautiful photo sitting still and quiet in the centre of my brain like it sits in the centre of that window display that stopped me from going back i didnt want to defile that image in all its purity and essence its the way of the warrior wilkins would know what i was getting at cunt though he was he was still a warrior old bowtie wouldnt have a fucking clue what bushido meant oh he probably knows the word all right but its one thing knowing the word knowing its meaning its another thing altogether living your life by that code hed be too soft around the belly bowtie too fond of his sherry and port and fundamentally too lacking in discipline to really get where i was coming from bushido is all about denial all about putting up with what other people would call discomforts real physical and mental discomforts until they arent discomforts no more until you have stood in the freezing rain for hours and you dont feel the cold and the wet no more you cant have a baldy notion what im getting at only then do you and your weapon become as one cos you forget you have a body that is weak and vulnerable you forget that you are bone covered with skin cos you see yourself as an extension of your blade like a long extended armourplated killing blade and you see your enemys death before you make a move just like i was seeing bowties execution in intimate and vivid detail all played out in the hushed screeningroom of my brain ive entered the shop at a rush the little bell is still tinkling at the end of its rod and bowtie has hardly had a chance to see that its me when i jump at him across the counter and stick my underpants on his face making sure to rub my shit in his mouth i hear wilkins the warrior shout out before i see him i know hes somewhere at the back of the shop all the same i have no time to lose and i throw myself away from the counter and lunge toward the window to grab the sword ive just got hold of it when i feel wilkins take hold of my right shoulder and the next thing i know is im flying back into the shop and landing with a thump on my arse i bang my head against the side of another counter running at right angles to the one bowtie hides behind fuck my heart is racing like a gerbil on a wheel but ive got the sword in my hands ive got both hands around that black silk handle good fucking thing too cos wilkins is coming at me with a real killer look on his face i dont know how i do it cos im feeling fucked as it is but i struggle to get up on my feet and manage it just before wilkins gets to me i thrust the sword at him but its still in its sheath and now we are struggling the two of us like demons possessed breathing like a couple of wrestlers he holding onto the red sheath me onto the black handle when i get spun around by his superior strength and i sort of fly off from him which releases the sword from its sheath and for a second he has such a woebegotten fucked look on his face like he doesnt know what to do next so he throws the sheath at me and tries to make a run for it to the shop door i catch him there right under the bell and dispatch him with a thrust into the small of his back the sword goes through him easier than any blade ive ever used and his cry dies as i twist and pull out the sword watching him slump to the floor i turn away from him at once and scan the shop for bowtie but he isnt anywhere to be seen an inner radar tells me he isnt very far away i feel a touch of the errol flynns coming on and with a leap and a bound im up on his counter looking down at the cunt who is lying in the foetal with his face a mess of shit and tears i jump down on his side of the counter and stand over him listening to him whimper like a baby hes got his hands up around his head for god knows what reason cos it isnt gonna stop me doing what i want with him the cunts mine and im gonna make him pay for his treatment of me when i was in earlier please please dont hurt me please you can have anything you want is it money you want you can have the sword you can help yourself to anything in the shop please just please dont hurt me i put the tip of the sword against his throat and tell him to shut it christ ive listened to some whinging bastards in my time but he was taking the biscuit get up get up i tell him and give him a boot up the arse he starts to struggle to his feet and i grab him with my free hand and yank him to his feet his bowtie is all twisted and i can see in his eyes that he is scared to death what is it you want what are you going to do with me i give him a dig in the ribs and push him out from behind the counter so he can see what id done to wilkins youve killed him he says holding his side and practically blubbering he had guts which is more than i can say for you then i take three steps back from bowtie and raise aloft the sword holding it ramrod straight above my head bowtie screams and covers his face behind his hands he is mumbling something that sounds like a prayer the old mumbojumbo about the lord is my shepherd and i cant hold it no longer and like the assyrian falling on the israelites i fall on him and cut an arc through the air and slice his guts open then im whooping round the shop like a red indian when i feel this hand on my shoulder i come to a complete standstill so fast that the shop with the dead bodies of wilkins and bowtie just flies from me i cant explain it no better pouf its gone like smoke and im spun round by this copper who blots out the sun hes that fucking tall and just what do you think youre playing at he says and i want to tell him that ive just rid the world of a couple of useless cunts a couple of ponces who peddled overpriced tat to twats with too much money and not enough sense but im standing in the middle of the kings road with a small crowd of onlookers gawping and laffing at me and for the life of me i cant explain why i am where i am you cant carry on like that in the street charging around like a bull in a chinashop you could do someone an injury if youre not careful hes a bloody hooligan thats what he is and i sense the crowd is not with me the crowd is out for blood id like to see what theyd do if i had the sword in my hand itd be a different story then all right i could chop one of the coppers arms off for starters and then id run right into the thick of the crowd slashing all around me course i wouldnt be able to get every last one of the cunts cos theyd fan out like a fucking disease and the quickest could probably get away but id sort the others out no problem itd be a regular bloodbath i could just see the evening papers full of it massacre on the kings road in less time than it takes to boil a softboiled egg twenty people ranging in ages from children of ten to old age pensioners of eighty five were brutally and mercilessly cut down by a lone assassin wielding a noboguchi samurai sword the sword would appear to have come from a local anteek shop where the owners a couple of faggot ponces had been savagely slaughtered earlier in the day the unknown swordwielding ronin would seem to have been stopped in a routine search by a local constable a crowd of onlookers gathered quickly at the sight of the encounter between an instrument of the law and one who sees himself above the law after a short exchange the ronin would seem to have taken exception to a comment shouted from the crowd of onlookers and exacted a cruel but just revenge upon them the constable despite suffering the loss of an arm due to a blow delivered with lightning speed by the ronin had the presence of mind to pick up his severed limb and go after the ronin not only did he go after him but he actually managed to stage a counterattack upon the ronin beating the latter about the head with the aforementioned severed limb this however only served to enrage the ronin who decapitated the constable with a single masterstroke this was a wound from which the constable had no chance

13

of recovering with the constable taken care of the ronin went unimpeded about his bloody business and made off according to reports by survivors whooping like an injun are you listening to me sonny did you hear what i said you have to take more care when in a public thoroughfare hes bending down to me peering at me to get a reaction christ what i wouldnt give to have one of my blades on me even a stupid breadknife would do id let him get so close let him lord it over me and then when hes within striking distance id catch him just below his chinstrap where his adams apple bulges he wouldnt know what hit him the poor cunt hed be on the ground gasping for breath and spitting up blood but hed lose so much of it and his windpipe would fill with blood so fast that hed be a goner before any of the cunts looking on could raise a finger to help him not that any of them would just look at them they make me sick the pussies course i havent got a blade on me not even a breadknife and hes still giving me that look so i nod once down and then up again and he seems to accept that and suddenly i have a notion hes a bit of a warrior himself under that uniform and that maybe hes just putting on a show for the crowd hiding his true feelings his respect for a fellow warrior in another time and another place it might have been different between us the sun beating down on two figures in a courtyard with all the windows shuttered like the eyes of the blind our shadows clinging close to our bodies our swords at arms length and casting their own thin shadows upon the ground baking beneath our bare feet i would win of course he knows this but the code forbids him to step aside from the challenge and the call to duty his acceptance of the code and of his inevitable death raises him in my eyes to the level of one worthy of combat with me worthy of my best efforts and i would kill him with an artistry reserved only for opponents of the highest order and with a sadness and solemnity that leaves a lump in your throat at the end of every bruce lee film knowing all this without the necessity of putting any of it into words he puts a hand on my shoulder and nods once down and then up again and tells me to be on my way and to take it easy and then he waves me away with the back of his hand i leave then feeling better for our unspoken exchange knowing that underneath that uniform he isnt really such a cunt after all hes just a warrior who has had his sword taken from him and his balls cut off i have to feel sorry for him its the uniform thats turned him into the useless cunt he is today i know hed rather be dead in that blind courtyard under the impartial eye of the sun having duelled with a master and died as he lived according to the code of the warrior the only code worth living or dying for and before i am out of earshot he gives me proof as he tells the crowd to move on all right now the shows over theres nothing more to keep you here thats what he says but there is something in his voice that he cant disguise it is something like a weariness and a disgust and i know what he is really saying to them is fuck off you pack of useless wankers dont you have anything better to do with your pathetic and meaningless lives than to stand around on street corners pointing fingers and making fun of a noble spirit you arent even fit to lace his boots you should all be ashamed of yourselves you should lie down prostrate yourselves before him and let him walk all over you with his dick out and if he should feel the urge to piss in your mouths you should open your mouths as wide as possible and drink his piss with a passion and feel grateful for it for you will have been drinking the nectar of the gods i can feel that sadness and solemnity coming over me i am bruce lee and theres a lump in my throat thinking of how i have been treated by the kings road ponces and i know i am going to break down if i dont stop the film in my head so id better do something or i will make a complete cunt of myself out in the street in front of any cunt who happens to be passing the thought of it practically drives me nuts and i can see the end credits rolling in chinese and there i am fucking bruce lee fucking dead and that copper did it to me and the cunts in the crowd but im not going to let them beat me and im breathing through gritted teeth holding in the emotion keeping it under stopping it from bursting through cos then i dont know what im capable of and thats when i start running i run and run and run until the houses i pass are a blur and my lungs are hurting i think theyre gonna burst they hurt that much and i have to stop leaning against a wall and draw in breath like an old donkey clapped out from years of carrying a burden clapped out and ready for the knackers and an old cunt stops in the street beside me an old granny about ninety years old and asks me if im all right but as soon as i show her my face she takes fright and fucks off doublequick as if her zimmerframe has a motor and i dont think i can hold it no more and thats when i realise ive forgot to take my drugs this morning and everything is beginning to float and hover in front of my eyes even the fucking footpath is buckling rising and falling like theres a earthquake a fucking 8 on the richter scale and the next thing i know im down on my hands and knees crying and yelping and howling and screaming and kicking out like a bucking bronco frothing at the mouth and spitting up gobs of puke from the lining of my stomach and i dont remember a thing after that all i know is i wake up back in my room like it was all a bad trip i had and none of it was real except dr death is there standing over me with a hypodermic in his hand and he injects me before i can even get a word out i have no resistance anyway the room is spinning round me slowly bits of it part of a wall or a chair or a window frame coming toward me and then receding like a concertina and i feel as fucked as a choirboy and in no mood to challenge the dr or take the piss out of him youre a very lucky young man he tells me did you know how close you were to home when you had your attack i havent the strength nor the will to answer him and let out a sigh like an old fart on his last legs and dr young who looks like death cos hes a walking cadaver just smiles as he rubs the spot where he injected me with cotton wool soaked in methylated spirit you get some rest now youll feel a lot better when you wake up and my eyelids suddenly feel like lead and i close my eyes and the darkness pulses with shades of grey and black with lots of white dots coming and going like sparks from a sparkler or like the stars in the heavens on a cold night i dont actually remember falling asleep but when i wake up the room is still the whole house is hushed like everyones out or asleep but its still daylight still early evening the light soft in the room through the curtains this is what i imagine death to be like you wake up in a room thats just like a room you lived in but you dont know that you dont recognise it you dont have no memories and you dont want for nothing theres no one else in the world and you may as well stay in the room as go out cos you know you will meet no one and you dont want to anyway and you could sit on the edge of your bed thinking of nothing and a minute or two might pass or it might be a whole age like a thousand years and you wouldnt know the difference it wouldnt matter one bit to you and you wouldnt be happy or unhappy happiness wouldnt enter into it it wouldnt have any meaning for you youd be above it beyond it beyond all cares and worries and all the other things that drive you nuts and give you the gripe in this life fuck im off on one again i get like this after one of my attacks i start thinking about a load of old bollocks and before i know anything else im imagining myself in a completely different world in a completely different fucking universe sometimes like im floating outside the space capsule doing repairs and i can see the earth all blue with beautiful swirls of snow white cloud and i feel like god then on the first day of creation i try to get inside his head to think like him but i cant do it i dont think anyone can so i try to come down to earth you know literally come down through the layers of cloud and touch the earth then i think of something really hard focus on it a tree or a huge rock or one of the bigger animals i get inside the skin of some weird animal like a rhinoceros with a great big horn sticking out of my forehead i could do some fucking damage with that all right take that fucking anteek shop for a start id stand snorting through my nostrils glaring at the window display with its loveliest of swords and then id begin to paw the ground with one of my front hoofs you know sort of working myself up into the right mood for a charge i can just imagine what old bowtie would be saying over the counter to wilkins mr wilkins hed say i may have overdone it with the sherry at lunchtime but unless my eyes are deceiving me there would appear to be a rhinoceros out in the street opposite our display window im not so sure what wilkins would say in response in fact i dont think hed say anything at all being a man of action and few words he would move from the back of the shop to the display window perhaps giving bowtie a certain look as he draws level with him any exchange between them would all be done with the eyebrows but one thing is certain that as soon as wilkins looks out through the window he sees me and he recognises the danger at once and i feel on pretty safe ground when i say that he would say something to bowtie at this juncture along the lines yes that is a rhinoceros and if i know my rhinoceroses he looks to be in a bit of a mood a bit of a mood mr wilkins pray elucidate do but wilkins is wiser than bowtie cos he knows this is not the time to stand around and chat so with no further ado he turns on his heels and heads back into the murky gloom that is his habitual abode at the rear of the shop whatever are you doing mr wilkins there is something in bowties voice to suggest that an element of panic has overtaken him but mr wilkins is calm itself and without looking back at bowtie he shouts over his shoulder im getting a gun sir ah capital idea wilkins if i might make a suggestion sir says wilkins i would remove my person from the vicinity of the window but it is sage advice given too late for i have started my run and before i even smash into the plate glass of the display window i have set things vibrating and shaking on shelves and counters i have set the bell above the shop door jangling all of which sets bowtie quaking and roots him to the spot and when i hit that display window why youd swear a fucking bomb had gone off the window shatters in an almighty explosion that can definitely be heard out on the kings road a shower of glass fragments erupts into the shop interior hitting everything in a split second studding floor ceiling walls and counters im through to the centre of the shop before i even know it carried there by my own momentum and a shitload of adrenaline like ive never known before neither bowtie nor wilkins are anywhere to be seen and i wheel round throwing off shards of glass like solidified sweat and aware that something is dangling from my horn and banging against my chin with every turn of my head its the noboguchi and im going nearly crosseyed trying to see it well i dont need that any more loveliest of swords though it is ive got my own weapon pointing out of the middle of my forehead so with a defiant toss of my head i fling the noboguchi into a corner of the shop and start my search for wilkins cos he is the dangerous one and a rhinoceros will always go head to head with his strongest opponent first i know hes at the back of the shop but the gap between the counters is far too narrow for my bulky frame i dont stand there like a dimwit thinking about the problem too long the problem of how to get through to the back that is i just put my shoulder to the counter and rip it right off the floor and shove it back until i can get through the gap comfortably and thats where i find him wilkins covered in glass and blood and twitching the length of his body i dont even think hes got the strength to stand up but im not waiting for him to get to his feet am i i stand over him snorting through my nostrils smelling him smelling the fear off him and watching his face for any sign that he might be playing possum that he might only be faking being fucked but no he cant be faking it not the way he looks hes a spent force the warrior is fucked good and proper and im going to have some fun with him i lower my head until the point of my horn is pressing against his stomach just below his ribcage and then i ram my head hard into him and my horn goes clean through his body and strikes the wooden floor beneath him course hes screaming like a cunt but that only adds to the fun i back out through the gap i made between the counters until im standing in the centre of the shop once more wilkins is raised aloft on my horn and the screams coming out of him are only to be imagined he hardly weighs a thing for a big man its like hes a rag doll and now i start shaking him around on my horn this way and that banging his head and legs off the counters and im spinning round and round in the shop area until i get a bit dizzy with it all and then i put the brakes on all of a sudden and give one last violent toss of my head and the rag doll that was wilkins the warrior flies off and smacks into the wall at the back of the shop id piss myself laffing if i knew how to but it seems ive lost the knack which doesnt seem to bother me none what does bother me though is my vision is somewhat impaired due to my spinning round and round the shop is turning round me in slow circles and i seem to have the impression that bowtie is standing with a rifle raised and pointed straight at me i cant be sure whether or not im dreaming or hallucinating cos im thinking this is probably the closest a rhinoceros has ever got to the feeling of being drunk sure enough as the shop finally slows down and comes to a stop bowtie is there all right and he has a rifle pointed at me and his hands are trembling the rifle is shaking badly he gets one shot off but i dont feel a thing he must have missed me by a mile and i start to steady myself and stare at him breathing through my nostrils building up a head of steam to rush at his counter and bulldoze it out of the way so i can get at bowtie and do the same as i did to wilkins to him but i dont get any further with this thought cos i see bowtie squeeze the trigger again and its like i feel suddenly very strange theres a horrible ringing in my ears and a pain dull and intense between my eyes theres a trickle of black blood oozing out and flowing over the base of my horn and i dont think i can stand up no longer and then my front legs give way and buckle and i have to fold my forelegs under me as all my weight wants to drag me down and then the funniest thing happens is im not a rhinoceros no more im bruce lee and im kneeling in a blind courtyard and ive been dealt a sword blow that has knocked me for six and im just waiting for the coup de grace and ive got a lump in my throat just thinking of the sadness and solemnity of it the dignity im showing in the face of death and how deaths victory is stolen away by my very act of nobly surrendering to this death sometimes the old woman wont call me bruce or if she does she always uses the name in some way to be sarcastic or ironic with me i dont know why i bother my head going down to see her only that its no big deal to go down one flight of stairs and shes an interesting old bird i always knock when i get to her door i dont know why somehow she commands my respect i cant figure it out really i mean its not as if i couldnt kill her with my little finger she must be about ninety years old and shes got some interesting clobber worth nicking i could flog it to those fuckwits who run the anteek shops off the kings road thatid be fun seeing some of her old tat in the window of bowties anteek shop and some stupid nonce paying way over the odds for it i could even follow him or her and do a bit of gbh a bit of persuasive retrieval and then sell it on to another anteek shop nearby course im not gonna do anything of the kind cos i cant be fucking arsed and like i say i like the old bird gracie come in martin she says and it beats me how she knows its me each time i call on her unless she hears me coming down the stairs or my knock is distinctive or should i say bruce and somewhere under all those bags and wrinkles shes having a laff at me i try not to react to much of what she says but she knows shes rattled me and for the life of me i dont know why i let her get to me its just i dont like my given name much im not a martin i dont feel like a martin and bruce suits me much better you know like when you try on some clothes and they just fit right well thats the way it is with bruce ever since i first saw enter the dragon and was just blown away by the majesty of bruce lees presence on screen i identified with him right off i became one with him and i was kicking and punching my way through shitloads of evil bastards anyway as i say i know shes gonna have a go at me and still i cant stop myself from feeling hurt i can actually feel my face getting longer and sort of settling into a sourpuss expression why so pale and wan fond lover prithee why so pale she does that all the time quoting bits from books and poems i just give her my brando look head to one side and chin tucked in and eyes narrowed but all she does is laff at me even more but all the same i know shes glad to see me she dont get out of her room much now on account of her age and shes frail and all that and she dont get many visitors shes got her whole world in that room all her bits and bobs a whole lifetime of collection all sorts of knickknacks and books floor to ceiling books books books what was it she said the other day to me theres no end to the making of books and i shrugged and she got sort of funny with me a bit off and shirty and told me i was too intelligent to be playing the fool and that i was wasting my life and i turned it right back on her and said and you havent wasted yours i thought shed be gutted but she smiled and said touchee and then poured herself a little drop of brandy into her coffee and said thats the spirit and i didnt know whether she was referring to the drink or what id just said sometimes we have talks about language laff for example she says it should be written laugh and i say why its a flat a and you can see her rolling up her sleeves for a good old intellectual dust up not in this part of the country it isnt and i say why should this part of the country dictate to the rest of the country to the rest of the world in fact and then she says that historically it comes from the german lachen and the gh in laugh would once have been pronounced like a k but got softened through time and usage and anyway why didnt i write larff because some people put in an intrusive r when they say the word and why dont i just use one f to be completely consistent so that it should be laf in my book and not laff by which stage im just looking at her like shes a demented old loon and shes nearly crying with laffter or laughter or even fucking lafter if you prefer gracie likes nothing better than an argument a spot of mental fisticuffs and sometimes i give her what she wants and other times i cant be arsed and i just let her rabbit on about whatever just sos i dont have to go back to my room or out onto the streets the more ive seen of her the more i think how alike we are you probably think thats about the stupidest thing youve ever heard but think about it for just a moment i was lying on my bed one time when it come to me like an epiphany i didnt hear no choir celestial or nothing but the knowledge of it entered me like a feeling of bliss and calmed me and the strange thing is i think shed been getting up my nose that very day id gone to see her and wed had a bit of a barney and id got pissed off and gone stomping back up to my room and thrown myself on the bed and at first id had a flood of really murderous thoughts about her and rehearsed all the ways i was gonna do her in you know along the lines of garrotting her and smashing her head in with a hammer or just waltzing into her room with a switchblade concealed behind my back and as soon as she called me bruce in her teasing sarcastic way i was gonna stick the knife in her heart and give it a twist and there was plenty of other things went through my head that day lying on my bed and i let them run on until id practically exhausted myself and then i saw her the time she give me a book a copy of the canterbury tales in the original middle english she said she wanted me to have something of hers to remind me of her when she was gone she said id find it interesting if I could apply myself and i give her one of my brando specials and then she said these words that i hadnt understood at the time you and me we are not so different you have a sensitivity you want to hide all the time because youre ashamed of it you hide it behind a mask of violence you give in to violent thoughts because you dont want to deal with

19

thoughts that might make you appear weak in the eyes of others but these other thoughts are the really important ones the ones that need nurturing and protecting look at me im an old woman and you might think ive never had a violent thought in my head oh but i have when i was married i had lots of violent thoughts mostly against my poor incompetent husband and you with your hard body think youre the antithesis of me a rundown ancient hag but you have breasts like me why even your wedding tackle is the same biologically i have a part that stiffens though not as prominent as yours i dont actually know how i looked right at that moment but i suppose i cant have looked too clever cos she was rocking back and forth and practically wetting herself she was laffing that much when she calmed herself she wiped her eyes and offered me a turkish cigarette all wrapped in lavender and goldtipped when youre my age you will understand that frankness is not only a virtue but one of the few privileges that age confers its a sort of return to the openness of childhood not quite the same thing because theres too much knowing going on but what can i say one has earned the right to abandon ones shame ones hurt even ones pride after all theyre only a sort of protective armour and what are we protecting ourselves against she doesnt allow me to answer i dont even know if i have an answer cos im not sure if i understand the question but she has another question for me anyway what dyou think of my turkish cigarettes can i be frank i say and she says certainly i expect nothing less and i pause and take a long drag and blow out a small cloud of blue smoke im holding the cigarette away from me now in a gesture at once theatrical and intimate im thinking i would cut a fine figure down on the kings road with a turkish cigarette and a copy of the canterbury tales too good for them martin she says theyre really a bunch of pigs ignorant armies of them clashing by night they know only money and what money can do for them but the things of the spirit elude them because they cannot go into a store and buy themselves a soul or happiness they have style but little content i dont know why you want to spend so much time down there be careful you dont let their brash materialism rub off on you im about to take another toke of the turkish cigarette when i know i have to tell her about the noboguchi she sees something in my face and asks me what im thinking about a sword i answer oh you and your swords and knives no this is different i tell her and i relate the whole thing to her of standing out in the road and not breathing for about a minute a minute she says a whole minute well maybe half a minute i dont know thats not important whats important i tell her and i can hear im almost shouting whats important is that it alone in the whole world was what i saw everything else the shop the street houses cars people everything else just sort of vanished while i looked at it and i told her about wanting to break into song or burst out crying did you go into the shop she says i shake my head why not i dunno didnt seem no point they wouldnt have let me look at it anyway which shop was it the one with the queer couple oh that could be any number of them she says and reaches for the brandy bottle hes got a bowtie the owner ah i think i know the one youre talking about a man of hebraic extraction yes ive bought and sold one or two things through him over the years an educated man which is always a bonus when transacting business oh im sure he would have let you look at the sword if youd asked him nicely actually i didnt want to ask him nicely or otherwise i didnt want to speak to anyone about it except you i mean he mightve let me look at it he mightve even let me handle it but thats not the point cos the point is hed have filled my head with a lot of crap calling the sword a noboguchi one minute and something else the next taking the piss out of me i mean it doesnt matter who made it to me what matters is its beauty its unique quality like you martin youre unique youre one of a kind i dont know about that yes you are oh for christ sake cant you just take a compliment without getting defensive just this once i left her then just got up and walked out going for a sulk are we and i turned in the doorway to see her raise her coffee cup in the air and give me a mock salute before sticking her tongue out at me i closed the door on her and walked off down the corridor more sad than angry more weary than sad she gets to a point where the brandy starts to have an effect on her she just gets niggly about small things and i can see the signs i know when shes gonna start getting funny and id just as soon not be around her when shes like that shes probably not even got any coffee in her cup any more gone on to straight brandy by now and then she starts to sing or roar and maybe even recites some chaucer before falling asleep ive heard it a hundred times if ive heard it once its most likely what brought us together in the first place me lying on my bed and hearing her spouting off in the room below and then going tippytoe down the stairs to listen at her door i dont know half the people behind the other doors i know old dr young has his room further along the corridor and sometimes i put an ear to it and if hes in i can hear him mumbling to himself i think he might be dictating into a machine but i cant be certain but i definitely think hes talking about me sometimes and the old woman i think he talks about others too but i cant make out much of what he says i suppose its only part of his job and to be honest i dont even mind him that much hes not bad as cunts go tweed jacket and pipe kind of twat that he is now ive reached the area between the stairs i could make a bolt for it but i dont think i can be arsed so im going back up into my room once im inside it i get that familiar feeling come over me like what am i supposed to do now its like i want to crawl out of my skin and maybe blend and disappear into a wall like wilkins but i know i cant do that so i flop down onto the bed and just stare at the ceiling i can hear the old bat below reciting chaucer she doesnt even need to look at the book she knows huge chunks of it off by heart sometimes lying like this on my back staring at the ceiling i try to imagine what some of the others are like the others who live in this house whose doors i pass or listen at actually i think i met one of them once bumped into him by accident in the corridor he was pretty ordinary looking just dressed in jeans and a sweater had about three days growth of beard could have been mid thirties i dunno anyway he looked at me like i was something freaky and unreal and he asked me what i was doing there and why couldnt i just fuck off and leave him alone and then he just vanished he opened a door and disappeared into his room i really wanted to go and kick his door in and threaten him and if id had the noboguchi on me he would have been dead meat for certain but i didnt bother doing any of the above i didnt even tell the old woman about him seeing as she never goes out of her room shed probably tell me id seen a phantom and shes probably right i sometimes think all others are phantoms creatures of our imagination we only have to think of them and we summon them from the depths christ i wish i had the noboguchi with me now i could practise moves with it thrusts and slashes and sweeps and arcs the beauty of it all reflected back to me in my mirror im standing in front of the mirror now i dont think i have a bad body but maybe my rags could do more for me she down below has a go at me from time to time about my appearance when she first saw the mohican she said it was a fright and then when i dyed it pink and orange she said it was a fucking awful sight im taking off the t-shirt and the bags i probably havent taken off for at least a week to stand naked not quite as mother nature made me cos apart from the hairdo i have a cock ring a ring in each nipple and a bolt through the soft tissue at the nape of the neck what i like about my body is the flatness of my stomach my chest is a bit hollow but you cant have everything as far as im concerned the stomach compensates me for the chest ive got nice tight arse cheeks too i nearly had bolts put through them but the girl who did the rings and bolts wouldnt go for it which beats me seeing as she put a ring in my foreskin like i say i wish i had the noboguchi now id stand just as i am naked with the noboguchi clasped in both hands and held out in front of me or else raised high over my head id hold my stomach and arse cheeks as tight as could be cos i read somewhere that warriors going into battle are in a state of heightened awareness their whole bodies are in a state of tension and to achieve this tension they practise clenching and unclenching their buttocks and stomach muscles they even clench and unclench the hole between the buttocks and in this way they stay alert and prepared for anything the enemy may throw at them and i would take such care of the noboguchi i would sit on the edge of the bed and i would pour a little oil down the edge of the blade and taking a tissue i would rub the oil gently into the blade with little circles i would start slowly very slowly and delicately working the length of the blade gradually build a rhythm until i was rubbing in bold strokes up and down the length of the blade up and down and up and down until the blade was glistening all along its length and the motion had made me and the blade become as one i didnt hear the door open but i heard a laff and turned to see lester blocking the doorway his skin is so black it makes the white of his shirt stand out and i can see the brilliant white of his teeth hes laffing all openmouthed youd better put that offensive weapon away now cos if i report to the doctor what youre doing hes gonna up your medication and then he shuts the door and leaves me alone but i can still hear him lafffing at me as he walks off down the corridor and the metal heels of his shoes striking the concrete floor i can feel my cheeks all aflame theyre burning after what he just said and i have to control myself i want to shout out or scream im standing in front of the mirror again and i look so fucking pathetic i could cry my noboguchi has gone all limp and all i see is a shitty little stick of an excuse for a human being i feel so low that if i had the sword from the shop id turn it on myself right now and stick it in my guts i can hear her below speaking out some of her chaucer and im staring hard into the mirror so hard something strange is happening right in front of my eyes my noboguchi is shrivelling up and disappearing and my tits are growing into little sacs little dried out dugs more like flaps of skin than breasts my stomach is sagging and my shoulders drooping and my face is all fallen and grey and full of lines my hair is thin and white and i lift an ancient trembling hand to move rebellious strands away from my face that hand dotted with brown age spots and the skin wrinkled and paperthin and i look at myself calmly feeling my hand becoming still at my side once more no need of armour now that i can just let go and i want to tell martin that there is no running away there is no hiding place this is all there is a frail body certain to decay and there are no need of heroics i have known for a very long time that i shall die and i may not be a bruce lee or a warrior but all the same i have been preparing all my life for the moment when i can let go when all will fly from me and leave me the shutters will not open and no one will enter the courtyard all is still and hushed not a breath of wind stirs the leaves on the trees i am alone quite alone now and i am ready

Chapter II
Song of a Ragged Man

they moved me to this new place the pricks way out in the country far from the madding crowd alright far from anything and everything all i could hear every time i stepped outside the door was a caca cophony of birds i couldnt see them for shit for all the trees and bushes but i could hear them it spun me down into a dark pit of depression like i was that fat chick in silence of the lambs waiting for buffalo bill to get me to the right size so he could bump me off and skin me and make a dress out of my skin i took to lying on my bed to avoid contact with any of the others ill tell you about them all in good time but dont get too excited with the anticipation of it all theyre just a pack of loony wankers and youd run a mile from them if you saw them coming towards you in the street so i just lay on the bed staring at the ceiling feeling sorry for myself cos i missed london and my walks in chelsea and all them twats i used to stalk you dont realise when you was living the high life when life was sweet on the stalk until its gone and thats when i started thinking about my mother i recalled one of the last times i saw her she already looked like a corpse her skin had turned ruddy and gone dark with a sort of purple bruising but her face was gone a light shade of yellow you know like old pages lain too long in the sun i would go in to see her in her bedroom i didnt know if she was asleep or merely resting she was lying on her right side her left eye partially open she never acknowledged me or give the least sign she had seen me so i call to her softly twice *mother mother* perhaps too softly cos there was no response i thought about rapping with a knuckle on her skull but i just touch lightly her forehead and she starts opens her left eye fully and recognises me lifts her head from the pillow i can see that her right eye is shut she is almost deaf in her left ear and every time she wants to hear me she has to lift her head from the pillow poor mother a shadow of the woman who brought me up almost like someone else but she is not pathetic in her travail she keeps her chin up despite the pain she tells me it is pressure on the brain making trouble for the eye ear and mouth yes the mouth is closed on one side though i forget which for the moment beneath the brave front she knows this illness will be her last today her blood count is very low chris tells me the doctor can give her a blood transfusion but if she lapses back to her present poor state she might be doubly depressed susan calls in on mother says that mother looks like a candidate for madame tussauds fuck her envy and hatred of mother know no bounds but even while i contemplate sticking a meat cleaver in my big sisters noggin i know she is right mother does look waxen she is so frail and feeble and i can think of nothing to say to cheer her up my brain is numb i want her to die peacefully for she must die soon there is no way she will pull out of this illness i want to remember her as she used to be when i was small coming down to the kitchen in the winter when the only heat in the house was from the oven and she was there giving us porridge and love i want to hold on to this faded image even as i watch her slip slowly into the grave mother talks of how it will be after she is better and how things will be in the summer this is the brave face she wears ababbling of nothings i want to pick her up and hold her and protect her there seems so little of her now i turn my face to the window i just want to gaze at the sky at the slow drift of the clouds i cant think of my poor mother no more cos i feel i want to howl out my pain and hurt and thatid give them all the excuses they need to stuff me into a straitjacket and shove me into a padded cell lock the door and throw away the key the slow drift of clouds you can almost feel the traffic of your blood slowing down to keep pace with the clouds and your heartbeat sounds less like the drumbeat in the finale of a ludwig van beethoven symphony and more like a stately procession in a chorale by bach funny i never saw at the time how much the old bird gracie back in london had an influence on me but she did before her id never have known what ludy and j s sounded like and i complained like a fucking child when she sat me down and made me lissen to them records of hers but fuck when the fifth started with its four drum beats repeated i was sucked in hook line and sinker and i could see death himself in all his dreadful majesty pounding on a door with the hilt of his sword and there aint a thing you can do to stop him from getting through the door hell have you no matter how hard you fight and twist and turn and all the rest of the fifth is like a great battle between you and the ruffian on the stairs and you can be stinking rich as the duke of westminster and draw your troops up in good order but theyll be smashed and crushed by the minions of the lord of misrule until you are dragged down weeping and sobbing and gibbering like an idiot it wont matter you wont get off with a caution its curtains for you and me my mother the old woman back in london the king of thailand the president of france and every single one of us here on earth as we spin and weave our pathetic little webs and dance our dervish dances twirling and turning faster and faster and faster to escape and all to no avail i dont know when i drifted off but i know i was dreaming i was in a long dark tunnel and the walls were of brick running with water and i was crawling along the floor of the tunnel which was slimy and covered in shit and pools of piss and there were rats the size of small dogs and i was naked and i was sore afraid they were going to bite my willy off or chomp away my buttocks fuck think of that think of explaining that away to a dr now tell me once again how you came to lose your penis and get these bites around your anus it was the rats i tell you really i have something of a problem with this story of yours you see the bite marks are more consistent with the voracious incisors of a prostitute or indeed prostitutes plural i dont know what youre on about i was in a dark tunnel like a sewer and these rats were all over the shop and they were massive like dogs small dogs i mean not fucking alsatians or dobermans or irish wolfhounds and did they have names like lulu or jessie or miss whiplash said the dr i was getting more and more worked up by whitecoats

25

foureyed professional sarcasm and i seriously considered strangling him and cutting his head off and sending it in a box to the british medical association with a note that said dr doolittle hereby tenders his resignation and then i heard a rustling which sounded very close to one of my ears and the sound grew louder and louder like it had moved right inside my brain i awoke to find i had turned over in my sleep so was now facing into the room and my face was inches only from a ferrety little face the mouth of which was opened wide to receive a gobstopper or some such sweet and the ferret himself was rustling a plastic wrapper practically over my lughole you was jibberjabbing thats what you was doing did you know that no course you didnt you was asleep im certain sure of it sweet dreams was it then he laffed and i could see the gobstopper sitting at the back of his mouth in a sort of groove formed by his tongue then suddenly clamping his mouth shut he sucked in air and saliva with a kind of short sharp rasping sound care for a brandy ball at all i had no time to answer this it was a bad dream wasnt it i could tell you was making involutary inviolently you know what im getting at you was making movements you had no control over twitching like a goodun you do that in front of the guards and theyll put you in a high density unit i must have looked a bit confused what i mean is the high sensitivity no no no no no no thats not it security high security unit and then my son your goose is well and truly cooked i sat up suddenly and ferret started back with a look of concern on his narrow face his ferret eyes were darting this way and that i uttered two questions to him in quick succession who are you and what are you doing in my room he stared at me a third question formed itself will you stop rustling that fucking wrapper what wrapper says he and gives it a rustle i swiped it from his fingers the look of concern and shock on his phiz was worth the price of admission to this loony bin in the wilds then his bottom lip began to quiver and i had the weird feeling the munchkin was going to cry what mental age is this retard anyway i thrust the wrapper back into his eager little mitts and he smiled even as a single tear rolled down one side of his nose i stood up at this point thinking along the lines that i could bundle him out of the room and boot him up the backside or maybe dropkick him into a field outside and it was only when i was standing looking down at him that i realised just how incredibly short he was he only came up to my belly button i suppose i wouldnt have minded if hed been a woman some men are into dwarves they can twirl them on the end of their knobs and carry them round a room while holding a book in one hand and reading about the next position for carnal pleasure what they call you stumpy thats not the least bit funny came the reply wasnt intended to be funny cos i already assed you what your moniker was and you didnt tell me my name is not monica he shouts and his bottom lip is all aquiver once more steady on dopey i didnt say monica i said moniker he stared hard at me though his eyes were in rapid motion darting all over the place trying desperately to find a still centre miraculously the rustling of the wrapper had stopped lissen up shortarse this conundrum is easily settled if you would be so very good as to tell me your name its that simple he gave a shifty look over his shoulder at the door then turned back to me like he was going to confide a great secret at the exact same moment the brandy ball he had been violently and noisily sucking on popped out of his mouth and fell on the floor swiftly succeeded by a line of drool which he let hang from the side of his slack mouth before wiping away with the back of a hand this short sequence of events elicited a strong emotional response not from me i was as unmoved as desperate dan after hes stuffed his craw with a dozen cow pies but there was a sort of explosion from the dwarf fuck bert its bert well fuckbert itsbert you still havent got round to telling me what youre doing in my room no no no no no thats not right thats not my name i grabbed him by the throat my thumb one side of his adams apple and two fingers on the other side his tongue protruded over his bottom lip stained a ruddy brown he made a hissing sound from the back of his throat like the sound of an angry swan just tell me how you got in here i fixed him with a look a bruce lee special and slowly took my fingers and thumb off his throat door was unlocked i threw a glance at the door i was sure id locked it but stumpy bert the fuckbert itsbert seemed to read my mind you cant lock the door none of our doors can be locked the suspicion of a smirk played on his lips as he studied my face im sure i wore the look of a victim of an attack by the great bruce stunned and disbelieving at what i had just heard they can come in here any time they want night or day and theres not a thing we can do about it isnt there i said he shook his head slowly from side to side i know its against the code of the warrior to kill an unworthy opponent but i really did want to go to town on the dwarf mutilate him at the very least for his uninvited visit and for his unwelcome bit of news instead i just lifted him by the collar of his tunic which advertised what he had had for breakfast lunch and dinner for some considerable time some of those stains would have been of historical interest and dumped him in the corridor outside my room with a curt fuck off turd features then i slammed my door in his face and stood glaring at the door handle almost daring him to be so stupid as to come back into my room cos i knew exactly what i would do if he did that i would defenestrate him on the spot thats not another way of saying id cut his goolies off assuming he has any no id chuck the little cunt out of a window and watch gravity do its work on him as he plummeted like a mangy little cutprice icarus to his death but he didnt come back in to face the consequences of any rash and unconsidered action i heard him padding off down the corridor mumbling to himself and most likely justifying his world view from the lofty height of four feet nothing i turned now from the door and walked over to my bed sitting on the edge of it i had some thinking to do i knew i didnt want to stay where i was among mental cases like stumpy bert and the thought of anyone just wandering in on me like a guard in the middle of the night made me feel uneasy in a way i hadnt felt for a very long time not since i was little and susan was my big sister she was quite a stumpy brute herself but when i was only six or seven she was bigger than me and struck me across the face out of spite and i ran up the stairs so she wouldnt see me cry and i took one of her lipsticks and wrote across her mirror susan is a pig she told me later it cut her to the quick i was thinking of that and a lot of other things like maybe these fuckers of guards would come in to my room and piss on me while i was sleeping and i knew then i had to leave i didnt have nothing just the clothes on my back and that book the chaucer and i could carry that with me and so i waited till dusk had fallen and a gloom had settled in the room making pockets of shadows and there was only a pale light above the trees beyond my window and i walked out of my room into the corridor that led to the stairs and the entrance hall the place was quiet enough save for a distant murmuring and chittering like baboons settling down for the night i reckon old attenborough balls would have a proper commentary to fit this place here among these walls the baboonlike colonies of dwarfish halfwits and drooling imbeciles who make up the inmates spend the fagends of their days wiping excrement on the walls and preening themselves by picking lice from their pubic hairs and scratching their genital warts i confess to having a soft spot for stumpy bert and his ferret face i dont know why neither do i david which just goes to show that even the great panjandrum who has sat down with gorillas doesnt always get it right anyway that passed the time i know it passes willy nilly but sometimes it is carried like it has no weight at all and other times it burdens you like a deadweight and every second makes you grieve that you were born i was now at the head of the stairs and i could hear voices down in the reception area i lay down on the floor and contorted my body so that i could peek out at the reception counter and not be seen there were two big blokes two gorillas having a colloquy over the counter one seated behind the other leaning on the counter itself they had on white trousers well the one leaning over the counter did and grey jackets there was a lot of grunting and laughter going on hoo hoo hoo the one seated went and he was practically crying at the same time with lafter youll be the end of me you will hoo hoo you gotta laff aint you said the other wait a minute look whos wandering in the night i gazed beyond the counter to a dark corridor and could make out a thin emaciated scarecrow of a man shuffle into the light with half steps and quarter steps his body shaking and trembling with every movement he made you want to go wee you old shitsack shouted the gorilla standing the scarecrows face lit up and a gummy smile forced his lips apart he had the look of an ancient innocent backward child as he glanced from one gorilla to the other a french horn sounded a long sonorous note from his backside and then the front of his already soiled pyjama bottoms dampened yellow as he pissed himself fuck said the gorillas in unison the one in front of the counter moved to the old scarecrow and turned him to face back into the gloom of the corridor he had come from ill leave you to swab the decks was shouted back at the counter and the shuffler and guard moved away into the depths of the building the one behind the counter now stood up and peered at the place where the shuffler had stood he muttered to himself it sounded like no rest for the wicked he picked up a phone from the counter and stuck in ear phones and came out from behind until he was standing over the tiny pool of piss on the floor suddenly he began to move his head and arms and upper body in a jerky rhythm and i understood he was dancing but his talents didnt end there cos as he drifted round the reception area he now began to make sounds distorted and offkey so that they couldnt be described as singing as such more like the moaning of a lovesick donkey this man was a puzzle he looked like a gorilla he moved like a wounded bear and he sounded like an ass quite a specific set of qualities i thought as i lay watching and lissening from my hidden vantage point all the while i was wondering when he would stop arsefarting around and leave the reception area so i could get down there and fuck off into the concealing night he must have read my thoughts cos the next thing he straightened up and marched businesslike in the opposite direction to the other gorilla the reception area was mine and i didnt need a second invitation i slid on my arse down the length of a banister and tumbled off at the bottom of the stairs i glanced nervously round me to make sure there was no one about and then i bolted for the front door fuck jesus fuck it was locked there was a heavy bolt below and one above i had to exert myself a bit but i got them undone didnt do me no good cos the door had a heavy duty lock and the hulk wouldve struggled with this one i was thinking could i smash a window and clamber out into the night when i focussed on the reception desk it might be there the fucking heavy mother of a medieval key to unlock the door i took a peek back along the corridor that the scarecrow had come from then darted on tippy toe over to the desk and sure enough it was there a large brass key on a chain with a ton of other keys i didnt even have time to pick it up when i heard the songsmith come back moaning and groaning to some tune in his headphones i was down under the desk now concealed for the moment by the support for the counter i could hear the swish swish of a mop as caruso the gorilla cleaned up the puddle of piddle then i could hear the clack clack of metal heels faintly at first then getting louder and closer and i didnt need to peek out from my hiding place to know that the two big apes were back together any moment now they would find me and then i would be like a seal when two killer whales get hold of it just tossed this way and that for the sheer fun of it and i had no blade to defend myself be a different matter then for sure just think about it they pick me up by the scruff of my neck and they think its gonna be a fucking walkover but thats cos they aint seen the blade i got in my hand i flick it open and stick the blade into the guts of the one with the metal heels he never had a chance i twist it round his guts and pull it out he drops to his knees all glassyeyed and his gorilla accomplice is gobsmacked he goes slack jawed and its me going hoo hoo hoo and chasing him round the reception area hes even forgotten that hes just mopped up and slips on the wet floor sliding on his enormous haunches and clattering his bowling ball of a head against the metal bucket he brought with the mop i could cut his head off and stick it in the bucket then fuck theyre standing leaning on the counter now its only a matter of seconds and theyll find me shit maybe i could put up with the ferret bert and the scarecrow and their like ive been too hasty thinking i wanted to escape ive been premature in my analysis of the move to my new home but providence comes in the oddest guise even to miserable sinners like me cos i heard a faint wailing and hooting coming down the corridor that led off the reception area metal heels grunted and forced a loud puff of breath out of his lungs what is this the night of the living dead looks that way replied caruso and stretched a hand out towards the bunch of keys on the desk leave em there said metal ive got my bunch lets get these dirty stopouts back into bed and then lock up for the night with that they set off down the corridor and were met by a wailing and gnashing of biblical proportions as soon as the sounds had died away i came out of my hiding place grabbed the keys and opened the front door i went back to the desk and placed the keys just as i had found them then i scarpered closing the front door behind me and running across a huge lawn to the edge of the estate which enclosed the building i had just escaped from it looked dark and forbidding in the failing light gloomy and menacing i walked along a road until i reached woodland and then entered the woods and felt as if they had swallowed me and plucked me out of existence things were so pitchblack at first that i stumbled this way and that stubbing my toes against roots that clutched i had to stop though i had not gone far a few miles in daylight i could have walked the distance in less than an hour but it seemed as if i had been walking for half the night i sat down on a carpet of pine needles and rested my back against the trunk of a pine tree i gazed upwards to see some pale stars overhead and clouds made luminous by the light of the moon it wasnt cold the month was june the month of my birth though i never celebrated my birthday it seemed pointless to celebrate alone i pulled the collar of my jacket tighter round my neck and felt the copy of my chaucer in an inside pocket that would serve as my pillow when i felt it was time to put my head down and sleep i wondered what she was doing now the old bat back in london was she still alive amid her memories of distant times her youth and the days of her marriage to some feckless waster people are such a fucking trial it isnt a brave new world with such people in it its a hell or a purgatory with demons and imps for companions who want nothing more than to torment the life out of you the clouds separated and let the moon shine down on me among the trees and i saw how thin and insubstantial i was how much of nothing i was made i came from nothing and to nothing i will return i felt a sudden passing wave of remorse for my poor mother that she should have gone through all the pain of bringing me into this world and for what to see me here in this woodland a zero a cipher adding up to nothing a resentful festering sore on the face of the world it came back to me then the whole atmosphere of my aunts house cloying and choking like the heavy scent of candles in church it was where my mother was as she lay dying she was forty and my aunt was her younger sister but she was an odd ball that aunt small of stature tiny really and without an eyebrow bald as a plucked chicken above the eyes i skulked around the town in those days friend to no one and lost abandoned discarded by one and all and only hunger would drive me to my aunts place it would get a grip of me and suffer me to place one foot in front of the other and put up with the drivel that poured forth around my mothers supine figure it was the baby drawing all the nonsense from my aunt chrises baby the wunderkind christine must have been all of fifteen when she was shagged up against some wall at a party but thats all brushed under the carpet now conveniently forgotten as visitors coo and cluck over the little bundle of joy i watch him bawl his lungs out feeling like i want to join in with him he protests loudly his right to life demands attention and food while his grandmother suffers and slips away minute by minute in the bed beside it was only yesterday i was in the babys place mother nursing me talking to me and about me with aunts and uncles at times mother talks about the future and i have to hold myself together when i feel like im coming apart at the seams for there is no future and i could see the time when chris and me were little and mother went into hospital it was at the edge of a park and there were ducks and geese in the large pond and we were bringing fruit and chocolates to mother but we stopped in the park amid the cries of peacocks and ate up the chocolates every one i was never a good son never the son my mother wanted me to be the moon passed behind a cloud and i was hidden there in the woods feeling myself wrapped in a cloak heavy with the sadness and melancholy of that time when my mother was passing from this world and my nephew was protesting his right to a place on the dunghill of existence its a mercy we know nothing of the world and its ways when we enter it cos the knowledge of the pain and struggle we will face would make the staunchest refuse the breach i was now so weary that my hands were round my chaucer before the thought had fully formed to lay me down to rest and when my head was on my hard pillow it was the hooting of an owl that serenaded me towards the land of sleep and forgetfulness and it was in that night in the woodland that i dreamed a dream most strange and full of uneasy sights and sounds i was lying on the ground with my head on a large slab made of stone i could make out some words above my head here lies the body of but then i could not read the name as my head and shoulders covered the rest of the slab a rabbit was eating grass at my feet and as it moved towards my head chomping on the grass it got bigger and bigger and the sound of its chewing and chomping sounded loud and angry then it was over me looking down on me big as a fully grown man and it had stopped chewing it was staring at me and its bottom lip was quivering beneath its two large front teeth its eyes were red and it looked full of fury and outrage you shouldnt be here thats what it said you shouldnt be here and youre late where should i be i said and what am i late for you know you know then it looked away from me as the sound of something crashing through the undergrowth came closer and closer it was a rhinoceros with one of the gorilla guards on its back the gorilla had a meat cleaver raised above its head the rabbit had time to tell me youre for the chop little man before it loped off behind a tree and then i heard the slow beat of wings and a gigantic owl swooped down from the moon and took the meat cleaver right out of the gorillas huge mitt i awoke in the pale morning breathing hard with a small bird a robin on a branch its head titled as if it was lissening to the calls of all the other birds in the woods i sat up and startled the robin it flew off i blinked and looked about me my tummy rumbled and it sounded like a ball bearing sliding down a groove in a helter skelter fuck what was i gonna do i could have eaten a dan dare breakfast 5 cow pies and a foot long black pudding all washed down with a pot of tea i stretched and pulled myself to my feet as i looked down at where id lain last night i could see the imprint of my body on the bed of pine needles and a small damp patch at the edge of my chaucer where id drooled on it i picked it up and wiped the book off on my shirt tail christ if gracie could see me now shed be shaking her head and clucking her tongue at me what sort of a state are you in martin you have to present a better face to the world than this drooly unwashed hobo i tucked my shirt in and stowed the book under the shirt next to my skin i ran my fingers through my hair and tried to take a reading of where i was it was hard work what with the birds getting all up about nothing just throating full throttle their warbling notes and then there was the baaing of a mass of woolly fleeces it started off with just a handful away in the distance then they started shifting over towards the woods and got joined by all their inbred cousins and backward rellies until they seemed to be surrounding the woods what was it like to be sheep theyre not that fat at all cos i could see some had been got at by jason and his argonauts cos they were bald and white and odd looking their heads so small compared to their bodies like they had that illness brought on by being bitten by mosquitoes but at least they had a plentiful supply of food all around good thing too cos all they do the live long day is eat and poop and poop and eat in fact doing both at the same time you wonder what on earth they think about do they look at clouds and think they are supersized sheep do they look at us and marvel how we get about on two legs do they even know what a leg is cos first off theyd have to know the word for leg you couldnt get nowhere in a conversation with another person if you didnt know the words for things i mean imagine you go into a shop and say two big things from the large thing please theyd know you were asking for something but theyd definitely be on their guard okay humour him and keep him talking while i ring the local loony bin to see whos escaped and all you really wanted was two litres of milk from the fridge i scratched my head these morning thoughts pass the time and i must have farted a good dozen times while i pondered the existence of sheep we dont do enough of that putting ourselves into the skin of an animal and trying to think its thoughts for one thing if you were a sheep your head would be closer to the ground and you find it harder to gaze upwards but on the plus side you wouldnt care about mincing around trying to avoid stepping in your poo pellets which brings me to my major gripe with the state of nature you see once i cleared the woods which didnt take me long and then parted the sheep like moses parting the red sea i then had to keep a good watch on where my feet were going cos those woolly baskets shit just about everywhere they feel like it chewing the cud and staring off into the distance and pushing out another little packet of black pellets mind you cows are worse gracie had told me she went skiing in switzerland back in the day and the locals there call cowpats alpenpizzas she thought that was fucking hilarious and when i didnt laff she had one of her goes at me about not taking myself too seriously thing was i could never be right either too serious one moment or not serious enough the next anyway cowpats or alpenpizzas they attract fuckloads of flies and it was early yet but the flies were all over the place and landing from time to time on the back of my neck and drinking my sweat i felt like i hadnt got a proper nights sleep like i was all scummy and gritty and i probably had zombie breath fuck i had not thought this escape bid through it was definitely not the great escape and i was no steve mcqueen on a hotroad fleeing the nazis no i was climbing over stiles and flicking flies off my forehead wiping drops of sweat off chin and nose and plodding one foot in front of the other over and over and weaving my way between stinkpiles of festering shit you could take your country life and stuff it up your crusty arsehole i was all at sea i knew that it was like i was the boat and the crew and the sick man at the end of the boat who was doomed soon to pop his clogs and be eaten by the rest of the crew christ i was thirsty it wasnt that hot i just felt overheated and dry in the mouth i wanted to stick my head under running water and the land was changing even as i stumbled onwards i looked back at the woods i had slept in and they seemed tiny and far off and there were no sheep or cattle around i was among hills now and birds with large wingspans and broad tailfans one moment they drifted without moving their wings then they would stop and hover flapping their wings swiftly i felt they were waiting for me to drop to the ground and croak my last then they would swoop in for the kill plucking out my eyes and tearing the flesh off my bones my tongue was cleaving to the roof of my mouth and i was breathing hard it seemed to me that it was someone else now who had run through the chelsea streets whooping like an injun and creating havoc where was he this wild boy in his place was a sick man hollow eyed and consumed by thirst and hunger and just when i thought id had it you know i was gonna have to drink my own piss i could hear running water i could hear it gurgling and gushing though i couldnt see it but it spurred me on i was don quixote on his thin nag rocinante both of us with our tongues hanging out and without the strength to put one foot or hoof in front of the other but i practically charged towards the sound of the water a bunch of thirsty ayrabs in the desert wouldnt have fallen upon a watery oasis with any more violence than i stumbled and lurched towards the gurgles and gushes of that water and as i forced apart some prickly bushes there it was like a white and silver and green rope slicing through grey rocks i fell face forward into it gulping at the cold water and catching my breath until i could drink no more i turned then and lay gazing up at the sky and blessing nature in all its infinite beauty but a thought buzzed into my head that there might be a dead sheep lying in the very stream that i had just slaked my thirst in and i would die some godforsaken miserable death with my guts twisting and turning inside me like a nest of vipers and i would pray for some vagabond ronin to finish me off put me out of my misery by cutting my head off and setting it on a rock for carrion crows to pick at it would be a sight to behold the eye sockets all bloody and dark and the lips and nose bitten off so that my teeth would show in a snarling grimace i started to laff even as the sky began to swirl above me and clouds drifted and collided in the blue what was i worrying about i hadnt seen a sheep for an hour at least and as soon as that little thought took hold you can guess what i heard nothing but the collective baaing of a flock of sheep i sat up and looked with dismay and despair upon their innocent and murderous blank faces o christ i couldnt hardly take one more step my whole body was aching to have a drink my tongue was sticking to the roof of my mouth and how good that water tasted and now to be mocked like this by a bunch of nancy prancers in sheepskin fuck the lord works in mysterious ways to fuck you up i scrabbled up the rocks to see if i could find the carcass of a dead sheep lying in the stream i was huffing and puffing and feeling that i wanted to heave my guts up saliva dribbling out of my open mouth when i looked back at the sheep they seemed like little offwhite smudges on the landscape i had come further than i thought driven on by a manic passion if i was gonna die i wanted to die of my own hand by throwing myself from a height and dashing my brains out on some monstrous boulder below i would defy gravity for some moments time would slow and i would be as graceful as a butterfly until i plummeted like a stone to my death it would be like the younger monroe daughter in the last of the mohiccans with hawkeye looking on approvingly hed have a lump in his throat the size of a walnut fuck that hed be choking back the tears no doubt saluting me and telling me it was a good day to die and hed mark the spot where i leapt to my death by placing a series of stones in a configuration that would confound anyone else but he would know thats the point and his ancestors with whom i would be spending eternity i realised i felt better after all that scrabbling about and thinking about hawkeye i definitely didnt feel i was gonna kick the bucket right there and then imagination is a great thing a solace at times but then again a burden at other times like you can imagine all the world is against you plotting your downfall and conspiring to bring about your end like kit marlowe brought to a great reckoning in a small room he was a violent roister doister if ever there was one being stabbed in the arsehole or stabbing but thats not how he died a petty squabble over a bill in a pub in deptford and he gets stabbed above the eye imagine if theyd had tv back then how that would have played out on the box weve just had a report in from deptford that the wellknown man about town and serial bum bandit christopher kit marlowe has been killed in a brawl in a palace of low repute with another possible bum bandit who has been named as ingram frizer it has not yet been confirmed that this last name is a genuine name or a false one given to protect frizers family from the shame of association with marlowe who had something of a reputation for fighting and stabbing marlowe was well known as a man of letters a university poet and a scribbler of plays another scribbler from the sticks a man of warwick a bill shakeshafte was asked for a comment upon hearing of marlowes demise i doubt hell be writing any more plays then was all that he had to say well not quite all cos he added that he was nowhere near deptford on the day of the incident that led to marlowes death and furthermore he had witnesses to testify to that effect i felt so much better for thinking of marlowe and his erotic life and even more erratic death that i lay down in the lee of some rocks and closed my eyes i was smiling up at the sun that warmed my tired body and a weight seemed to lie on me like the air itself had grown heavy pressing me into the earth i felt i could not move under any circumstances each limb like a heavy log or branch and even though i knew my eyes were closed i could see the scene before me painted in bold colours and full of sounds and the breath of wind i heard the trill of a flute there on a rock flute in hand was a shepherd come live with me and be my love he said then he stood up and used his flute as a conductors baton waving it in front of him and raising his other hand to exhort the sheep in the valley below to cry out as one and we will all the pleasures prove that valleys groves hills and fields woods or steepy mountains yields but all at once the shepherd stopped waving his fluty wand and a fearful baa went up from the mob of sheep the shepherd turned and pointed beyond me i turned to see a giant a cyclops with one eye in the middle of his forehead and a huge boulder raised above his head kill kill kill kill the giant cyclops chanted and slowly moved to blot out the sun and a cold wind swept over me i awoke to see the giant with the rock over his head and standing between me and the sun and i heard him say on his breath once more the word kill the rock was inched higher lookout i shouted hes behind you the giant hesitated and lowered the rock glancing over his shoulder i rolled away from the lee and stood up in one swift movement and it was now that i could see it was no giant that had been standing over me but a weirdo in a tweed jacket and camouflage pants he was shorter than me and much older he looked terribly confused and his arms now began to shake with the effort of holding up the rock above his head what are you doing i said you dont wanna go around holding rocks above your head i dont he said i shook my head slowly from side to side put the rock down and i gave him the full warrior look all at once he cracked and the rock fell to earth with a small thud it barely missed his toes that would have been justice i suppose of a poetic nature if hed smashed in his toes with his own rock you tricked me he said and began to cry jesus its odd the things that set some people off well what dyou expect me to do you lunatic were you really gonna drop that rock on me i dont know he replied the voice was telling me to what voice i said the voice i hear in me and around me not all the time but sometimes so insistent it frightens me and makes me do things i dont wanna do can you hear the voice now no of course i cant you chased it away i smiled at that and tweedy gritted his teeth and moaned through them why are you laffing this is not funny he gritted his teeth again and kicked the rock he had dropped then let out a yelp of pain and hopped around on one foot with tears rolling down his cheeks i was shedding tears too tears of lafter dont make me pick that rock up and smash your head in cos i could do it i gave him another warrior special and he looked away unable to hold my bold gaze he went and sat down on a boulder and put his head in his hands he stayed like that for most of a minute then wiped his face with a sleeve of his jacket and blew his nose into an ancient looking snotrag he pulled from the breast pocket of his jacket he seemed to be calmer now calmer and in control ill tell you about myself if you like i shrugged i dont mind i told him ill be your audience captive and attentive if you tell a good story

Song of a ragged man

how old dyou think i am you probably think im 70 or more but im only 60 i know a lot older than you you think youll be young for ever i thought like that once im young and fit and healthy and ive got all the time in the world to do whatever takes my fancy thats an illusion son thats the dance of illusion in the flames of eternity you think you wont get burned but what needs to get burned is your sense of the fantastic the longer your illusions last the longer you will stay lost i was a god you hear me or i thought of myself as a god not the god almighty but just a minor deity you cant believe looking at me now how i made heads turn cos what you are looking at is the ruins of a magnificent temple my father was a war hero of sorts common or garden sort no knocking out german machine posts or singlehandedly destroying a panzer tank or two but definitely carried that aura with him all his life to his dying day that he had been a part of history had done his bit for the cause of freedom and democracy big words somewhat tarnished now and encumbered with caveats you follow me ive never felt even like a bit player in the great drama of our age ive never been much of a joiner you see always stood on the outside looking in and as ive got older ive been dragged by a sort of centripetal force further and further away from the centre i was the last squeeze of the bag from dearest dada as i said dada is dead well if i didnt actually say it i implied it hes gone into the eternal flames all his vanities and illusions and fancies have been burned away theres not much left of a body after it has been burned in an oven ashes to ashes dust to dust are you given to poetic urges does poesy swirl around your heart and give you dyspepsia heres one you might try on for size penned by yours truly a long time ago ill give you but the first stanza fitting as it is for where we are on gods good earth on this outcrop i am weathered bitten blasted hacked by wind like these stones exposed where earth has drawn back my bones are worn smooth filed down returned to dust what dyou make of that then not much i would guess poetry is a cloak of many colours best suited to an old bird like me whose feathers are ruffled and no longer a thing of beauty do you believe in god ah the big question but no better place to pose that question than under an open sky with sun and wind and plashing water all the elements are here and if not here where then can we feel the majesty and awe of existence we only pass this way once my friend life is an experiment and we are its guinea pigs we burden ourselves with false burdens all the time pettiness and inconsequence will bring us to an early grave eating us up from the inside out until we are but ravaged shells of the pure forms of energy with which we entered this world under what circumstances does a man ever know of anything whatsoever which he himself does not directly apprehend or has apprehended this this is the kernel of rationalist ideology and it leaves so much unspoken and unanswered perhaps unthought for there is more in heaven and earth than rationalism such a paltry down at heel walking dead way of looking at the world you wanna suck the marrow of life right out of the bone and give a big smack of your lips and fart into the wind with a smile on your face a big broad foolish grin cos what do we know of life and love and the real meaning of existence you know what it says in the bible do you read it son not many do now a bit of a farmers feast to sit down and tuck into the bible but the story of job is a helluva story then the lord answered job out of the whirlwind and said who is it that darkeneth counsel by words without knowledge gird up now thy loins like a man for i will demand of thee and answer thou me what dyou think of that gird up now thy loins like a man well ill tell you straight i havent done much of girding up my loins for a helluva long time you look at me now at this shipwreck of a life and you think no wonder who the hell would want to kiss this old face and suck on these parched lips but there was a time i remember i was living in hampstead well the garden suburb you know with my wife yes i was married once upon a time and we were having problems the usual worries over finances she wasnt working at the time japanese you see and she hadnt got a work permit sorted out and i took a job as a telephone salesman surely the act of a desperate man for one whole weeks work i made £200 before tax i could see my life panning out like a car crash i had left japan to get away from teaching but i was gonna have to go back to it and felt sick at heart what was worse was london the old seedbox of lust and frustration i could barely walk ten yards on oxford street without putting a hand in my trousers for a spot of pocket billiards and i went for an interview and got a post as an auxiliary teacher in some ripoff language school and i was heading back to hampstead waiting for the tube on the platform at charing x when this old fruit loaf approached me and gave me the glad eye would the next train be going to highbury he caught me off guard the simpering ninny cos i answered that i didnt know i was edgware bound how many minutes till your train i still hadnt caught on at this point so i searched an electronic board and told him 2 minutes then the little shit disputed with me saying it was 6 i looked again at the board and dyou know what he was fucking right now he had a certain advantage which he pressed home by asking me where i was from i told him with as much equanimity as i could muster under the circumstances ireland you can hear the oirish lilt in my voice now cant you i mean ive never striven to kill it off or mask it entirely he came from dublin and started to liven up in a coy diverting way hed come over for a jaunt he next told me giving me the full smile and laffing eyes staying with friends did i live by myself no i told him im married oh yes said he and whats that like the things you have to put up with on lifes path a great pain in the balls and the rectum most of it but you can enjoy a little laff sometimes even through the mist of tears and the howl of recriminations i dont personally think marriage is all that its cracked up to be and why i ever married is a good question and one that i pondered deeply in a hindsight that was more like a depression or a psychotic episode it may have been both and more than that i entered the state of matrimony far too fucking lightly this is something i can tell you from deep and painful experience getting married should be looked upon in the same light as undergoing a life threatening operation i mean would you happily unconcernedly and absentmindedly put yourself under the knife to have a pimple removed from your penis there you are you didnt come round from the anaesthetic youre dead as marleys doornail but you have a beautiful pimple free penis which is of absolutely no use to you now you are dead its stiff alright but not in a good way by the way dont get me wrong i dont blame my wife for the demise of our marriage well not entirely i think it would be only fair and decent of me to own up to 50% of the damage the fact of the matter is we hardly knew each other when we got hitched now ignorance isnt a sin or a crime not necessarily anyway but i had had a biking accident about half a year before i asked yuriko to tie the knot i didnt know her at all at the time of the accident i hadnt met her and the little that i did know of her was not encouraging in the sense to which i thought she would make a good wife and bring fulfilment to me perhaps i expected too much from her i dont know all i can say is that when i popped the question she gave me a certain look but didnt demur i know i was in a dark place and was suffering from complications brought on by the accident but whats her excuse she could have looked me in the eye and tittered holding a hand up over her mouth in that very japanese way and told me that my gaijin humour was strange and odd baka dayoo i could have accepted that and saved both of us an extended holiday in hell there we were two not entirely stupid and insensitive human beings who voluntarily submitted to putting on blindfolds and stepping out to cross a minefield with no idea where we were going it could have been worse i suppose i could have murdered her and cut her up into bits and dissolved her remains in a bath of acid but the funny thing was i liked fucking her i could characterise our relationship as one built on mutual distrust we were on a raft on a boundless ocean and half the time i wanted to kill her and the other half i wanted to make love to her in the end i just fell off the raft and kept swimming as i said i dont blame her completely but she should take 50% of the blame for the failure of our marriage i know the accident put the willies up me and gave me this undeniable fear in my guts that i wasnt long for this world and i should think seriously about leaving a seedling behind but then i didnt kick the bucket and the stronger i got the further i moved away from her not that we were close to begin with theyre a funny old lot the japs if youre a foreigner a gaijin you havent a mission of being included in their society not in a month of sundays and it wasnt even that i resented being given the cold shoulder by her family i just realised one evening as i took my post dinner stroll among the carrot fields and small factories in the neighbourhood where we lived in the urban sprawl out of tokyo that i had brought this purgatory upon myself i had set my feet on the path to the day that will live in infamy when i tied the knot with the ungrateful bitch and you know i used to brood on this a lot who did i really blame me her japan no none of those yeah they all played a part in the theatre of the absurd that was my existence in the land of the rising yen but i knew deep down in the innermost recesses of my gut that it was my father who was the real culprit he had bequeathed me such a fucking low opinion of myself that of course i was gonna end up like this in a loveless relationship half way across the world up a fucking shit creek without a paddle or a compass and with a grinning conniving psychopath in a kimono at the other end of the boat he stopped talking breathing in short gasps with his mouth open and he looked like he was gonna burst into tears you alright i said and immediately regretted opening my mouth he stared at me and his eyes were unblinking the veins on his neck were throbbing his face was flushed like a boiled lobster alright alright he screamed no im not fucking alright you gobshite if i was alright dyou think id be out here in the middle of nowhere with a loaded gun what was he talking about a loaded gun but then he put a hand inside his jacket and fumbled about for half a minute he pulled out a revolver is that real i said he began to laugh in a throaty kind of fashion is that real he says yes its fucking real its a webley belonged to my pater and its got a kick like a donkey on steroids he raised the gun and pointed it at me i must have had a look of dismay on my face it wouldnt even have done me any good to have had a sword in my hands a knife maybe cos i couldve thrown it at him like in the magnificent seven and caught him one before he pulled the trigger would you like to find out what that kick is like he said i was shaking my head and inside i was shouting of course i dont wanna find out you fucking nonce but my throat was all closed up i couldnt even swallow let alone speak my words were eaten up by the crushing silence that pressed down on me he pulled the trigger and the loudest click i have ever heard came like a hammer blow im surprised i didnt shame myself by fainting i did however pee myself and let off some ferocious wind which put the nonce into a fit of hysterics you should see your face its a picture i felt an anger rising in me and he must have noticed the change in me cos he told me to chill out it was only a fucking joke i must have made a move towards him so he put a hand up to stop me and told me there was a bullet in the chamber but was it the next one or the one after that or even the one after that i stopped moving i must have looked wary and ill at ease dont think you can hurt me he said i will shoot you if you try anything you understand i started to back off then but kept looking at him he never stopped looking at me and always pointing the gun with a terribly steady hand that bullets for me you see he shouted when i was about twenty feet or so away from him that bullet is my ticket to the afterlife cos i have made such a fuck up of this life dont you fuck it up dont fuck up your chance of happiness you find yourself a good woman and shag her till it hurts shag her till your dick drops off and have children lots and lots of children cos thats what you were put on this earth for ive understood it all too late but its not too late for you i was fucked up before i had a chance to know i was fucked up i saw my old mans cock once yes i did he never locked the door of the loo and i pushed it open one day and he was taking a piss and he half turned with that habitual scowl on his face and glared at me but i had just enough time to catch sight of his hose it was thick and red and angry looking and the thought passed through my headspace faster than he could dismiss me with a curt expletive that that was the passageway down which a part of me had travelled to this world a fucking marvel a miracle nothing less though wasted on the likes of me he lowered the webley and his expression was torn between laughter and tears between mirth and morose abandonment he sat down then on a rock and the gun slid from his grasp he brought his hands up and covered his face as his body shook with the emotions swirling within i needed no further invitation to depart but turning on my heels i ate up the ground to put furlongs and acres and miles between me and that dangerous loon i thought i still could catch his whimpering snivelling on the wind as i made towards a village which i saw on the horizon as i came down onto the plain the other side of the hill where i had encountered the sadsack with the gun i ploughed on now i had the wind in my sails i was heading back to civilisation it might not be london but it would have life and people and cafes and shops i realised i didnt have a bean to my name but i could binhoke or nick some food from a convenience store i was getting a good feeling about this there was a definite spring in my step and then i heard a gunshot it brought me up short i looked back towards the hill and i could picture him now blood and brains dribbling down onto his tweed jacket his pants soiled brown at the arse and a hole you could put your fist through at the exit wound jesus i could hear hounds barking now from the far side of the hill they couldnt be there on account of his suicide it was too soon but maybe those gorillas had found out i was gone and had called out the police and there was a manhunt for me they could sniff my bed those dogs and theyd be able to find me across a wilderness shit i had to get into the village and blague a lift out of the area well ill tell you what fear is a great mover and motivator it put wings on my heels i was like some poor sod in a greek tragedy pursued by the furies and i staggered into that village feeling like i was on my last legs and reading every sight and sound like they were auguries of my doom a gull wheeled in the air over my head as i crossed a road and its cry sounded like malicious laughter the gods are cruel when everything is going against you the sky wheels indifferently overhead the light from the sun will take 8 minutes ive been told to reach earth and it breeds maggots in a dead dogs eye or the bloody black hole in the blasted temple of a madman on a hill i dont know how i got there but i was standing at a cafe window staring in at the food on the tables my stomach was growling like an angry badger down a hole and i was salivating so much that juice was coming out the side of my mouth there werent many in the cafe and a couple near the window got up from their table and went to the counter i saw my chance there wasnt much left on their plates but i was going to have it i went in trying to look as casual as poss there was a girl behind the counter talking to the couple whod left the table i gave them a quick glance as i sashayed across the floor like i was a competitor in a dance competition all nimble footwork all twinkletoes and plenty of cha cha cha at the last moment i showed the judges my back scooped up a napkin and swept everything that was edible into it there was a half eaten fried aubergine a sad looking tomato a nice crusty roll some scrags of ham and eggs i could barely stop myself from stuffing all of it into my mouth right then and there in the cafe but i held it together if bruce lee could hold his fist over a flame without whimping i could make it out into the street so i clenched my jaw gritted my teeth and held my breath as i forced myself to move to the entrance i pushed the door open and stepped away from the cafe i thought i heard a shout behind me back out on the pavement i lost all restraint i took a vicious bite out of the crusty roll and stuffed the manky tomato in after it i dont think i was walking straight cos i bumped into one or two passersby and they give me filthy looks which if id been less tired and hungry id have given them swift justice for there comes that shout again its lack of food thats giving me the paranoid shakes thats all and i stuffed the aubergine into my mouth which was half full of bread and tomato fuck i could do with something to wash it down some fucker gave me a look like i was a huge turd to be avoided at all costs then there was a hand on my shoulder and i was spun round to see the girl from the cafe she was a wild cat spitting and hissing at me i wasnt lissening to her not really i was just aware that she was angry and people in the street were stopping and staring i suppose they dont get much entertainment in their lives suddenly i couldnt take any more what had i done after all taken some food that was gonna be scraped off a plate and thrown away so i shouted out im hungry dyou hear me thats all im just fucking hungry it was like the world stopped and everyone around me turned into statues birds hung in the air motionless defying gravity cars were stalled half in and half out of junctions and everything was silent but for the slow beat of my heart like a steady drumbeat then the noise and movement of the world came soaring back around me and the wild cat had me by the collar and was pulling me back to the cafe i was too weak and shaky to resist she dragged me into her cafe and sat me down at the very table i had pilfered from i could hear my breathing now as she stared at me i ought to turn you over to the police she said that but she didnt look so angry any more what would you like to eat this had to be a trick i shook my head i aint got no money i know that she said which is why its your lucky day i still couldnt believe what was happening and i couldnt force any words out so she pointed a finger at me and told me not to move then she went out into the back leaving me alone i dont know how many minutes passed i sat in a daze unable to take in what was happening was she gonna return with a meat cleaver and chop me up and feed me to her dogs she looked like she might have a pair of great danes who would need some feeding well they would make short work of me the way i felt right now but when she returned she brought a plate of spaghetti and meatballs i could almost have cried but i couldnt let my inner bruce down so i sucked it up and bowed once very formally to her she smiled for the first time and watched me eat she didnt have any food herself no one came in and disturbed us while i was eating and she didnt speak she just watched me and didnt take her eyes off me once when i was done eating she told me i was lucky she was on the cafe was her fathers but he was away on business and if he had been here it would have been a different story why did you feed me i said cos you looked hungry and the simplicity of her answer nearly undid me once again plus you looked like youd had a shock of some kind well she was right about that i struggled for a bit whether or not to speak about the ragged man i had encountered out in the hills it all sounded a bit far fetched now that i was back in civilisation and i didnt want her thinking i was a liar or making up stuff but i neednt have worried cos i hadnt got very far into my tale when she started laffing her whole face lit up like a parade peter stuyvesant thats who you met i dont think so i said he wasnt dutch or nothing like that he sounded irish yeah yeah thats him alright and she was nearly crying with laffter he is irish youre right coyle or doyle is his name we just call him stuyvesant cos hes always popping over to amsterdam to have a break and chill out with bob hope the actor but hes dead isnt he o she nearly fell onto the floor with that one o youre sweet she said no you know bob hope dope i must have looked a right twat who was having his mouth clamped open and pissed in now and im sure i blushed cos my face was on fire but she didnt seem to mind she told me stuyvesant had met tarantino in amsterdam cos he spends a lot of time there tarantino the film director yeah she was nodding her head up and down as if this was so well known that only a prime twat would argue against it then she wrinkled her nose well thats what he says i mean theres only so much you can swallow from the stuyver i think hes dead i announced she looked at me as if she now didnt credit what id said and i had to go into the whole bit about him pulling out this revolver and scaring the shit out of me she shook her head and laffed under her breath look he does that all the time he takes his gun out into the hills and fires off a round or two hes a harmless idiot really course the gun belonged to his father my granddad knew him 60 years ago stuyvers father they were in the war not in the same regiment but he was a madman too he used to go up into the hills as well the father and fire off a few rounds i must have looked a bit strange at this point cos she asked me if i was alright the thing is id seen a copper out of the corner of my eye talking to some of the people whod been standing around in the street when id been brought back to the cafe i didnt have time to answer i didnt even have time to ask if there was a back way out of the cafe when there was a loud knocking at the entrance fuck i must have forgot to put the sign up that were closed she got up from the table back in her serious mode and padded to the door i thought should i make a bolt for it but i couldnt see the copper at all and the talk at the door sounded friendly enough so i was just a sitting duck when the copper come round from the doorway and stood looking down at me is your name martin he said and i didnt need to answer cos i knew in my bones he knew who i was and i was not gonna fight a fight i was bound to lose

Chapter III
A Mad Mad World

the gorillas had fun with me when the police brought me back as soon as the constabulary was out the door it was tag team wrestling and it attracted no small audience ferret face stumpy bert had a ringside seat one of the gorillas picked him up and placed him on the counter in the reception area so he could enjoy my comeuppance anything youd like to see bert grunted one of the gorillas give him a twirl and his wish being their command i was twirled round faster than a ceiling fan until the reception area was spinning round and i could just about make out in an upside down wobbly turning sort of way that other freaks had joined bert of course i could tell the freaks from the gorillas cos the freaks were dressed in nightgowns and soiled pjs and they were leering and laffing at the proceedings in a toothless twitchy kind of way as if they all suffered from epilepsy and degeneracy i couldnt tell with some of them if they were male or female there was one they called janet but she was over six feet tall with the body shape of a sumo wrestler and gave off a stink of rotting fish and urine she was enjoying the sport more than anybody else even stumpy bert and when she started shouting drop him and pulled on her chin whiskers all the freaks joined in and a swell of sound filled the reception area drop him drop him drop him screamed the pinheads who all had small heads on deformed bloated bodies i had absolutely no control over the situation and when the drop came i howled with pain the big gorilla didnt just drop me onto the floor he dropped me onto his knee and hit me in the small of the back i lay on the floor then with pain radiating out from my spine to every part of my body feeling like id never walk again and too disabled to move or respond to the whooping applause that filled the room i must have passed out cos i thought i was on a plain in africa i was a rhinoceros like the one that had smashed up the anteek shop in chelsea there was a storm raging and i wanted to call to two figures in the storm but my voice was weak my tongue cleaved to the roof of my mouth i was weak and i lay down on the parched and cracked earth it was my son out there with his mother and then the boy was standing over me much taller than i remembered and with a splendid horn i thought of him as my own i wanted him with all the strength left in me to go on and never look back upon this desolation he came close to me sniffing my scent then he leant into me and said in dreams we are foretold and our lives are the remembering of our dreams then he released a strong jet of piss and it landed in my ear which woke me up and i bleary saw i was sprawled out on a smelly old sofa and some ragend was taking a pee over me a shout came from behind him

43

and then he was pulled away i tried to sit up but it was an effort beyond me the one who had shouted came to me and hauled me into a sitting position which action caused my body to scream and protest in a series of violent contortions never lie down like that specially not in the daytime youre lucky he didnt shit on you where am i came out like a long whimper there was no answer there was a banging on a door and across an open space i could see the two gorillas through a glass panel laffing and pointing at me youre in the ward dingus this was the one who had pulled the ragend away from me she was fierce looking i mean she was dressed like the others who were standing around the edges of the open space they were like cattle but she was switched on what ward i said trying to stop myself from looking at the gorillas what ward she spat the words out and glared at me her forehead lined and puckered you mustve done something to piss them off she gave a twitch of her mouth in the direction of the glass panel where the gorillas were pointing at me i ran off thats what i done clever boy she looked at me like i was backward and morally degenerate did you have a room on the other side the other side yeah the other side of the door yes i did can i get it back thats not for me to say but likelihood of a second coming zero and ditto for you and your room being reunited she leaned over me so that her upper body was between me and the view of the glass panel this is the ward for the lifers theyre not all morons but there are those here theyre not all schizos and paranoid junkheads but youll find those too the quiet ones you should watch out for i dont know you who you are or what youre capable of im martin i volunteered well martin you watch your step around here im block commandant thats a madeup title made up by me and i operate on very straight and uncomplicated lines you fuck with me ill fuck you over so be nice to me and well get on like a house on fire capiche i nodded that i understood she straightened up the names gloria or glory but dont come crying to me if you get hurt its every man and woman for herself she smiled and walked away giving ragend a clip around the back of his head he swore and started to sing glory glory haleluljah but she gave him a look that silenced him what sort of a shithole had i landed in i was like a wildebeest on the serengeti i was wounded and watching for the jackals begin to circle but it was only ragend staring at me scuse me scuse me scuse me he was working himself up to something and i didnt want him near me in an excited state in fact i didnt want him near me full stop if you dont fuck off you little cunt ill bite your cock off and stuff it down your throat this had the desired effect he moved away from me casting furtive glances at me over a shoulder till he came to a corner gave me the fingers and scooted out of sight thank fuck for that all i wanted now was to be left alone so i could rest and save my strength for getting better the commandant returned after a while with a couple of tabs and a glass of water she told me to swallow them theyd do me good and she didnt hang around for no small talk she only wanted to know if i was hungry i didnt answer hunger was something that made no sense to my body right then it was a word like drought and famine never mind she said youll feel hungry soon enough once the pain goes i dont know what pills she gave me but they were strong i must have gone off to sleep quite quickly cos i dont remember a thing until i came to in a fuzzy dim way i heard voices close by me before i made out a man in a wheel chair and a tall man behind the chair the one in the chair was maybe 40 give or take and the one standing behind could have been 60 or older hes dead i tell you said chair no hes not said standing he looks dead no he dont im sure i saw his eyes move the sun tell you that and he laffed in a sinister way standing didnt want to show any emotion but he was narked at some level his voice had a bitter edge you look now you can see his eyes opening chair leaned into me and studied my face youre right youre right the sun tell you he was gonna live or die now standing grinned in a strange frightening kind of way you dont understand because you cant speak to the sun we all gotta die under the sun all life is corruptible all decays everyday people live and die under the sun you think the sun is sending packets of light little packets of light but he is sending messages which i alone can hear like what shouted chair o you you havent been given the equipment to receive the messages you cant understand youll never understand all this climate change its just the sun telling us that what were doing is wrong the nerves of the sun and the nerves of human beings are linked but we are too stupid to see this great truth this outburst from standing was followed by silence then chair rocked with lafter and i sat bolt upright which made chair sit back and standing start cant a man get any peace around here i thought this was a very reasonable question but neither chair nor standing seemed inclined to give a response they turned tail and took off disappearing round the corner where i had seen ragend vanish with a flourish of his fingers i felt weak and groggy but perhaps a little less sore i feel screwed by life life and me we just dont get along ever since i can remember ive thought that i was taking little bites out of life but now i see that life has been taking huge lumps out of me what have i been doing but sticking my head in a bucket of shit and swallowing hard jesus when am i ever gonna be free fuck ill end up in a wheel chair pushed around by some freak who talks to the sun or has a beehive up his fucking arse christ i had a case of the blues alright any more of this and id be blubbering like a baby commandant gloria returned just then pushing none other than a wheel chair what the fuck could she read my mind like standing could talk to the sun she saw the state i was in im taking you into supper she said i can walk i said she shook her head anyway im still not hungry nothing i could have said would have made the least difference cos she just hoisted me under the arms and dragged me to the chair and dropped me in you need cheering up and i want you to meet the gang no more words we were off down corridors and past walking wrecks who shuffled and shambled along under their own feeble power the thought passing through my brain that they would reach wherever it was i was going only in time for breakfast but before long the buttery as it was called was announced before i set eyes on it announced by sounds that seemed to come either from a kiddies playground or the chimp enclosure at a zoo high frenzied screeching interspersed with howls and lunatic lafter the scene that greeted me was like a marx brothers movie on acid this one was stealing the food off that ones plate and the responses varied from shrieks and tearful displays to violent threats and even some retaliation in the form of spitting and banging of knives and forks on tables just a normal evening gathering in the alcatraz of loony bins this i would learn in the fullness of time but speaking of that particular time i was reminded of a picture by bosch which gracie had shown me back in the good old days of just a week ago fuck i never knew i had it so good the garden of earthly delights all these crazies struggling and beating themselves up and pursued by imps and demons gloria pushed me against a table and cuffed a man who was leaning over a table and cramming food down the inside of his shirt she cuffed him so hard he staggered away and collapsed onto the floor that caused a stir she knew she had their attention and she shouted to drown out any pockets of noise telling everyone to go back to their places or shed spank their botties and twiddle their knobs this was followed by general lafter but everyone did what she said all the same and the place became quiet and still with only a murmuring like bees in a summer garden i wondered whose arse they were coming from and had a quiet laff to myself i caught the eye of an ancient wrinkled hag seated across from me fuck i could see her dried up dugs cos her nightie was open what a sight this wasnt all cos she only had a few strands of grey hair left up top and then she opened her mouth and gave me a winning smile except her teeth fell out and landed with a loud plop in her soup someone down the table stuck out an arm and pointed at her the whole arm shaking and trembling like it was a divining rod she spat them out she did the agitated man shouted spat them out like she has no use for them well give them to someone else you great cow then he leaned back made a mooing noise which started the whole table and the next table mooing fuck i really didnt know if i could take much more of this but everything went quiet again just like a sunny day can go grey and cold all of a sudden when a rain cloud covers the sun it was the return of the commandant i didnt even know shed left the room but she must have cos she had a tray which she placed on the table in front of me and told me to eat it wasnt so much of a concerned request as a command you gotta keep your strength up was added then she ruffled my hair and moved off to sort out some fractious border dispute between two tables i looked at the food set in front of me food btw is one word for it shitswill is another it was half liquid half solid my best guess was it was supposed to be minced meat mash potato and carrots but everything was so soft and runny you needed a spoon more than a knife and fork i could only think that most of the inmates didnt share a full set of teeth between them and would gum and suck the infant pap or simply lick it off the plate which was exactly what my neighbour to my left was doing leaving remains of it on his nose eyebrows and chin he looked well pleased with himself as he raised his face from the horizontal he was a hunchbacked bald creature with bug eyes and i named him eyegor at once to myself at any rate cos i didnt wanna start any nonsense by inviting him into my world by parleying across the no mans land of rat holes and bomb craters that represented the vast distance of mutual incomprehension that was bound to reveal itself at any attempt at communication but he spoke first though he avoided eye contact in fact he was looking at gummy granny opposite me i suppose theres always something out there we want to torment ourselves with or torment others with the eviscerated entrails of our least half thoughts but why do we have to terrorise ourselves and others just steamroll over them with a fucking tsunami of trivialities and nonsense best shat into a toilet bowl and flushed away was it because i was trapped in a wheel chair and on his radar that he chose me as his victim well i was tired and weak both mentally and physically and imagined he could go apeshit on me and i wouldnt be able to fend him off christ the shame and disgrace of it i mean if that ever got out that i was rolled over by a bald hunchback fuck i wouldnt be able to show my face anywhere south of the watford gap it wouldnt matter up north or scotland cos theyre completely inbred and degenerate there anyway so i let eyegors words float in the air for a moment just in case id misheard him or there was more to follow she likes you who likes me i pointed across at gummy granny who was even now finishing her soup with the bowl raised to her face and her false teeth sitting on the bridge of her nose no came the bald hunchback shout no no no and a furious eye met mine i thought you was just a cripple not backward too fuck me now i was getting insults from a creature who would have been in the vanguard of a troop of freaks not her gloria i must have worn a strange look cos eyegor drew back a little the better to take me in youre lucky cos she dont go for cripples normally sometimes shell stretch to someone on crutches but youre in son you watch if i thought he was talking about what he was talking about my face obviously hadnt caught up with my thinking cos he leaned back in and said not in a low conspiratorial way whatsoever shell give you a blow job thatll make you explode then he picked the one remaining half eaten crusty roll from a basket on the table mimed pulling a pin from it and lobbed it at a far table with a shout of grenade incoming the roll hit an ancient crone on the back of the head and bounced off she was none the wiser wherever she was in her head but it caused an uproar at her table and suddenly there were bits of roll and dirty napkins and catapulted mash and mince flying everywhere i sunk down into my chair watching projectiles flying overhead and hearing the heavy pad of the commandant and others on the floor of the buttery as they arrived to quell the idiot baboons and restore calm and order that was my first supper and my introduction to the gang of drooling misfits who inhabited the ward i didnt touch my food i didnt get the opportunity but as i said before i wasnt hungry anyway when things had quietened down and a few heads and botties smacked i was trundled off and put in a bed in a long room which had around thirty beds in it the grunts and sighs and groans and mad mad lafter coming from the loonies who were going to share my nighttime repose reminded me again of the serengeti plain i was still that wounded wildebeest and i was anxious about what the hyenas and jackals would get up to while i was in the land of nod there was a team at work orchestrated by the commandant battening down the hatches and manhandling the loons an ancient hag approached me and threw something on my bed i looked at her she didnt look much different than the ones getting into bed she dressed just the same as they did and she was just as emaciated standing on stickthin legs she had a scarf tied around her head from under which poked strands of whitegrey hair her face was scored with lines and her eyes were dull and dead as the eyes of a shark she didnt look the type for small talk but i had to ask her what she had thrown on my bed pad was the one blunt word barked at me pad i repeated back to her she fixed me with a look of reproach intolerance and defiance incontinence pad i shook my head stammered i wont be needing that why would i need an incontinence pad so you dont shit and piss into the bed and she moved away then to dispense more caring advice to my neighbours how did i end up here amid lifes rejects and controlled by brute force ignorance and intolerance what had i done to deserve this so id had a few fantasies about cutting nonces up or pissing and shitting on them but i hadnt done much of anything i hadnt even begun to live properly what chance had i had to do that id just been caught and torn by traps like a wild animal stumbling unawares i dont suppose none of us escape them all we can do is realise that a trap is a trap you dont con yourself it aint so its the ones who dont realise it who are fucked theyre finished for good and all i looked round the room and it seemed such a misery that none of these halfwits and idiots would know that the jaws of the trap had them in a tight grip christ they were fretting over nothings all day long and all night too look out the commandant was coming my way you settling in okay what sort of a question was that i gave her a weak smile she didnt press the matter i see the major has paid you a visit she pointed at the incontinence pad you just slip that under you in case of any little accidents in the night and heres a couple of painkillers to see you right she put them down on the covering blanket next to one of my hands then she stood watching me i havent any water ill need water to swallow them she passed me a bottle she took out of a deep pocket in her dressing gown i felt like my choices were few and far between and boiled down to this it was either i took the tabs voluntarily or i had them rammed down my throat by the commandant i unscrewed the top of the bottle and popped the tabs in my mouth when i had swallowed she took the bottle back and pointed at the incontinence pad before having her attention drawn to an outburst at one end of the room she left me to investigate as soon as she was a safe distance away i put a finger in my mouth and hoked out the tabs i didnt care about not getting my beauty sleep i wanted to be awake in case of any nighttime movements including bowel movements the thought of passing a warm shit into a pad and then having to manoover the pad around so i didnt plaster the shit all over my bum and balls fuck i wish id hung around with old peter stuyvesant he was a bit ripe and fruity but they probably wouldnt have found me if id stayed out in the hills too late for that kind of thinking i was momentarily lost in a swamp like bogie in that film where he was the captain of a river boat he never give up and neither will i even without the painkillers i somehow drifted off to sleep i had a couple of dreams that interrupted my sleep and gave me some concern the first one took me back to the buttery gummy granny was pushing her false teeth around her soup bowl with a wooden spoon and as i watched her i felt one of my teeth was loose and i waggled it back and forth with the tip of my tongue suddenly it came completely free and i rolled it around in my mouth then i picked it out and stared at it i know i must have looked a bit weird frightened or shocked or something cos there was a loud cackle of lafter from across the table and gummy granny was rocking back and forth with her mouth wide open and her blackened gums gaping at me i woke up with a start and didnt know where i was for some moments i could see ghostly figures moving about the room gibbering and jabbering to no one in particular i gripped the bedclothes cos suddenly i felt terribly alone and weak and sad if any of them had come near me right then id have screamed the place down but as the seconds passed and turned into minutes i got calmer i found my equilibrium again the old bird back in london she was always talking about equilibrium she was possibly the most equilibriated person i ever knew i was in a bit of a sweat when i first came round from that dream my pillow was drenched and my breathing was rapid and noisy i could feel the blood coursing through my body like a powerful current i lay on my back to get my heart and breathing back to normal just staring at the ceiling it didnt seem real that just the night before i had gone off to sleep under a blanket of stars to the hooting of an owl and now i was banged up with the maddest bunch of retards in an institution stuck in the middle of nowhere i dont know when i flaked out again but now i had a problem in the back passage i could feel a large turtles head poking out but the good news was i could move much better than when i had gone to bed i was hurrying down passages trying doors which were all locked the pressure was building in my back passage i had to find a toilet or i would explode i could see a write up in the papers a grenade must have been secreted up martins arse and when it went off it sent shit flying all over the shop this happened in harrods on a busy day thousands of priceless items were damaged and a couple of chelsea models were drowned in excrement but brave gals they just carried on as if nothing had happened sipping their g&ts and throwing their heads back shaking the shit from their manes and laffing lustily i turned a corner and found a group outside a door my face was a picture of agony by now no 2 is it someone said i nodded and a thin yelp of misery must have escaped my lips well youve got no chance of getting in here cos weve all been waiting for hours weve all got impacted stools and well have to dig the shit out of our bottoms with our fingers i felt like fainting felt decidedly queasy and at odds with the world the floor was getting wobbly and the walls were floating towards me and away from me i was having to clench my buttocks so hard that my face was getting redder and redder i stumbled off with lafter and ironic shouts behind me but i hadnt gone very far when i found a toilet door open i rushed inside and practically threw myself on the toilet pulling my pants off with a shout of joy and relief but in my haste i had left the door open and in poured a straggle of people who bunched around each other with gleeful expectant expressions firmly fixed on their faces mind if we watch i froze the pressure was unbearable in my bum hole and im sure my face was a picture of agony and despair which only made the group at the door howl with lafter i woke up then breathing hard the old heart going like the clappers and sweat running down my face and back and pooling in armpits and crotch there was a little man sitting on a chair a few feet from my bed watching me he was a grey haired sallow sort of little man unthreatening inoffensive i thought but what was he doing sitting there you were making noises in your sleep he said was i he nodded im norm norman what they call you martin i replied and at the very same time i felt a movement in the back passage can you help me norman i said i could hear a pleading tone in my voice ill do my best though usually its me asking other people for help i need to go to the toilet can you help me get there norman sat blinking considering it seemed decisiveness was not a part of his make up even as the movement became more violent and the turtles head inched out of my bottom something twigged with old norman eventually perhaps the increasing volume of moans and groans escaping from my throat i managed to get myself to the edge of the bed i put an arm round little norm and using him as a crutch we set off for the lavatories ill give the man his due he was no complainer he bore up as best he could and the pain in my anus seemed to dispel the ache in my back i shed a little lump of turd on the way to the loo i dont think norman noticed least ways he didnt say anything i wasnt wearing any underpants under the gown they had dressed me in and the turtles head just slipped out without any effort i was barely on the bowl when the rest shot out of my arse like shrapnel from a cannon fuck it was like my whole innards got pooped out then norman waited for me like a good soldier and we were just leaving the lavvy when there was a howl of anger and hurt coming from the ward whos that i said to norm thats the major he replied she does her rounds in the middle of the night sure enough when we come back to the ward she was there with a look of thunder on her face what you two doing out of bed he needed to go volunteered norm and the major fixed me with a bayonet of a look so you are the fucker who shat on the floor i tried to smile but it had no effect on the major i stepped in that you fuckwit i should have made you clean it up sorry i said but it sounded so pathetic she stormed off then muttering to herself and norman got me back into bed i thanked him and hoped he wouldnt get into trouble over my unappreciated gift he smiled and shook his head he told me not to worry you should see this place in the morning its like a human sewer the major doesnt hold grudges shell have forgotten all about it she wont even remember who you are as it happened he was wrong about that cos when i come to in the morning i was groggy as hell and my limbs felt sore and heavy i could hear all this jabbering going on around me a sort of rumbling commotion and something was poking me in the chest it was the major spitting fire and brimstone at me digging into me with two bony fingers when the morning stars sang together and all the sons of god shouted for joy where were you in your indolence dyou understand me shitboy no i dont fucking understand you you old witch fuck off and leave me alone course i only said this to myself i wasnt exactly in a position to defend myself what is it you want i blurted out what i want no what i need is you to get up get out of bed get dressed washed and go to buttery for eat 5 minutes no more you still here we throw you out of bed onto floor i could see why she was called the major she didnt hang around to help me but was off at a brisk pace poking other halfawake denizens in the chest or the ribs and prodding them out of bed i sat up and stretched a bit there were a lot of walking dead shuffling about going round in circles twitching and shaking and trying to take their clothes off the commandant was there with her helpers steering the shuffling zombies this way and that well i had my marching orders so delicately and with great effort i pulled myself to the side of the bed and swung my legs out and sat there breathing i looked across the wide aisle that separated the beds on my side from identical beds on the other side there was an old bloke he looked near 90 if he was a day and he hadnt a stitch on he had little man boobs and a saggy belly like a halfdrained wine goatskin i wondered if he felt as shitty crappy as i did right then perhaps he had nothing going on in his head it was every day the same for him sleep eat shit sleep eat shit sleep this mantra was getting stuck in my head when one of the helpers a burly girl like a russian shot putter on steroids lifted him up to a standing position removed a crumpled pad from between his legs and dumped same into a black binliner which looked stuffed with pads already and was responsible with other stuffed binliners for the rank reek that hung in the air it was a smell like 5 day old cabbage mixed with stale urine and vomit and meat that had gone off and of course shit the funny thing was i felt really hungry and was looking forward to breakfast no matter how bad it was i was just gearing up to launch myself to a standing position when the shot putter wiped the old boys arse and sprinkled talcum powder liberally down his arse cheeks before sitting him back down on a fresh incontinence pad she then turned away from him to deal with his neighbour i was feeling it was just about the time i should attempt to stand when colonel talcum stood up lifted the pad from under his bum and somehow separated the layers of paper from the plastic base he stepped into it then like he was putting on a kilt and wandered off from his bed holding his newfangled skirt up with one hand i creased up with lafter id seen some funny things but this was a good one and almost worth the admission price to this loony bin of course the shot putter was rabid with rage and hauled him back to his bed when she saw he had made his great escape but he wasnt the only one facing a reprimand cos the major had returned with another gold medallist from the russian shot putt team i was yanked off the edge of the bed faster than you could say feedor dostoievski and then i did a wonderful impression of bambi on ice tilting forwards and backwards watching the floor slide this way and that whats wrong with him said the shotputter whose name i soon learned was jess the major didnt so much as look at me she dismissed me with a mumbled comment jess forget about him he shits on the floor so people can stand in it hes a dirty dog i hadnt the strength or desire to respond all my strength my willpower was focussed on staying upright and steering clear of flailing arms and bodies that seemed hellbent on careening into me and sending me for 6 like a last skittle in a bowling lane that you just have to knock down or the world wont function right itll all be topsy turvy with the rain falling upwards and fish falling from the sky until you send that skittle flying somehow anyway i made it to the showers which unbefuckinglievably were open and for one and all so i saw some tragic sights there of hanging flaps of skin from arms and waists and old cocks that hadnt been in pussies for longer than id been alive and i cant even describe to you the ancient pussies cos i really really tried not to look at their brillo pads i was holding on to the idea of breakfast so strongly i just had to grit my teeth close my eyes and take the quickest shower in the history of the guinness book of records i used my gown to dry off and found a store with clean gowns by the time i entered the buttery i was feeling quite a lot better the shower and the nights sleep had definitely restored some movement and strength back to me it was the same chaos at the meal as the previous evening i didnt care i stuffed as many bread

51

rolls into me and spooned the pap while the monkeys jabbered and the loonies raved and fired missiles at each other afterwards i found norman all by himself in a room with a view he looked normal to me sort of like his name and i watched him staring out the window for a little while before going over to him i plopped down into a chair next to his and he turned to me with a gentle smile you feeling better i nodded i told him i had some lethal bruising in the small of my back and the top of my bum he didnt react he seemed different to the others and not that old maybe early 60s what are you doing here norman oh i like it here i come for the view and not many people come here i looked at the view myself then in the distance i could see the hills where crazy peter stuyvesant had shown me his revolver what did you do before before said norman and turned a concerned face to me yeah before you came here i worked for the bbc you never i said without thinking it was an automatic response cos i couldnt get my head round what someone who had worked for the beeb was doing in this nuthouse questions were beginning to buzz around inside my head like bluebottles trapped in a jar i worked in research for a current affairs programme i did a lot of research about maggie i must have looked a bit uncertain cos he repeated the name maggie mrs thatcher oh yeah i said my mum hated her lots of people hated her said norman did you ever meet her norman shook his head no of course not i worked in this little room with two or three others and we all stayed very much in the background good work was it interesting oh very said norman what happened to you i mean whyd you end up here norman gave a sigh he looked out of the window again and stayed that way for some time i didnt feel like pushing him he never turned back to me but he opened up about himself in a quiet matteroffact voice i lived with my mother all my life until she passed away just going into the bbc and back home we didnt do a lot together sometimes went to the theatre or took day trips to the coast but when she passed away i felt very lonely it didnt help that i was at work in fact it made it worse i couldnt cope with the job any more and i just stopped going i cant really explain it very well even to myself my doctor told me i was depressed and one thing led to another and they put me into hospital for a while to see if it would help and one day they brought me here i tell you i felt very strange lissening to normans story it sounded downright fucking nuts norman i said you dont belong here not among all these loonies he turned to me and there was a sadness in his eyes its no use i cant go back out into the world you walk indifferent streets under an indifferent sky nobody cares for you and i cant take care of myself i thought he was gonna start crying then and if his waterworks had started mine wouldve too you know you mustnt think of them as mad or lunatic theyre just people who lost their way somewhere sometime and they never found their way back into the world they all have stories to tell they all have heartaches nobody gets a free ticket to happiness in this world fuck that knocked the wind out of my sails i couldnt think of a solitary thing to say to him cos i knew in my heart of hearts in my inner being that he was right he was right all the way down from the top to the bottom and i think the only difference between him and me was that somehow from somewhere i had been given the strength to fight back against that indifference in fact often it had been

more than indifference it had been downright undiluted hostility from teachers
and policemen and just random strangers out in the street or on a bus giving me
the evil eye as if to test me and see if i was strong enough to stand up for myself
i think that must be why i began to watch all them kung fu and samurai films
they seeped into my soul and gave me strength to look the indifferent world in
the eye and tell it to back off and watch itself the world wasnt no sound of music
for me it was the sound of one hand clapping cos the other hand had been severed
by a single blow from a tempered steel blade describing a precise arc with a
swish like a sudden intake of breath all the same i couldnt help but feel sorry for
norman he was truly one of the wretched of the earth ekeing out a living death
in an institution full of other wretched souls i thought hed finished his little
homily but he opened up a bit more to me maybe he felt i was someone he could
talk to i dunno if that was the case maybe i didnt know myself so well maybe the
old bird gracie back in chelsea hadnt been so far off the mark when she told me
one day that there were mysteries and ghosts and whole continents to be
discovered deep within myself i couldnt fathom what she meant at the time but
maybe i was just getting a tiny inkling of what she was on about like a chink of
light penetrating the dark of my cell i missed her right then and there if she had
somehow miraculously appeared to me id have thrown my arms around her and
hugged her half to death id have thrown in a couple of kisses on her lined and
ravaged cheeks french fashion which she wouldnt have liked in the least cos she
had no love of the french on account of they were a bunch of collaborating
wooses in the war she didnt actually say wooses but i cant recall now the word
she used she had such a monumental vocabulary that sometimes i thought me
and she were speaking different languages suddenly i was aware that norman
was saying something that fellow opposite you the old boy colonel talcum i said
norman looked confused his names mcfarlane robert mcfarlane now it was my
turn to be confused the old boy with the saggy belly and the man boobs i ventured
he must be nearly 90 there was a flicker of a smile on normans serious face i
suppose you could describe him thus he said the decay of the flesh is not a sight
that edifies hes 92 and you look at him now and all you see is a façade destroyed
imagine coming upon the ruins of a great city in the desert the winds and the
sands have worn down the edifices over the centuries and it is impossible to
construct in the minds eye the great and bustling metropolis of a bygone age its
the same with us you see robert served in the korean war i dont know exactly
what he did but he marched to the beat of the drum of history youre far too young
to understand this youre only creating your history now but one day you notice
that you are getting slower as the world speeds up and you are forced to the
sidelines whether you like it or not the major stuck her head in and peered at us
for some moments before ducking out again shes a strange bird who said norman
cos he hadnt seen her the major i could see immediately from norms face that he
hadnt a baldy notion who i was talking about i have a habit of making up names
and attaching them for no particular reason to people i dont know or havent been
introduced to i used to do it to some of the cunts in chelsea that i stalked like
dribbly arsc or burning dick anyway after id established with norm who i was

referring to he told me she was called helena and was originally from latvia or lithuania one of them baltic countries and shed come over to here a few years after the war when she was about 12 she still had a touch of an accent and even id noticed that she still hustled and bustled about for an old gal in her early 80s shes tough as old boots said norm and his face brightened a little as the words flew from his lips it must run in the family he said next and before i could pose a question sos i could get his meaning he laid it on me that gloria was helenas granddaughter what the fuck howd that come about i was so disturbed by this new information that i was certain the floor was beginning to shift and wobble and then i saw how stupid it sounded what id said howd that come about what i meant was what was gloria doing in here but old norman must have got hold of the correct end of the stick cos he explained that the commandant was in here on a voluntary basis she could leave whenever she pleased but she wanted to stay on account of the major cos helena had brought her up after her parents glorias had just upped sticks and fucked off into the night when gloria was around 10 norman didnt know much more but one thing he was sure of they were thick as thieves the pair you didnt want to offend the one cos then you offended the other and they didnt need to speak much they just knew what the other was thinking and feeling ive seen helena standing over glorias bed in the middle of the night just watching her as she slept i understand that you see said norman i sometimes went into my mothers room when she was still alive and just watched her breathing you ever thought about how many breaths we take in a lifetime martin how many beats of our hearts one day it will come your last breath and the last beat of your heart and it doesnt matter if you live a hundred years or more in the end its but a drop in the ocean of time you know you hear of some man or woman lived to be over a hundred and you think that was a long life there was some woman died a few years ago and she remembered seeing vincent van gogh in his cups almost every evening this was in arles and she was only 7 at the time its this connection with the past that speaks to us it conjures up a lost world before the motor car and the aeroplane and computers and mobile phones but its not so long ago when you think about the passing of the ages a sapling grows in a forest in california as the normans and the saxons fight it out at hastings and nine hundred years later it is still standing was it your lot then at that battle the normans id stopped norman in his tracks he blinked at me and then smiled it was a stupid silly joke but he didnt mind ta ta norman im off for a lie down and i really needed a lie down i was still pretty weak but also mentally i was spent i hadnt talked to so many fuckers in all my days norm was alright norm was good but i missed my solitude my peace i had it perfect and cushty in london and right now i regretted running off from my room would i ever get it back and even if i did my card was marked by the gorillas in the main part of the building as i stretched out on top of my bed i could feel a heaviness descend on me weighting me down and closing my eyelids before i knew it i was off to dreamland i was alone on a boat in a vast ocean or rather i was the boat and the waves were moving and pushing me from below in a monstrous swell towering over me like great hills of water bearing down on me they were so big they blotted out the sky and the sky and the sea became one i was so small and frail i felt really afraid that any moment i would be swamped the water come crashing down on me and break me asunder but i knew i wanted to go on i had to weather the storm and reach the safe haven cos far off there was a small light i could just make out when the waves plummeted down i was struggling towards that light but being beaten back the light was growing dimmer and receding and the sky was now dark as night and a wave was climbing higher and higher and i the small craft at its base was going to be drowned i woke up in a tangle of bed clothes it was growing dark had i slept so long i was bathed in sweat the ward was strangely still and quiet i noticed that many of the beds were empty then i thought i could make out the distant clamour of feeding time in the buttery at one end of the room there was something going on there was a screen round a bed and the shot putters were coming and going i managed to disentangle myself from my bed clothes and struggled out of bed i was still wobbly on my feet but i was curious to find out what was going on step by precarious step i closed in on the screen and i could hear hushed voices behind it he was a cunt anyway said one and another added i hated the way he expected you to bow and scrape to him whod he think he was when i was only about 10 feet from the screen i heard heels clacking on the floor and before i could turn round to get a look at whoever was approaching a doctor passed me and pulled back the screen with an authoritative flourish there was a thin man lying on his back on the bed with his mouth open he already looked stiff as a board and his colour was a sort of pasty offwhite apart from mother in her coffin id never seen a corpse but i was looking at one now the doctor did some perfunctory tests he sounded the dead mans chest yo ho ho and a bottle of rum and shone a light in his eyes and that was about it then he signed a form on a clipboard turned and marched past me without so much as a how dyou do or a nod of acknowledgement but one of the shotputters noticed me alright and sauntered over to me seen something interesting she said but it wasnt friendly and it wasnt kind i turned to go but she caught me by the arm and led me over to the bed youve come this far you might as well get your moneys worth and then i was standing at the side of the bed looking down at this stranger from whom the last breath had departed in whom the final heart beat had stopped everything had closed down all the internal organs switched off and the traffic of the blood stalled forever his mouth was a black cavern in which some yellowed stubs of teeth could be glimpsed above a thin bluish lower lip meet mr waugh the commandant said i confess i hadnt even heard her approach mr war i stammered this produced cackles of lafter all round not war you idiot waugh w a u g h i felt like i was back at school he was a misogynist you know what that is dont you i must have looked confused and uncertain cos one of the shotputters pointed at a book on a small table it was a copy of miltons poems he hated women just like milton but you dont hate women do you cos you know what we do to women haters we come in the middle of the night and cut off his willie thats enough now said gloria leave the boy alone and one of the shotputters came over to me then and ruffled my hair he knows were only fucking with him gloria took hold of me then and pulled me away from the bed as we walked off down the ward i could hear the shotputters talking about the unfortunate deceased misogynist thats when most of them go they take a shit cos they havent gone for a day or two and he was one who held on to his shit forever he was a miserly old sod and then they have to strain so hard to push it out that wham bam its too much for the old ticker and its like a grenade explodes there glad you found him when you did cos any later and hed have started stiffening up in the loo well wed better get started cleaning him up for the morgue i cant bear the thought of even touching him well wear protective goggles and double up on the marigolds this grumbling went on in the background as gloria guided me down the ward and out of it she took me to her office closed the door and stood looking at me for all the world like she was assessing and appraising a bullock in a pen lift up your gown she said in a voice with an undertone of sly adventure but ive got no underpants on i stammered to tell the truth i was feeling a strange mixture of feelings i did feel threatened it was true but at the same time excited my heart was churning like a concrete mixer and my chest was rising and falling as my breathing grew more rapid i wasnt even thinking no more as i lifted my gown i had a semi on already cos my imagination was running riot turn around she said i wanna take your temperature i did as told now bend over the desk i was curious and tense with excitement now wheres she gonna put the thermometer that was the question and i didnt have to wait many seconds for the answer cos i felt her tongue licking my undercarriage fuck my eyes were goggling now but i blinked fast when she stuck a pinkie up my button she turned her finger this way and that and i reckon i must have looked very japanese right then all buck teeth and slanty eyes do you like that she said as she cupped my balls and started to massage them i now sounded japanese as a high pitched tone escaped my open mouth and rose and fell in response to her twirling about in my arse button and without removing her finger she eased me round so that i was now resting a hip on the edge of the desk my noboguchi was fully out of its sheath her lips were on it swift as a sparrow hawk on a field mouse little yelps and moans were rising up from throat and lifting into the air like champagne bubbles from a swanky glass she was sucking me good and proper this wasnt any old run of the mill vacuum job this was a supercharged dyson with turbo attachment gloria mumbled something with my cock just about to crow in her mouth i really shouldnt have cared what she was saying but i heard myself say what she stopped sucking and playing ping pong with her tongue on my knob released me and looked up at my face heavy with sensuality yeah i must have resembled a pig with heavy glazed eyes but her response awoke my other faculties for a brief moment isnt death such a turn on i just get so fucking horny when i see a dead body even with a fierce erection the part of my mind that reasons and connects the dots between me and not me could see the funny side and i fired off a bit of wit i guess it wouldnt be such a turn on if i was a dead body gloria had a giggle at that and clamped her mouth around the jolly roger sucking it like a demon woman and kneading my ball sack till i fired off like big bertha on the western front cos i was in no way quiet about it i came like a noisy parade with a throaty growl and a high pitched hats in the air triumphant yelp and stood trembling and flooded with ease and joyful fulfilment even as the artful dodger was pulsing and vibrating like a high board after the diver has executed a half pike with gyroscopic twist i was spent i definitely needed to lie down again suddenly the door opened and a man with a pained expression was standing looking at my deflated dripping willie i covered up as fast as i could gloria got to her feet and barked at him yes jimbo what is it didnt i tell you about knocking before you open the door he blinked this jimbo blinked and screwed up his nose a number of times i thought i heard people in here gloria took a deep breath yes obviously there are people in here i was just examining martin here who had a nasty accident the other day what is it you want jimbo said nothing but stood blinking and wrinkling his nose ah the infinite patience of imbeciles who have lost the why and the wherefore of their lives i thought i heard people in here i could see it was going to be impossible to move jimbo from his entrenched position it was a one statement fits all arguments for him but the commandant knew this all too well and she moved to end the excitement and thrill of this standoff by moving to the door and turning jimbo round booting him up the backside and closing the door firmly i took to my bed after this all spunked out and dithery fuck maybe i wasnt no errol flynn cocksman after all or maybe i was still recovering from the giant haystacks drop and knee to the back that the gorilla guard visited on me anyway the elation of the bj wore off sooner than i thought it would i fell into a troubled sleep i was back in my aunts house and up in my mothers room the whole atmosphere of my aunts cloys and chokes like the smell of an undertakers jesus i have never been much of a son but i feel useless sitting next to my mother wasting away and eaten up by cancer i haunt the town most days until hunger gets a hold of me and my feet lead me along the beaten path to my aunts another aunt my mums older sister is there with her stiff of a partner billy they sit expressionless on the other side of the bed fuck it reminds me of every sunday evening the worst of times for family dropping round the worst of times to hear the greatest load of drivel how billy tunes his bikes and keeps his car in good nick cant decide as i look at them if they arent already dead and im in an antechamber of purgatory they have their baby with them and he starts up bawling his lungs out and making me want to join in with him id be protesting against life itself the unfairness of it all the randomness and the hurt but ian michael little hooligan is protesting loudly his right to life hes booked his ticket on planet earth and he demands to be noticed he wants his food well it gets rid of laura just leaving billy the mechanic and me i cant even look at him its all i can do to think of the suffering my mother is going through slipping out of life it was only yesterday i was in the babys place mother nursing me cooing to me surrounded by aunts and uncles i woke up then with a terrible feeling in my throat and chest it was an anguish i wanted to expel from my body with a scream out of the corner of my eye i could see there was someone sitting at the end of my bed it was norman my face must have been twisted into a greek tragedy mask with the effort to stifle my scream you alright asked norm and i stared at him until a single tear began to flow down one of my cheeks whats the matter norm pressed me quietly and i didnt say nothing just sat there breathing in little gasps with the ward out of focus as if seen through a stained glass window christ what was going on was someone putting some fucking drug into my tea i felt like i didnt know myself no more i was just a quintessence of dust a whirligig of atoms in flux why was i feeling all this now it was like i had a deep wound and someone had peeled off the bandages exposing flies and maggots crawling all over a raw and bloody hole norman was nothing if not patient i could imagine him beavering away for decades in a bbc cupboard digging up data for some ponce in a suit and tie to read out in a news bulletin in a clipped eton accent i began to smile through my tears and right there and then i knew i couldnt put no blame on old norman for the lies the beeb had put out over the years he was too soft a target for that anyway hed paid the price for having his gonads in a corporate vice for so long theyd fucking emasculated the poor sod and i felt drawn to him he was the only friend i had in the world at that moment and in spite of my usual reluctance to drop my guard i was gonna do it with him cos he was alright was norman he wasnt a cunt like most of them on the outside i was thinking about my mother norm she wasnt even 40 when she died just eaten up with cancer she was the best thing in my childhood you know what im talking about when she put her arms about me it was like the world was a better place she was gonna keep all the hate and the hurt away from me and i didnt even know how lucky i was when i was very little she would hold me tight against her so tight i could hear the beat of her heart and that was all that mattered the world was far away then the world was not the place she was the centre of my world of my universe and when i fell asleep in her arms then it was bliss to me and a happiness descended on me like ive never known since norman was crying now his face contorted into his own version of an attic disposition you know something norm were a right pair of nonces you and me look at us carrying on this way he smiled i smiled it must have hurt his face cos it was killing me to smile wed better not let the loonies catch us like this we wiped our eyes and looked about us we were fortunate indeed that hardly anyone was about to witness our display of emotion there were one or two floating about lost in their own world of dementia and vacant emptiness you know whats my favourite memory of my mother i said we were now composed and calm norm and me i was about 10 it was only a couple of years before she passed away it was a sunday and she asked me to go for a walk with her we went down to the beach it was about a mile from where we lived and we went on further to a headland full of gorse bushes with a winding path over rocks and on the way back the weather turned around and it began to rain we sheltered in the lee of a wall with buttresses we didnt talk we just waited for the rain to pass over and at one point i looked at my mother as she studied the sky for signs of change and i felt at one with her i wanted the moment to last and last so that we never went back to the house and resumed the life that goes on every day and every day takes something away from you until there is nothing left but a picture in your head and a feeling that you will never recapture that moment of lost content norman was smiling now in a quiet dignified way on na coon mare he said his eyes bright and full of warmth i must have shown some small sign of not knowing what the fuck he was talking about it was all greek to me thats from kamoo he said have you read any of his novels i shook my head one only has one mother thats what it means thats what what means i said what i just told you in french i sat and blinked at norman thinking it wasnt worth the effort of going any further down the road of explication or elucidation it couldnt make any difference to me if i never found out what hed been referring to there are plenty of mysteries you just have to take to your grave without ever getting to the bottom of them its like the mystery of life itself the more you find out lissening to old attenborough balls the more you know theres so much more the sly old dog hasnt told you and you could live as long as methuselah and youd still croak feeling short changed and wanting to experience one more episode of life of being in the world a living loving sentient being jesus it was like someone had just slipped me a happy pill we smiled at one another and then i saw a frown cross norms face just like a cloud passing in front of the sun i followed the gaze of his eyes and saw the major with a nasty scowl screwing up and squishing her features before she moved off out of the ward whats with her i said norman studied me for some moments as if he was weighing up whether to speak to me or not she knows he said at last knows what i said about you and gloria i tried to act casual but i could feel my heart rate going up i could feel the blood throbbing in my ears i dont know what youre on about i lied in my most convincing manner though it didnt appear to convince norman he shrugged and for a moment his lips were pinched together but then he opened his mouth and uttered the one word jimbo well id no comeback there so i asked him if everyone knew not that it really fucking mattered what a bunch of halfwits thought of me except why was i feeling apprehensive and a bit down yeah jimbo come round everyone telling them how you were the stuffing and gloria was the turkey gobbling you up i sank back into my bed this was about as bad as it could get i was randal mcmurphy and id been seen getting a bj off nurse ratchet i needed a chief to bust me out of this hole cos i had a feeling things were not in my favour gloria was gonna use me as her sex slave and the knowledge of that didnt fill my heart with joy and the stupid thing was i should have been over the moon in a rocket about it i mean imagine some years down the line i could be standing at a bar telling a mate about it yeah i was banged up in this mental ward with all these mental cases and it was run by this wellbuilt girl with large handfuls and she was crazy for it and drained my dick nearly every day and he would look at me this mate and tell me i was one lucky lucky bastard in fact i could probably dine out on this saga in years to come i could maybe even turn her into my sex slave but why then was i feeling like shit and wanting to break out of the loony ward there was a story gracie had told me about this warrior odysseus who was clever as clever in fact too clever for his own good and at the end of a long war he set off for home which was a long way off across the sea he had loads of adventures like escaping from a oneeyed giant by covering himself in a sheepskin and pretending he was a sheep i dont know if its a welsh story but i reckon theres loads of welshmen would go for that up in the hills with no one else around one of them playing the shepherd and twiddling on his pink oboe anyway this odysseus gets shipwrecked on this island where theres this really fit bird called circe and she uses him as her sex slave and he stayed on her island for years and yet he wanted to get away and when you first hear the story you think whats wrong with odysseus 3 squares a roof over his head all he and his merry crew can eat and sex on a plate but there was something missing in this paradise his happiness lay elsewhere and i was beginning to appreciate his point of view i couldnt even tell myself what life i wanted to live but it couldnt be this one the life you want to lead is one of your own choosing and i definitely had not chosen to live in dementialand with the fairies my gloom and doom seeped into me like a virus i got more intimate with the commandant but there was a coldness about our fucking even when i was rampacked up her pussy so that i was sure i was tickling her tonsils with my bellend i had a sort of outofbody experience and my better angel was sad watching the horny little demon thrusting like zorro with his fine blade she never noticed gloria she was indifferent to my feelings she knew how to get me aroused and ready for intergalactic penetration of space capsule into space station and she was as cold as interstellar space what i was afraid of was that one day i would be unable to get it up and perform and even during some frantic exchange of fluids when her mouth was running off like a burst water main with all kinds of fruity talk i had to focus real hard on the task in hand cos otherwise id have slipped out of her and shrunk back to a wrinkled peanut and god knows what her reaction would have been one day i was having a doze in bed when i was prodded awake by bony fingers i think i knew who it was even before i opened my eyes there she was the major standing over me with narrowed eyes i know what you do you think i dont i sat up wondering why she had decided to have a go at me now there was a man in a wheelchair at the end of the bed it was the man who had come to take a look at me when i first arrived on the ward make yourself useful shitty boy and push desmond around desmond by the by did not seem entirely enthusiastic concerning this notion i wondered where the tall man had got to the one who had been pushing him around as i lay on the stinky sofa feeling bruised and battered and sorry for myself what seemed like a small age ago of course i said nothing got up and stood behind desmond looking down at a bald patch fuck wheelchair bound and with a bald patch i felt a bit sorry for the man mind you in short order any sympathy for him soon evaporated as i got to know him a little better where to your highness ill admit that wasnt the most sutile of remarks to start with the major walked off and left us to our own devices and she was barely out of earshot when desmond told me to keep my comments to myself and push him round the ward any particular direction i said no replied desmond you follow your nose its big enough well that was tit for tat and it should have warned me desmond wasnt the docile and forgiving kind hed probably been harbouring a grudge against me from the moment he set eyes on me of course i didnt know this but it makes sense him in a wheelchair and me ambulatory with a big conk anyway i whisked him round the joint a number of times with a running commentary this is the buttery where we stuff our cakeholes and this is the khazi where we eject the pap out of our arseholes it was along these lines the commentary with some nice acid remarks about fellow inmates i wasnt exactly having fun but it passed the time though i knew the time was fated to pass willy nilly one thing i didnt notice on my travels with desmond was how he was looking and when we came by the commandants office and i heard raised voices i put the brakes on to have a good lissen the major and gloria were having a decent barney and i could hear my name being dragged into it fuck youd think i was the one responsible for starting the war the way they were getting on i happened to glance down at desmond to maybe give him a conspiratorial wink as if to say women what can you do mate but i was taken aback by his look his face was bright red and his teeth were bared like a furious chimp and then i did the stupidest thing cos i leaned into him as if that was gonna help he tried a straight uppercut and it only missed me by a whisker fuck he was wired up and so angry he started to cry and carry on greeting like a manchild and drawing all the loons from every corner of the ward it was like a scene from frankenstein somehow i was the monster and they were the inbred villagers if theyd had pitchforks they definitely wouldve used them the commotion brought the commandant out of the office and she quelled any insurrection with a single shout and a look that brooked no reply i could see the major on tbe blower in the background and i had a funny feeling she was talking about me a few days later this suspicion was confirmed by the entry of these officious looking twats who brought me my clothes and my chaucer and led me out of the ward and the institution and took me to this car they barely spoke to me and i couldnt help but feel i was jumping from the frying pan into the fire the gorillas and stumpy bert and the major all wore triumphant smiles as i departed and the only downer was a last glimpse of norman staring out of one of the big ward windows with the forlorn and lost look of a lonely child

Chapter IV
The Dance of Illusion

i was driven back to london it was almost too good to be true all the riotous hodgepodge of buildings the constant toing and froing and coming and going of cars and vans and bikes and buses the constant noise of engines and wheels rolling on tarmacadam and honking of horns and squealing of brakes and people people everywhere of all ages and colours and sizes and dressed up and down in the city and in camden town i was having the most drugged up drug free high i was so nearly purely happy i could have kissed the twats who had pulled me off the ward if the major thought she was putting one over on me she wasnt i was brer rabbit and i was back in the briar patch of course i didnt actually go ahead and kiss the twats i was too much at peace to violate the space between them and me they seemed happy enough to ignore me for the most part just keeping a wary eye on me as we sped past parks and gardens to an anonymous block of a building and turned into an underground cavern of a car park i was brought up into the bowels of the building and made to wait in a room with an ancient secretary who shot me the odd look of disdain down her nose as she typed away at her computer she was the conservative party type all starch and tight sphincter i held tight to my chaucer cos i didnt want ms carruthers worrying about the precious books and magazines on display on a low table i wanted to tell her in no uncertain terms that i wasnt interested in the horsey set in berkshire except i could rig up a dummy fox with explosives and blow a hunt to kingdom come i suddenly remembered watching this film on tv with my mother it was an old one but it had this fit girl and she was having an affair with this landowner he fancied himself alright as a ladies man he was always polishing his noboguchi inside some high class tart but this was different cos her nobility was a nobility of character and at the end of the film she was running across his land and there were horses and hounds but she had hold of this fox and was protecting it how we willed her to get away from the hounds and she did she fell down an old disused well the shock of that ending brought my mother out in tears and i was hugging her and couldnt stop my own flood cos i knew right then that the world was a cruel and indifferent place and you only have a moment in all eternity a single blessed moment of love and happiness in the arms of someone you love before you fall down that stupid well and break your neck are you alright there it was ms carruthers peering over the top of her glasses at me she didnt look particularly concerned or anything and i seriously doubted she had a concerned bone in her body but i realised i must have made some little noise while i was reliving the memory of watching that film with my mother im alright i said in fact im more than alright and i dont wanna touch none of your glossies i indicated the country lifes and the anteek catalogues on the low table and with an air of im better than you though you think youre better than me i raised aloft my chaucer and opened it fuck some malignant tumour of a twat had drawn a cock and balls and scrawled my name beneath it is nothing sacred in this putrid armpit of a world i had a fair idea who had perpetrated this indignity stumpy bert or one of the gorillas fuck theyd better not send me back to them or ill burn their institution to the ground just like the first mrs rochester you can go in now said the tight sphincter and i snapped my chaucer shut and stood up mustering and composing my limbs for battle while a bloody insurrection was being quelled at hq how dare they deface my chaucer i know exactly what old chaucer chops would have thought about it he would have had their collyons in his hand and hed have given them a right old squeeze anyway with this riot going on upstairs i went into this big room not much in it apart from seats round the walls and a huge desk with a woman who could have been ms carruthers mother or spinster aunt behind it and flanked by two suits whose names were johnson and johnson i cant remember what name the battleaxe gave but i more than half suspected she had a johnson too cos i imagined she was concealing something a lot more sinister than a fox they didnt do things by halves this trio of pofaced bureaucrats for as soon as id plonked my posterior on the seat in front of the desk they all smiled in unison it would have taken a hispeed camera to pick apart which one cracked their face first i havta tell you it wasnt exactly a pleasant experience them all smiling cos none of the three was smiling with their eyes i was waiting for them to turn their heads through 360 degrees and vomit green bile all over me and for starch and sphincter old sourpuss carruthers to come running in from her little cubby hole with a large butchers knife to stick me in the back martin how are you feeling now this was sourpuss mater i found it strangely difficult to answer such a simple question cos id got so used to keeping my feelings to myself before twats in authority and i suspected a trap these bureau types string you along so far and then when your heads in the noose they tighten it and dangle you like musso the wop from the nearest lamppost im alright i heard myself say and a tiny voice inside me told me to not give anything away youve been through a very troubling time this was the thief or the murderer to one side of the weird jesus in the middle that wasnt a question so i didnt feel like i needed to answer i could feel a slight movement in the lower part of my face it was an attempt at a smile i think though i dont know how it came across the cynic who sits in a loft conversion in part of my brain was smoking a cheroot and telling me not to overdo it that was good son you didnt overplay that smile you keep it up maybe throw in a sigh now and again but dont milk it cos they get a whiff of that of you putting it on and theyll turn on you like a mutinous crew of sea dogs i bit my bottom lip thats the spirit said the cynic and put some dave brubeck on his swedish hifi deck fuck hed gone back to vinyl and i suspected i would if i had the money and lost what little sense i still clung to the other johnson plucked the cheroot right from between my lips with his question how did i find grangemount i must have raised at least one eyebrow that was the name of the hospital you just left there was so much i could have said in response to this little bite of information such as i never got settled in enough to find out what the shithole was called nor did i care cos no one else seemed to care and most of the denizens were lost in the labyrinths of their own minds turning and turning in ever decreasing circles the three smiles with each more like a cruel rictus than a smile the sort of cold smiles on the faces of mexcians in a spaghetti western mexcians who speak even without twitching a muscle in their faces with voices that seem to come from a back room in the cantina which is probably why the man with no name almost never replies to any of their stupid comments or when he does he lets his six shooter do the talking the three smiles switched off all at the same time on the faces of johnson & johnson and matron which was odd cos the next words from the lady in charge contradicted this return to the unsmiling status quo i wont bore you with the blow by blow account of what she said but the upshot was undeniably a turn up in the fortunes of a foundling or however else you want to romanticise my vomit ball of an existence she said id been treated very badly abominably said one of the johnsons at least i think thats what he said cos his lips barely moved and he may have been simply clearing his throat yeah id been treated very badly and it was the opinion of the committee that i was to be taken to a place of public execution there to be hung drawn and quartered at least thats what i decoded their mumblings and throat clearings to be saying cos i couldnt believe my own ears when they said i was gonna get a small flat to myself and a key to the front door id still be under supervision from a social worker but they deemed i fell in love with that word immediately it was uttered deemed i was fit to be given a measure of control over my life fuck me back to chelsea and all the old fruits in the anteek business great day in the morning but wait a mo they werent saying chelsea what was they saying hackney o fuck murder central if ever this was proof of the existence of god the old bugger was laffing up his celestial sleeve yeah welcome back to london but you have to be careful what you wish for you keep your nose clean and ill send an angel to watch over you but you fuck around looking for trouble and youll end up with your own peculiar rictus of a bloody smile opened up from ear to ear with a switchblade when i got into the flat there was this man called simon who called himself a social worker i couldnt decide straight off if he was bent as a wonky one pound coin or just funny in a middle class sort of way but he showed me around the place which didnt take a whole lot of time cos it wasnt very big it was functional and clean and totally devoid of any soul but who was i to complain when he left he said hed be in touch he gave me a contact number and said there was some cash on a table and some food in a cupboard and i was to take it easy at first get my feet and get to know the area and not to abuse this privilege cos these flats were in high demand gold dust pure gold dust and with that he was gone leaving me alone it was a very strange feeling eerie almost and unsettling i sat on the edge of the narrow bed in the small bedroom and looked round at the walls and the floor and the scant furniture and then i couldnt sit no more and i stood up and started to pace i paced everywhere in the flat like i had something wrong with me that wouldnt allow me to stay still and then i found myself staring out of a window that overlooked a scrubby park there were people walking dogs and mums with kiddies and teenagers on quad bikes fuck not a one of them knew of my existence i could drink some rat poison and die an agonising death right at this window and none of them would know or care mind you flip that coin over and they could all fall into a massive sink hole in the middle of that dogshit park and i would be well entertained but hardly moved to tears too many of us all strangers to each other ignoring those we dont know as the world turns and flies off into the cold interstellar recesses that woman there with the small girl she was practically yanking the kids arm off who did they go home to maybe she was bringing the girl up on her own but she didnt look like she had much love in her cos i never remember my mum treating me that way a hipowered rifle would do the job one shot take her out and run down and tell the kiddie it was all part of a plan to remove her pain of a mother so she could live a better life one where she wasnt being yanked around and screamed at just for being alive i didnt know if i could make it in this flat i was right up against it here just me and my defaced chaucer fuck if i didnt stop thinking like this the hours and minutes would weigh as heavy on me as marleys chains what was wrong with me i couldnt be frightened of stepping outside the flat thatd be mental for the past years now id been banged up in homes and institutions where they kept an eye on me and i was always looking for the main chance to get one over on them and flit out the door so i could run amok and do some damage to everyone and no none in particular was that the problem was i going soft in the centre like a jam doughnut i could just imagine what bruce lee would make of that hed strip me of my brown belt and tell me i was a disgrace to the world of kung fu and karate i had to go out just to see what state i was in and to get a gander at my new surroundings i scooped the money twatty simon had left me which wasnt a fortune but i could get some decent nosh with it cos i didnt really fancy cornflakes and biscuits and baked beans which was what was on offer in the shopping on the kitchen table when i poked my nose out of the block of flats it didnt seem as bad as i thought it might be no 6' 10" black guy was standing waiting for me to split my head open with a baseball bat or pop a cap in my ass too many blacksploitation movies i told myself as i walked towards a busy main street it was built up alright blocks of flats all over and low brick buildings covered in graffiti i didnt feel at home or nothing but who was i to complain i had a box to live in with other people in other boxes all just trying to get by yeah we were all strangers and all watching where we put our feet so we didnt stand in the dogshit but i wasnt being fucked around by gorillas or kept against my will on a ward of bedwetters and dribbling loons if life wasnt exactly sweet it wasnt bitter either it was what it was you dont want to be lifted and carried do you cos when it gets to that stage youve probably lost the use of your legs and cant wipe your arsehole for love nor money and just think of it youre being pushed around by a big butch girl on steroids and you get a real bad itch in the very centre of your bumhole button now youre in a quandary yes you is cos you really want to stick your finger in and give it a good old rattle but you know you cant cos you are totally and utterly dependent on butch for everything to do with bodily functions and once again you have to abase yourself and grovel to her you have to utter those demeaning words itchy bumhole needs scratched youve been brought to tears working yourself up to ask for this service and butch is beaming broadly youve made her fucking day and to her youre light as a feather she lifts you up with one arm lays you down on a latex rubber sheet and removes your incontenance pad shes already worked one of her mitts into a rubber glove and now she covers the raised middle digit with a liberal amount of baby gel you dont like to admit it but when the finger is inserted you almost swoon from the pleasure and you cant stop making little noises of appreciation and contentment but just be careful not to overdo it cos itll only act as a red rag to a bull dyke if you moan too loud shell strap on a monster dildo and ride you ragged you might end up with a bunch of haemeroids the size of a childs fist i couldnt recall how i had slid into this particular slough of anal despond but i was knocked sideways out of it by the sight of something down an alley between two buildings at first i thought it was an old cushion daubed with red paint and i was about to move on when something prompted me to take a second look the old brain was working overtime cos i could see legs sticking out and the more i looked it came to me that i was staring at a dead cat with a ring of dark blood around one of its eyes id always liked cats we had one when my mother was still alive and id buried it in a small plot of land out the back of the house when it died what sort of a violent death had this poor mog faced to end up like that i couldnt take my eyes off it poor thing a voice said close by me and i turned to see this old tramp with all manner of plastic bags fastened around his shaggy frame one of gods poor creatures sad isnt it to see it like this people are so uncaring these days and he smiled with a broken and chipped low palisade of grey teeth you couldnt spare an old alleycat such as myself a bit of change to get a cup of tea or a small bite to eat not likely i heard myself say inside but i surprised myself by inviting him to come and have a meal if he could tell me where there was a good caff he winked at me this bear of a man carrying his world in plastic sacks and off we set the weirdest thing being that i had a very good appetite in spite of the bloody dead cat we sat down together the tramp and i in a soulless burger joint and i treated him to a full family meal cos it comforted me not to have to eat alone richard was his name and he wolfed down what i placed in front of him he was good value cos hed lived a life and relished telling me about it he was not quite 75 years of age though it was hard to tell underneath all his clothes and matted hair he could have been a great uncle talking about the good old days of glam rock it was fun just to watch him light up and buzz as he talked about a time when my mother was only a baby we nearly got a record deal he said he was almost wistful as he looked back i was married back then with two little ones a boy and a girl theyd be in their late forties now if they was alive i heard this and wondered where he was taking me in his story we had gigs all over we called ourselves vanilla experience and the buzz when we went on stage was electric mauve eyeshade you cant imagine how it lights the eyes up i couldnt it was true and i just couldnt see this old stinker as a raver in west london or yorkshire cos he started yabbering on about clubs in bradford in the early 70s great time to be alive i was on the tip of telling him i wasnt around then so ive no idea what he was talking about but there was no stopping him we always ended up in some dressing room that was no bigger than a broom cupboard 4 big blokes all squeezing into our leotards and fighting over the mascara and i began to smile inside at the insanity of the picture he was painting and the stage was so close to the girls who came to see us and it was mostly girls and they was practically ripping their knickers off to get at us and then the most unreal thing came along we got invited out to japan to play to the teenies there you ever been to japan i shook my head o you gotta go tokyo is a real headfuck but just out of this world we couldnt credit it when our manager told us we were going he might as well have said wed been accepted as astronauts to fly to the moon none of us had ever been outside england at the time in fact we thought yorkshire was a different planet you know what was one of the funniest things that happened there i didnt and hoped he wasnt waiting for an answer we went into this department store in shinjuku thats a hip part of tokyo and there was this huge keyboard on a floor you know like the one tom hanks played in big and we jigged and pranced about on that riffing off one of our hits fuck i had hair down to my bum in those days and we got this huge crowd round us taking photos and wanting to have photos taken with us sounds wild i said it was it was for a while and then the bottom fell out one message from home and that was it i couldnt carry on i looked at him and saw that he was fighting with himself to stop from breaking down and a terrible calm and stillness came over him i was on the point of asking him what was wrong did he want some more food and then he told me my wife and kids were killed in a housefire and he sat there breathing still trying to smile i couldnt think of a thing to say nothing made sense after that the guys were great but i lost everything then and nothing made sense no more what did it matter playing to crowds of kids when my own kids were gone im sorry he said you dont need to hear this its alright i said im sorry for your loss it sounded so feeble he took a drink of tea and looked down at his plate funny isnt it we go on day after day not really knowing why we do its a habit thats all like breathing we just go on because we dont know any other way i tried to kill myself a number of times in the years after but i lacked the courage to go through with the act im not christian or nothing and i dont have a philosophy of life no peg to hang a system on so here i am wandering about the streets like an old alley cat whose lost most of his fur and depends on the kindness of strangers but youre a top boy he paused and i heard myself say martin youre too young to have any kids of your own but when you do youll see what it means to you my wife and kids were the best part of me he touched his chest theyre in here and they keep me going through thick and thin he started to gather himself together you aint going o yes he said ive took up enough of your time already i started to panic in a weird unknowing way and i put my hand in my pocket and pulled out a £20 note whats this he said its for you he shook his head no no no youve been generosity itself i thrust the note at him and forced it into his hands please its all i can do and he took it and before i could withdraw my hand he bent and kissed it god bless you son and smiled through tears he left me at the table feeling inadequate and forlorn but at the door he turned to me and said all things must pass youll see i dont really know if there is a god but im sure were put on this earth to suffer and endure be kind to yourself he slipped out of the burger bar and tramped off down the road i sat down to collect my thoughts and heard some whispering and tittering from the counter two youths not much younger than me who passed as servers in the burger bar were nudging one another and winking at me hes good value said one and his fellow wimp in uniform chimed in with hes up and down this road like a bad smell but their smiles disappeared when i stood up and glared at them cos i could feel a monumental anger building in me you alright i could feel my face was tight and the skin drawn back to my ears one of them moved away from the counter and sloped off into the kitchen the other looked down at the counter fuck i had to get out of there pronto or thered be blood the old noboguchi could have come in handy right then you fuck i shouted and saw a look of fear in the server then i turned on my heels like clint eastwood at the end of unforgiven any of you come after me and ill burn this town down and ill murder your wives and your children and all your friends fuck i had to get back to my flat and lie down or id be in trouble as it was i very nearly was in trouble and when i got back to the flat i was in a bit of a state there was a note from simon the social worker with a debit card in my name and a 4 digit password the note told me to be very careful how i used this card cos it wasnt dipping into a bottomless pit of money and if i abused it i could be out on my ear or banged up with some fruit and nut cases and the key thrown away he didnt use those exact words but that was the general tone of the epistle i was in such a state that i couldnt raise as much as a cheerful toot from my bumhole in fact i felt more like having a good old cry as i sat down on the end of my bed it wasnt just the dead cat or the old tramp richard reliving his glory days in glam rock and then spilling his guts about the deaths of his wife and kids youd think that would be enough for a first outing in the new hood and it wasnt even the shitty look of most of the houses and shops and streets and the gangs of black guys hanging around corners and down alley ways one or two giving me a look as i passed by as if to suss out what was inside me a pussy wimp or a nascent rambo bruce lee combo ready and able for a bit of a rumble in the jungle i wasnt stopping long enough to throw down or pick up no gauntlet and it really didnt bother me whether they slashed each other to death when they was high on some drug one of them had cooked in his bedroom at 3 oclock in the morning but when two guys are chasing another guy along a street in broad daylight and practically bowl me over like some rampant savage ozzie fast bowler whos snorted cocaine before a match and before i can react and cry foul or whatever they shout in a cricket game one of them draws a gun and fires at the guy being chased and shoots him dead right there out in front of a greengrocers in front of jamaican mothers and grandmothers who all scramble into the shops and huddle together in fear for their lives im not gonna tell you i played the hero cos i didnt i staggered back to my kip and took an age to calm down i dont know how long i sat on the foot of the bed i was like a comet whizzing faster and faster round the earth just not being affected by gravity or inertia my brain just wouldnt slow down i probably stared at the same spot on a wall for hours without seeing it it was dark outside when i finally made a move i went to a window and looked out at the dogshit park and could see a few souls walking their cockapoo spaniels or whatever mixed up cocktails of dog dna and i thought what sort of world have i been delivered into fucking ragged arsehole of the world shit i was gonna havta look out for myself better than some swiveleyed chameleon in an attenboroughballs docu about some remote island where everything was fair game for everything else fuck i had to tell myself to calm down and chill her out cos it wasnt me who had bled to death on the street and it wasnt me who was lying down an alley with a ring of blood around one of its eyes i thought about richard and hoped he was okay maybe got a bottle of something and was prancing around on that big keyboard in the tokyo of his mind what else could he do when life had hit him below the belt and poured poison into his mouth i didnt feel like leaving the flat after that i ate through the groceries that simon had left me it was mainly boxes of carbs in the form of cereals and pasta but i didnt care when they ran out which was only a matter of days though it seemed like weeks i slipped out to a corner shop which opened early and closed late and was run by a couple of silent pakistani gents who watched my every move flitting here and there sniffing at the different pongs in the shop id never seen some of the items they had on sale but i put that down to being an untravelled ignorant inexperienced lout at least i imagine thats what mohammed and his brother called me in their own language as soon as i had paid and left yeah they was silent when i was poking about on my errands but as soon as i made to go theyd start up like bbc world service in pakistani i tried to imagine the world theyd left behind or their parents or grandparents to come to britain i had no idea nor probably never would cos i knew how different the world in my head was to the world in other peoples heads and i knew mine was not better than other peoples worlds just different in fact their worlds were probably way better than mine what did i know head filled with violent images of death and destruction i so wanted to change that but i couldnt find the room to turn the projector off and people didnt help for every loving caring sane and sensible soul there had to be ten thousand complete and utter bastards and fuckwits trying to spoil your day and shit on your doorstep simon called round uninvited just to see how i was getting along i didnt go into details cos i didnt think he and i would ever get to be buddies but he could see i was down you getting out much he asked and i shook my head as if to say i had enough holes for breathing without wanting any more it can take a bit of getting used to hackney you dont say said a small voice inside me though i didnt let simon into my confidence on that score but lissen said the enthusiastic one the worlds your oyster speaking of which let me introduce your friend and companion on your travels i watched him as he produced a card out of his hand like a bad magician you know you dont have to limit yourself to just these streets around here and maybe i laid it on a bit thick about watching the spending on the old debit card but we have had one or two disasters with people odeeing on crack cocaine cos they handed their cards and passcodes to dealers but i mean what can you do its a good system if its not abused you just gotta take things slow and easy day by day step by step get to know a few people in the neighbourhood and settle in to a life that suits you i didnt think he was gonna shut up but then he paused and took a breath and smiled he maybe knew hed overstayed his welcome cos he was next thing at the front door and mumbling something about having put some money on the card for me then he was out of my hair and i was studying the oyster card in my loneliness of the short attention span fuckwit i had no intention of going anywhere except the paki shop for cornflakes and milk id watch the world go by outside my windows and marvel in a numb and distant manner at the dogs capacity for taking unending pleasure from the act of retrieving a ball from a mudpatch over and over and over again until youd think theyd have worn the record out and if they could talk they ought to say something along the lines cant you come up with something a bit more interesting a bit more demanding than just lobbing a spheroid object into the air and allowing gravity to pull it to earth i mean youre supposed to be the lords of creation im terribly disappointed in you naked ape youre not all youre touted to be some days passed in this hazy torpor and one day i woke up and though i couldnt really attach the word excitement to my general feeling i knew i wanted to push the envelope out and go visit trafalgar square which i equated with crowds and noise and a general holiday mood where this notion had come from was anybodys guess but i wasnt gonna sit and chew it to death in hackney so i took the no 38 bus and ended up in tottenham court road where i sprang off the bus near a redbrick theatre that advertised it was extending the run of a musical about a french rabble who were so unhappy that it was all they could do to sing about it forever and a day manning the barricades and chanting in frenzied harmony and ill bet they charged the punters a small fortune to hear their sentimental drivel fuck the frenchill do just about anything to get noticed i could hardly credit the atmosphere how different it was to hackney it was more like the kings road and chelsea though busier and i tried to work out in my head how short a time had passed since the days i used to stalk down by the river looking for trouble it wasnt that long ago only a matter of months and yet i was like the one telling the story in heart of darkness id gone looking for kurtz and thought i could change him but it was me whod changed i didnt wanna charge about the streets causing mayhem and slashing all over the place with some killer blade no that was someone else i wanted to watch and record everything all humankind in infinite variety passing before my eyes in endless procession everyone seemed so selfobsessed so much in a hurry that it seemed they were in a film speeded up and i was in a different fim which was slowed down and directed by a different director maybe even a silent film director look about you youre pleased with what you see even a little shocked but in a pleasant sort of way no not that shocked and just be a little careful not to turn round too much so as to avoid bumping into the oher actors on the street and watch out for that banana peel below you this isnt a mack sennet comedy you know and were not insured and indemnified against injury i got some money from a hole in the wall and it struck me then that i had landed on my feet i was back alright i wasnt living in a swanky area but i had a roof over my head funds and no gorillas to yank my chain this called for a celebration i found this little chinese restaurant which wasnt that hard since the whole place was coming down with them it was chinese eateries wall to wall along the street i was in i couldve been in a foreign country for all i knew anyway what would britain be without foreign food its a long time gone since you could drop into an eating hole for venison and ale yeah you can get venison alright but you have to search high and low for it and pay through the nose when you get it there wasnt much room in the joint it was a huggermugger steamy little boite if you can apply boite to a joint that doesnt sell drinks which are a neon blue and retail at greatly inflated prices i was sat opposite this ponce who had tortoiseshell glasses and a mauve shirt he called himself raymond and led the way with the chat he was very good at it it sort of rolled off his affluent tongue in an accent which reeked of an expensive education eton most likely and he had what i thought at first was a slim briefcase but turned out to be a manbag he was leafing through a book of poetry when i sat down but he tucked that away in his leather pouch and started his patter as if we was old friends from buggery days in 4th form im only painting this picture of him as a prelude to telling you that he wasnt bad company he grew on me so to speak and not like a disgusting fungus more like a mild dose of vertigo or pleasant fatigue i just ate my noodles and pulled duck and observed him i wasnt in hackney and he didnt seem threatening so i let him weave his long words around me like plaintive and egregious and wanderlust like it was a gentle spell i could undo with a snap of my fingers except i couldnt be bothered and when he invited me for cocktails at an insouciant little club in soho i should of course have declined with a silent and firm shake of my head as if to say i dont do insouciance or the like but instead i heard a small voice accept with a simple yes what was i playing at it was hard to say i think i was putting off the evil hour when i would have to return to staring out the window at the dogshit park and all the nonentities of hackney raymond was a sutile and benign guide through soho he made some allusion to virgil as we strolled along past stripclubs and porn shops i was still pondering that reference to thunderbirds when he said voila and waved a palm at the entrance to an establishment called cafe climax abandon hope all ye who enter here was said with a smile and a wink thunderbirds are go i responded and he clapped his other palm on my back and told me i was a good sport thats the spirit he was lucky i had agreed a nonaggression pact with myself or hed have been in the gutter with a broken nose for stepping over the line and becoming a tiny bit too familiar with the old etonian back slapping his finely coiffed hair would have been mussed up then and his expensive tortoiseshell specs broken into bits but i was determined to go with the flow and see what lay ahead what did i know this might even qualify as a mini adventure inside the climax it was dark and gloomy and it took my eyes some minutes to adjust there were cubicles along the walls and couples or groups chittering away as if exchanging dark secrets and throwing their heads back in sudden explosions of laughter some were hugging each other as if theyd gone to eton as well and one or two were giving mouth to mouth resuscitation but not from any medical textbook id ever looked into it didnt take me very long to gather the single most obvious fact about the place there wasnt a female in sight this didnt mean there werent girlish squeals and highpitched trills and i made sure i shifted my position in the cubicle raymond led me to so that my back was against a wall and i had a big fat cushion to put between me and any shrieking ponce who thought i might be of interest to him you alright said raymond as soon as wed settled i didnt want to appear as if i was ruffled so i shrugged theres nothing can happen to you here i guarantee that unless he added with a suave smile that would have done a 2nd hand car salesman credit you want it to before i could quite weigh those words with due care and attention a blinged up shellsuited nonce minced over to us and even before he opened his mouth i knew he would speak with a lisp raymond sweetheart so good to see you where have you been hiding yourself we thought youd deserted us for good is this your new boy raymond put up a hand to silence the mincer this is a friend martin weve just met and i thought id show him this aladdins cave of delights the mincer practically shuddered with a spasm of thrilled energy and gave me a look that a cat gives when its licked the plate clean such a way with words the poet laureate of soho ive always said that what can i get you boys i think well have a sheesa to share and a couple of mohitos that all raymond sweetie doubles inquired mincing boy and when raymond nodded the mincer looked at me and said with a serious little frown he old enough to drink get out of here shouted raymond and there was an explosive trill of giggles from bling and shellsuit for a moment he had turned into an exotic wading bird like a flamingo in a courtship dance he turned to go but shot a question out the side of his mouth flavour darling i almost forgot about that what do you suggest said raymond strawberry i always find strawberry so soothing on the palate o get you said raymond whered you get that phrase from nigella or nadiya i cant remember now i watch them work their magic though id never in a million years actually make anything they suggest far too labour intensive and lifes just too short he seemed to want to linger but raymond shooed him away with a waft of a hand what dyou think of the old place raymond said and i turned my head to one side like ive seen cockatoos do as they stand on one leg its a bit strange i offered after some moments i dare say it is to you ive quite forgotten my own first reaction to the place im so comfortable here now that its like a home away from home and by soho standards its pretty tame then he laffed though wait till you see the toilets theyre a porno delight that would not have been out of place in a symposium in platos athens the mincer returned with the drinks in tall glasses pale lime green concoctions with shrubbery then he set up the hubbly bubbly putting red coals on top under a lid and when raymond sucked on the end of the tube a low rumble like you get when you blow out air from your lungs under water or sometimes once in a blue moon achieve from a long fart in the bath was followed by a perfumed cloud pouring from raymonds mouth and momentarily shrouding our cubicle in a dense fog i loved it from the get go and didnt notice the old mohitos slipping down another one was ordered and i felt myself gently buzzing in the semidarkness of climax you had to keep drinking cos the smoke from the hubbly bubbly sheesa made the inside of the mouth feel parched with a hint of metal he was right too raymond about the loo it was like an art gallery done by a filthy minded banksy all these half goat half man creatures chasing naked men and all of them had boners and some were getting rogered behind trees and rocks so that a little bit was left to the imagination though not much and they all wore old etonian grins ear to ear cos theyd probably been excused latin and greek cos of bugger practice when i came back from the loo i was greeted by the dance of the trannies they werent actually dancing but they waltzed in like they owned the place and they were all kitted out in long silky dresses false hair false eyelashes and heels some of them had slashes down the side of their dresses and showed a bit of stocking and garter they couldnt hide the adams apples and the dark shadow showed under a thick layer of makeup i had a fit of the giggles and one of the trannies came over to me and looked down at me from a great height you find something funny junior even his nose was big and i was wondering where this was leading were we going to dance or rumble when raymond came out of the cubicle and pulled me away from the confrontation hes with me and hes a bit tight you know better than this raymond you bring your catamite to the climax you make him behave i was protesting in a halfhearted way as i was pushed towards the exit whatd he mean whats a catamite when i found myself out on the streets of soho with raymond or virgil or whoever he was and night had fallen thunderbirds were no longer go i was feeling a little fuzzy round the edges and stood staring at the neon and bright lights and the ghouls and goons drifting by in throngs somehow we ended up in raymonds pad he must have invited me though i dont recall any actual form of words passing between us it was neat and tidy with bookcases and books everywhere and we seemed to have floated there on gossamer wings so it cant have been far from soho we didnt go down into the bowels of the earth and travel by tube you really a poet i asked him amd he smiled of a kind he said what can i get you to drink just a beer thanks you sure i make a devilish cocktail myself if i do say so i stood breathing looking round the room there were some proper expensive looking bits of tat fuck he could have a good old colloquy with bowtie about anteeks he disappeared for some minutes and returned with a pink concoction for himself and a bottle for me we sat by a window and because we were in a mews it was fairly quiet he asked me to tell him something about myself well i didnt give him the full life story for one thing i was too jaded for all that nonsense but i told him enough to keep his interest what i found out about him wasnt a great deal either but i did learn he didnt go to eton he laughed when i said i thought he was a toff from money he did go to a private school in the west country and yes he did have a private income but money is only a means to an end and he considered it useful and necessary but also a great evil it set people against each other and the lack of it brought great misery to whole swathes of territory countries continents take the north south divide for instance the flow of wealth is east to west and west to east not north to south theres a reason for this or multiple causes i dont know if he was expecting me to take part in this discussion well it wasnt a discussion more like a monologue and i was zoning out fast and i only came back to life when i heard him say that when he left cairo and headed south into the sudan he had thought egypt a barbarous and uncivil nation but when he returned after months of hard trekking his views on africa and egypt in particular had turned 180 degrees did i know the poetry of cavafy i must have given him the blankest of blankety blank looks which didnt stop him or derail him from shunting the old locomotive of knowledge my way an alexandrine greek early 20th century marvellous poet very sensual the last faint echo of the cosmopolitan world of prenasser egypt sorry im waffling on i do this when ive had a few and the company is special lissen your final pleasure to the voices to the exquisite music of that strange procession and say goodbye to her to the alexandria you are losing thats cavafy i picked a book of his poetry up in an english bookshop in alexandria it was an oasis in a desert of monolithic gross conformity with that he polished off his pink lady or whatever it was he was throwing down his throat another one he proposed and i accepted and when he returned with the drinks i asked him about his own poetry he laffed and talked about a work in progress and though i did not press him to recite or read anything he sort of talked himself into doing just that from a low cabinet he extracted a jotter and leafed through half of it until his eye was detained by a short poem he gave me what might have been a shy smile except nothing about him had seemed shy unitl that moment greek nude he announced and i took a long swig of beer cos i wasnt sure where this one was going the fire in my loins will not be put out by the lapping of your tongue other tongues may wag let them the sweat from our backs is not dishonest nor will we hide our priapic pleasure with figleafs of hypocrisy we play our games as of old naked and unashamed and like ancient wrestlers we grasp each other in an embrace so close we breathe as one i dont know what sort of expression i was wearing when he finished but inside a little voice was saying that it might be time to be going down the road and i was working up to saying just that when raymond produced a spliff and lit it up we smoked for some time without speaking just him and me and nobody else in the world i felt weirdly comfortable with him considering we didnt know each other he told me how he liked to sit at his window and just zone out which he admitted was a bit crazy considering he lived in the centre of london surrounded by millions of complete strangers did i like a dare i looked at him and it was quite extraordinary how he appeared to be a 3d cutout of himself and everything else was background i couldnt even find a voice to ask him what the fuck he was talking about i suppose i must have been too chilled to care i shall take the part of john flamsteed first astronomer royal and you will take the part of the moon the moon i heard myself say how do i play the moon very easy said raymond you drop your breeks and stick your bottom out the window this brought on a fit of the giggles and the little voice inside me was telling me to to tell raymond to shove his game up his arse but the thing was i could hear voices somewhere outside the window not very close but close enough to make the dare worth doing and i could hardly believe what i was doing when i felt the cool night breeze on my arse as raymond told me to shake my arse cheeks and wobble my booty then there was a shriek from a short distance away down the mews i withdrew inside and nearly wet myself and raymond was choking on the spliff and coughing out a small cloud of smoke he told me that he had got a good sight of the moon this night and it was a red letter day for the astronomical society when i had pulled my pants up and calmed down he told me i was a good sport and that it was time for bed o boy i sobered up double quick with that and now the little inner voice was shouting and carrying on im not gay i told him and he looked hurt and disbelieving but we could make such sweet music together he said and there was disappointment and a sombre look in his eye are you sure im sorry i said and got out of his flat as quick as i could whatever was i thinking i beat myself up with that refrain as i walked the early morning streets of soho had i deliberately been leading him on i couldnt be sure but of one thing at least i was very sure and that was that i needed no salami sliding up and down my keester and as the cold light of day sobered me up i could tell myself that he had been leading me on in his sly way he was a very disarming and charming man good looking too if good looking men is what you want there is something strange and disquieting about shifting around soho before the world is quite awake its a hustling bustling nonstop carnival of a place and to see it closed up and still and quiet it just didnt sit right but i trudged on my anus and fragile self respect intact what i didnt want to do at that hour was slink back to hackney it would have been too depressing after the weird odyssey of the day and night just gone i wanted to find a coffee shop where i could get myself a fry up and take stock recharge the batteries and maybe take another part of london in before settling back into murder central and the old dogshit park a few men passed me like crumpled and dessicated versions of themselves that had been doused in alcohol then hung up on meat hooks to dry out they were hollow eyed and utterly wasted no one spoke to me and i spoke to no one in turn what could you say i avoided being buggered what about you no mate i was taking french lessons at the top of the stairs after bleeding through the nose paying the price of a good meal for some rocket fuel in the dark recesses of a strip joint what a tremendous waste of time and energy and i dont know where the fucking money went ive blown a packet on what some disease ridden pros who werent even fit or goodlooking they were fat and bloated like pigs in corsets shit my fat fucking cow of a wife better not find out it was a fucking works do well thats my excuse and im sticking to it i glanced up at a blue plaque above a restaurant called quo vadis which was of course closed like every other premises in the street and it said that karl marx had lived in rooms above the restaurant back in the day fuck i wondered if he had got his rocks off with some fat pig after scribbling in his rooms i doubted it i mean not everybody is a waste of space some people actually do something with their lives and keep the baser part of themselves in check fuck get me i must have been in a worse state than i thought with the way my mind was rambling on soon id be dreaming up all manner of alternative histories like queen victoria hanging out a window of buck palace by her garters being porked by prince albert from behind i came to a small park at the end of the street i had to sit down on a bench i was feeling that nauseous from lack of sleep there were other benches around a small central building in tudor style and these other benches had tramps or scruffs stretched out on them so i didnt need no great debate with myself to lay my bones down and make a pillow of my hands i must have sunk into sleep rapidly cos the next thing i remember was a feeling of warmth and then a buzz of different sounds all around me as i came to and blinked at the world there was a toffy business suit at the end of my bench he wasnt paying me the slightest bit of attention he had a newspaper on his lap and a coffee in one hand the smell of it was a perfect storm of olfactory revolution and i stirred and sat up aware that the world was busy now and people were passing in every direction like they was on fastmoving conveyor belts i arose like lazarus sloughed off my winding sheet and joined the living i had a serious job to do to wit locate an eatery place myself in it and eat i didnt have far to look as the little square was just off tottenham court road i come into it spitting distance from where id jumped off the no 38 less than 24 hours before i was too preoccupied with the thought of food to enjoy any drop of irony in the situation by scylla and charybdis by stripjoint and brothel by porn shop and ale shop closing the ears and tightening the sphincter ulysses had reached the happy isles once more and rejoiced at a feast in his honour in other words i got myself breakfast and i stinted not for this was the full english with a side order of toast and the biggest grande grande cappuccino they had to offer i had nearly wiped the plate clean when a girl came and stood in front of my table did you pay for that she said and she was very serious looking did you pay for the food youve just eaten she repeated the question i suppose because i was staring at her with knife and fork poised mouth slightly open i was wondering why she was bothering me and was she police and while i wondered at her she sat down and smiled you dont remember me do you i shook my head should i well i fed you she said and tried to save you from the police i must have looked like a gormless twat any second now she would start speaking very very slowly to me and i would lose the power of speech altogether and would only be able to moan and grunt like a retard you came into my dads cafe and made off with the leavings from a table my eyes must have looked like saucers as the penny dropped you stopped me in the street and shouted at me yes i did she freely admitted but you deserved it but dont you remember i brought you back to the cafe and gave you a proper meal what happened to you i told her without going into detail especially what the gorillas had done to me and the particular form of punishment the commandant had specialised in when i finished i realised i still didnt know this girls name nora she said grayson i dont remember much about that time in your cafe you look different now somehow its the street gamine look i had my hair long when i first met you you suit short hair the words were no sooner out of my mouth than i felt awkward and selfconscious whyd i say that the voice within had a quizzical even an interrogative edge to it fuck i was feeling strange first this nonce takes me to a gay club gets me to waggle my arse out of his window and then like zebedee from the magic roundabout tells me its time for bed and now a street gamine called nora is getting me to pass comments about her hair and its not even midday but i just realised like a morning epiphany that she had the most beautiful eyes nothing like the sun or anything but a shade of emerald that glowed when the light hit them we talked on about this and that and i found out that she was studying to be a nurse at tooting bec and she was living in balham i dont know how long we spoke but it was as if the world went away while i was with her all the people coming and going in the cafe and all the busy background out on the street the pedestrians the cars and buses and motorbikes and bicycles all of it faded and receded and there she was this nora talking to me and making me feel like i was the only other person alive in the world but then she stood up and said she had to go she might as well have hit me over the head with a stick i was dazed and uncertain what did it mean why was she going something about a lecture at ucl then she grabbed a napkin and wrote her address and phone no on it before i could say a word she was out of the cafe and had melted into the bustle of the street i sat on staring at the address on the napkin not wanting the moment to pass but feeling it was already fleeing from me like past time and memories of happiness i stood up i had to get out of there and back into the world of movement and people and things and time present she had spooked me that was all nora with her loveliest of emerald eyes had made me think of other things that weighed upon my heart perhaps she recalled to me my mother in some strange and hurtful way she didnt mean to hurt me i knew that it was the association in my mind and soul with the warmth of her presence and the strength of her character these things had taken me by surprise and opened a small door into the deeper part of me why should i feel so melancholy and down i had a girls address and phone no and i was a free man o free as a bird and i would fly to her when the time was right i moved with the crowd back out on to tottenham court road and considered my situation from different angles and from the top deck of the no 38 surely things were better than they had been just 24 hours ago and i could afford a degree of optimism despite the ruffian who stood always in the shadows and carped his disdain at myself walking in the sun in a linen suit and wearing a silver sombrero i still baulked at going back to hackney and got off in islington for its pleasant face and happy disposition it had the look of a slightly down at heel chelsea like the poor relation who has to go in by the servants entrance but it still looked a world away from hackney and the dogshit park i passed the time in a genial idleness somehow sitting over a bottle of beer in a dreary pub with pool tables and degenerates like myself it isnt as if time doesnt pass anyway we have no power over that if you think about it too much time will drag you screaming and kicking from the cradle to the grave in a blind instant so dont sit there thinking about it too much i could have made an approach to the pool sharks and asked for a game theyd have loved that and taken a real delight in fleecing me of every penny but i knew their game from start to finish and i had no need of proving a point with them or getting involved with any push or shove in a sordid joint on the fringes of expectations i wouldnt go so far as to imply great expectations but the meeting with nora had buoyed me up put wind in my sails and set my little boat on a journey there was something about her definitely no doubt about it i would leave it awhile so as not to appear too eager but i wanted to get to know her funny i found it hard to reconcile her now with her gorgeous green eyes with the spitfire who had dragged me back to her dads cafe and tore a strip off me for helping myself to leftovers well she seemed to have forgotten about it so i wasnt going to let it hang over our future together like a dark cloud get me id only met the girl twice and now i was hearing this voice inside me talking about a future with her i started giggling to myself as id heard about what a woman could do to a man id never put no credit in it like but maybe just maybe it was true i fished her address out just to look at it and convince myself that i wasnt making things up hallucinating or daydreaming or conning myself no there it was true blue and for real i looked up at the lads around the pool tables they looked in aspect like a cackle of hyenas ready to pounce on me they might have taken my giggle as a sign that i was getting drunk but i wasnt and i didnt fancy fighting off three or four from a pack of wild dogs like them so i tucked the address away and stood up i swear every last one of those hyenas glared at me as if i was a nonce walking out on a fair fight i got out quick from that den before my better sense deserted me and they pushed me to the point of no return it wasnt that i didnt think i could take them no that wasnt it it was just it wouldve been so stupid and pointless and i imagine a beak would have come down hard on me and asked me to explain myself to the court its difficult if not impossible your honour and members of the jury to explain to you my actions in the cold light of another day when that day i was provoked beyond reasonable measure by a gang of thuggish hyenas who were goading me and mocking me and showing that they thought so little of me that they was signalling to me that i was the nonce of nonces to them so i found myself running back into that black hole of calcutta of a pub grabbing a pool cue and breaking it in half over the head of the first yobbo i could lay hands on then i was fighting for my life as they all come at me at once but my training in swords come to my aid and i battered them left and right breaking heads and ribs and smashing the odd jawbone the best i saved to the last as the most villainous of the gang of hyenas i made drop his breeks and bend over as i stuffed the shaft of my broken cue up his arsehole there was a silence in the court above five minutes as the judge drank a glass of water cleared his throat and poured himself another glass of water his brow was as furrowed as a corduroy jacket and he was grim about the mouth the jury will retire to consider your verdict i took this as my cue to step down from the stand but i was arrested in my action by a member of the jury a very tall woman with a large bosom standing up and speaking in a strangely deep and commanding voice we have no need to retire for we have already come to our decision i had the weirdest feeling come over me that i had met this woman before and what is the decision of the jury the beak asked not guilty the beaks eyebrows raised themselves to the top of his forehead and his jaw went slack as a wellused cock indeed went on the amazon of the jury we commend the actions of the defendant too many cocky little shits hanging around our streets and public houses causing social mayhem and disruption this was followed by a spontaneous burst of applause first from the jury itself and then from the public gallery and the amazon smiled such a camembert grin that i knew then where i had come across her she was a he and was in fact the trannie i had encountered in the climax just the day before i was carried from the assizes on the shoulders of a policeman and deposited in a street off the main drag in islington for some moments i was a little disoriented and whirled around to get my bearings i couldnt fathom how id got to where id got to but it hardly mattered anyway as sometimes just drifting around a strange place with no particular goal in mind is the best way to travel you give yourself to the moment and let it reveal its secrets to you unbidden it was by now late afternoon i could see a pub at the corner of a street and it advertised a beer garden this was more like it a bit of nopressure relaxing over a pint or two before the inevitable undesired return to the base in hackney when i got that pint and got into a corner of the beer garden i could tell right off that i was in a friendly zoo there were chimps and orangutans a few bears and a contingent of koalas and kangaroos from the land of oz but definitely no troubling dingoes or hyenas or packs of wild dogs i could chill and people watch without fear of being challenged or intimidated i thought back over the weirdness of the night before and it began with a gentle smile inside but lead inevitably to me laffing so much that i was getting looks from one or two who probably thought id smoked some strong weed thing was raymond the dirty cock poet had tried to seduce me with flattery and arse waggling antics and drink and a spliff but none of it had worked cos i simply wasnt wired that way and if i had been it would have been happy days all round cos he was a goodlooker and he seemed alright he treated me alright and didnt get narked when i turned him down flat but then he did try and this is the funny bit to use logic on me he told me that being gay is a normal state in nature its a natural thing to do between consenting adults you take two bulls in a field and theyll go at it like nobodys business was they in a field near eton or harrow i thought to myself but i kept that one back from raymond hed been a sport and i had nothing to complain about and anyway hed already told me he didnt go to eton or harrow so how he ended up a fruity ponce is anybodys guess might have been spanked too hard by the old pater or denied the maters titty what do i know were all fucked up in our own way and i took that thought to the lavvie cos the beer i had consumed while pondering my tiny thoughts had put some pressure on the old bladder now are you shy or not shy cos these are the two camps that divide men im talking about bladders here see when i got to the mens i was a bit taken aback cos i thought id slipped through some timespace tunnel and landed in hackney it was right at odds with the look of the pub it was a stinky pissy ancient whitetiled urineandbleach pong hole of a toilet and im not that choosy its just if youre in a dump of a place you expect the khazi to be less than salubrious but not when youve come from a beer garden arbour where not even everyone is puffing like nutso on their personally engraved vape pipes i was just surprised thats all to enter such a stinkhole from where id come from no biggee really cos i had wazzed in some sinkhole stinkholes over the years but that still doesnt get away from the fact that i cant release a stream of piss no matter where i am if someone is standing close to me proximity is the problem hence i fall right in the middle of the boys who cant riddle when other boys are near there was a space at the urinal but there was no way under any circumstances i was going to step up to that plate and release the todger i would only get red in the face and painfully aware of others to left and right and behind me so i turned to leave thinking i could probably do a waz in some alleyway near the pub when i saw there was a single toilet door and it was narrowly open i needed no further encouragement to try there and the pressure seemed to build on my bladder in anticipation of releasing a wheatcoloured stream of piss into the undoubtedly filthy shitsplattered toilet bowl fuck i wasnt her masjestys inspector of toilets i just needed somewhere to pee and very soon but when i pushed the door open the sitdown shitdown was occupied but not by anyone taking a dump no there was a bloke and a chick doing drugs from what i saw which was all in an instant cos the bloke told me to shut the fucking door and get fucking lost she had a length of thin rubber hose knotted round an upper arm and he was injecting her with a needle i couldnt have been more surprised if hed been injecting her in a different part of her body with his cockaluigi i closed the door over fast and stood looking at the door itself for nearly half a minute just considering my options i wasnt going to stay in the toilet any longer thats for sure oddly the pressure had eased on my bladder but i decided to get out of the pub altogether i needed fresh air and a short walk to find that alleyway to bring release and relief what sort of a place lets women into mens toilets this is what i was thinking as i peed up against a huge skip which partially blocked an alley that i stumbled into just a minute from the pub youd think i was outraged from surbiton or flabbergasted from wimbledon but i was strangely outraged and flabbergasted i mean bruce lee wouldnt have condoned a girl shooting up if hed gone into a mens for a waz hed have made chop fucking suey of that idiot cunt fucker who had told me to shut the fucking door i gave my dick an extra savage waggle as i finished peeing and tucked him away before zipping up id just completed this delicate operation cos the last thing you want is to be thinking of something else and zip yourself up with the little man still outdoors that would put you out of action for some time not to mention the bandaging and the pus weeping from the lad for days and weeks and just for the loss of concentration of a moment i came round the skip then to leave the alleyway and i could hear someone else having release and relief in the shadows i couldnt see no one at first though i still heard the gentle hiss of passing water but this was on account of looking at eye level i expected to see another brother from a different mother the worse for an evening on the tiles with his hose out and his forehead pressed against the side of the skip what you looking for it was a girls voice coming at me out of the dark shadows and then this figure sort of materialised out of the dark pulling her knickers up and wiggling them into place under her skirt she stepped out of the shadows then and i could see it was the junkie from the mens toilet o its you i said before i could really think of anything to say she swayed on her heels then and blinked at me do i know you she said no i said not really what does that mean she said though i heard in her voice a total lack of interest in an answer i could have walked on then but something kept me rooted to the spot you were getting a hit in the john she started to laff what i said you laffing at me no she said and laffed some more is that your name john then she swayed so much i was sure she was gonna fall flat on her face i took hold of one of her arms what you doing there was no surprise in her voice and no fear or anxiety im saving you i said saving me from what a fate worse than death she swung her body into mine and an earthy druggy sweaty mix of scents and smells hit me wheres your white horse knighty hes in the stable for the night for the knight she quizzed her eyes rolling back in her head suddenly she put a hand on the back of my neck and pulled me into a kiss it wasnt so much a kiss as a fullon nhs examination of my tonsils her tongue waggling like a little snake and sending express messages to my trouser snake i had closed my eyes as we kissed and opened them expecting to see the heavens exploding with fireworks giant cartwheels and sparklers and rockets making flag patterns or portraits of the famous dead like mao or george washington or michael jackson ooo ooo but her eyes were open staring at a fixed point beyond the back of my head i pulled away from her and she smiled the goofiest smile which had me rock hard in the only part of my body that was fully alert to what was going on you seen my boyfriend she said next and not even this had any effect on my thumper of a stiffee was he the one giving you the hit in the john john she laffed again no thats just just how dyou know so much john it was my turn to laff its easy when you know i said how true how true what was the question the insanity of the situation did not pass me by even though i was only dimly interested in talk she couldnt help herself her mind was racing everywhere all at once and i was humouring her for one purpose only i was thinking of the possibilities in the alleyway the practicalities darkness was one thing that was a big plus but i couldnt see how i could muffle her constant chatter not to mention any sounds she might make in fragrant delight or whatever its called lucky for me she lived not far away though every bloke who passed by she called john and laffed and i had to smile and shrug my shoulders and act out with shakes of the head and rolling of the eyes that she was blitzed and didnt know what she was saying when we got back to her place we had first of all to get in at a narrow door between shop fronts that were boarded up and had layers of graffiti on them i almost felt at home at least i was going to be one more night out of hackney she fumbled around with her keys at the door swaying and teetering on the edge of collapse she dropped them and as i bent down i got a vison of the crack of her arse cheeks divided by the thinnest of thongs you like what you see down there john i was half in mind to straighten her out about my name but i convinced myself very quickly that this was not the time what did it matter who i was in that moment and in that time i had to get the key in the lock and turn it hard which was exactly what i did i pushed her into her hallway which was no more than a space covered in letters and junk mail in front of a steep stairway she fell against this face down and began to clamber up the stairs i was behind her all the way tugging at her thong and inserting my tongue in her crack i was right about her being a screamer and a talker she kept up a galloping commentary even as delighted squeals and shrieks erupted from her throat she was madame turrettes combined with the sounds of a menagerie at the zoo i flipped her over at the top step and stuffed my dong in her crack she had a body there was no doubt about it and it had even more tattoos than i had first thought one day i would take the time to explore them and kiss and lick every one of them but right now i was banging her so hard i thought i was gonna have a meltdown right there on top of her my brain was speeding and my donger was going like a piston into the wetness of her my heart was pounding like a bailiff pounding on a front door my lungs were on fire and my throat was dry as dry it was getting difficult to swallow i want your came the shout from beneath

81

me my cock i breathed out with sharp little breaths yeah i want him in my mouth i blinked and stopped pushing i pulled percy from the slick passage way she sat up and took him in her mouth she became a deluxe vacuum cleaner her head bobbing back and forth i wanted to cum with a big explosion in her mouth shooting the cum as deep into her throat as i could but she stopped and pulled away from me then said move back give me a little space i was so drugged up on sex at that point i couldnt think of what else to do but obey and then i couldnt believe what she did next she swivelled and did a handstand right there at the top of the stairs i caught her just before she was about to topple backwards and lifted her using my shoulders my face was right up against her slit and she was back gobbling my little man well he didnt feel so little right then it was as if the rest of my body had shrunk and i was more cock than body i walked her then into the first room off the stairs the living room and my tongue was right up her crack i swear it was tricky enough to breathe i brought her down onto the carpet and had her walking on her hands like a wheelbarrow with me standing and gripping her by the thighs of course it couldnt last for ever thank the fucking lord cos if it did youd wear yourself out in a single night a young man has just been reported dead in islington with a ridiculous smile on his face it would appear that he died of a massive heart attack because he couldnt pull out of a womans private parts his heart was so overworked and used up that it couldnt take the strain of 15 orgasms his penis on examination was red raw like a chunk of undercooked beef the sun newspaper in a typical banner headline put it this way 15 and out top order cocksman couldnt last the pace and had his middle stump ripped from his body by a woman with a square leg and a silly mid off police are pursuing various lines of enquiry and are particularly interested in hearing from cricket fans by now i couldnt take it no more i had her bent double with her feet behind her head and her tits squeezed together under her chin she was screaming at me to shoot my load and i thought it sounded a fairly reasonable request at that moment and my balls were aching to shed their cloudy essencce and when i did it was all fury and fire sweat pouring down my back and into my eyes and the stars themselves shot out of their spheres and lightning flashed down the sky over a desert landscape where no one was there to witness it her eyes were liquid and shiny like the eyes of a doe and someone was breathing so heavy that it took me some moments to understand that it was me my whole body was tingling and trembling i pulled out and collapsed onto the sofa where we had rocked the universe then it was all of a sudden lights out and me coming back to the world in a grey halflight alone on the sofa and naked and shivery under a rug it all seemed like a weird dream what was i doing on this sofa in this strange girls flat i sat up and looked about me in the immediate vicinity it looked like a hand grenade had gone off my clothes were scattered all about my underpants were hanging off the ceiling lampshade i retrieved them and collected the rest of my clothes and got dressed i went looking for the girl i wanted to know who was going to be the mother of my children i was laffing to myself at that one when i heard snoring coming from behind a door along the passageway from the stairs i had humped up the night just gone i opened the door as quietly as i could and saw a vison of total anarchy and disarray she was face down and tangled in sheets like tracey emin had personally arranged the disorder a snakes head appeared at her right shoulder and i was about to pull the door to and fuck off into the grey morning when the siffling little pig snoring stopped and she opened a heavy eyelid and stared at me who are you dont answer just go then the eye closed and i did just that closing the door and leaving her to her drugged out brain fucked morning i needed my space i needed time to myself and rest i didnt care that it was in murder central hackney they could knife and shoot each other to death in the dogshit park or off homerton high street it made no difference to me i was gonna sleep for a week a little atom of eternity undisturbed in my private mausoleum and the only people i would hope to see would be the people of my dreams plucked from the old subconscious and endowed with the power to move me to laffter or to tears i cant say but it was odd and not a little disturbing to be back in my own pad it wasnt like i had been there that long anyway i felt disturbed to my inner core like the quiet heart of my soul was not sure of its place in the world no more all my life i had been moved about pushed and pulled this way then that and i should have been a happy little bunny in my hutch but i wasnt i couldnt really believe that i was safe and secure and it wasnt nothing to do with hackney christ there were people dying on the streets who would have envied me what i had and it was my warped way to see the shitty disorder of it all under the still surface it was all compact and dense as a dream my life i had moments when i caught a glimpse of another world a better world but i didnt know if i would ever touch it live it inhabit it my soul was a wandering star and i had burned so bright burning up my energy so that it was a fierce and frenzied stranger a madman with a blade who wanted to terrorize the weak and foolish and what did that make me o christ i was lost and abandoned on a dark sea im gonna fucking end up painting my faeces on the walls of this hackney flat theyll find me that simon twat will find me bollock naked and stinking like a sewer hanging from a doorframe with some sort of knot tied to make a noose and my tongue all black and swollen and bulging out of my mouth fuck i really needed a long rest i crashed and slept ive no idea how long days but what does it matter bears hibernate for months and dont come back out into the world and think fuck ive just missed the whole winter thats a pisser i felt more able to face the world way less agitated when i woke up i thought about my mum and dad funny id thought about them almost like single people he had a pork pie hat and she wore tight skirts and she was the one i went to if i felt afraid of the dark or just something off the dial like the pattern in the wallpaper in my bedroom was moving and he was drunk a lot and swaying to the beat of some music in the living room but now i thought of them conjoined a couple giving each other a bit of tongue or a nibble behind the ear and it come back to me in vivid detail the rogering i give the junkhead up the stairs only now it wasnt me no longer it was my dad blowing like a grampus with my mum below screaming and fighting with and against him it was thus from the beginning of the world adam and eve in the garden of eden or at the side of a campsite in olduvai gorge when time itself was young i didnt feel bad thinking of the lusty work of the dear dead departed they had got me here got me over the starting line and i knew one thing i was gonna fill my boots and go back for seconds and thirds to islington it was about a week later i turned up on her doorstep i had a semi just hearing her pad down the stairs to the door id taken a chance she was in cos i had no way of making contact with her id even thought of a half clever line to throw at her when she opened the door remember me im the one who thrust you up them stairs on the end of my knob and i was smiling to myself when the door opened but smile and semi disappeared like the baggage train of a defeated army in disarray and confusion cos it wasnt her standing in front of me it was a bloke with lizard eyes cold lizard eyes narrow as slits what can i do you for mate trouble was i could think of a hundred things to say to him but none of them particularly helpful and all of them guaranteed to end up with one of us drawing blood from the other can i help you his tone had changed in the short interval between two blunt questions and i still hadnt uttered a syllable i was pretty sure he was just about to do the human equivalent of a lizard extending his tongue lightning fast and sticking me on the end of it and chewing me up attenboro balls was preparing the comforting speech for the nation about the film being slowed down by a factor of twenty so we could catch every grisly detail of the action but as it happened i was saved the necessity of defending myself by her voice at the top of the stairs who is it lizardman turned his head slightly and shouted dunno some mute boyfriend of yours she peered down at me and padded off into what i knew was the living room with a brief admit and that was that i was in the door and followed the lizard up the stairs i was certain then that she must have recollected something of our night of monstrous passion but as soon as i got in the living room she looked me up and down and a knot appeared in her forehead what dyou want she said which threw me and the lizard both you dont know him he said to her and she shrugged and answered should i i felt i was on a high board over dark blue water there are situations when you absolutely feel compelled to jump against everything that your body is telling you it just becomes impossible to stay on the board a moment longer and your fear is so great you want to end it before some heavy bastard gets on the board and starts jumping up and down and causing massive vibrations that will reverberate through your body and turn your insides to jelly i came here over a week ago id opened a toilet door in a pub near here and disturbed you she was blank as blank but lizard suddenly perked up clicked his fingers and pointed at me knew you looked familiar you gave me a minor heart attack that night i tried to look cool and laff but i knew it sounded nervous and pathetic you got any dosh on you mate john suddenly popped out of her mouth and into the room the lizard looked mildly interested you remember his name he looked at me youre honoured you know that she usually forgets everything if its more than two days old its martin actually i said why i cant say at this point in time but the john business had irritated me somehow she didnt seem to care or mind anyway to judge by her expression and lizardman was smiling and holding out his hand i gave him what cash i had on me maybe £30 he seemed satisfied i didnt even ask him what it was for i felt it was like the entrance price to some kinky club and i was sort of right in a way cos he produced a pouch and opened it up there were pipes and spliffs and powders and needles pattie i soon found out lit a spliff while he gerry lit up a small metal pipe hed filled with shatter it was party time in the tepee the pipe and the spliff changing hands and moving between us in a miasma of a drowsy heavy fog we were tighter than a cluster of chinkies in an opium den the talk wandered all over the place it wasnt important what was important was a spot on a wall that seemed to grow and shrink and move about of its own free will can spots have free will i was getting very anxious to know the answer to that all encompassing question though i had no idea what it had to do with a compass maybe it was following true north the lizardman old gerry was in fact a chameleon or a comedian anyway he changed hue looked more blue then more red and came towards me before shrinking down to the size of a child he was speaking a lot a hell of a lot but none of it made sense bits of his monologue went awol just jumped out of sequence and left me feeling very disturbed they were looking at me i must know something they needed to know and they were going to get angry and kill me then there was a silence all around pattie was looking at the floor and gerry was smiling and staring at one of his hands turning it this way and that in the light they seemed entirely unconcerned about me uninterested yet i could not shake the feeling of dark apprehension and foreboding there was somebody standing directly behind me and he wanted to do me harm i wanted to turn round and see who it was but i couldnt i wanted desperately to leave to go home but that word home rang hollow for fuck sake where was home it couldnt be hackney not hackney you had to be born in that shithole gutter to call it home i wanted to move but the will wasnt there the very thought of movement seemed a kind of absurdity if i tried to put one foot in front of the other i would topple over and laffter would grapple me from every quarter of the room the furniture would bend and sway and the curtains swish back and forth with giggles and chuckles and lights would flicker with coughs brought on by the strange dispensation of laffter we were three chimps at feeding time at the zoo and i really wanted to run up the back of the sofa and screech with delight but as i said my rootedness forbade any such hysterical behaviour you have been brought before this court for the crime of rootedness this was the terrible judge who was standing behind me and holding some bastard of an executioners axe right over my head but as i couldnt turn round i started to sing to drown out his speech about me being a cheeky chimpanzee who has lost his mirth for all it was worth i recalled from somewhere a memory of my dad in another sitting room singing a tom waits song the piano has been dinking the piano has been drinking not me not me not me i must have been singing along cos pattie practically screamed wheres the fucking frog croaking which started gerry on a musical pilgrimage to join in and croak along with me and tom waits and this really set the witch upon the broom cos she called us a pair of cunts and threw something which shattered against a sideboard with a boom like a glass grenade then she put on a disc and shouted this is real music you expletive deleted cos it was either piles of human turd or hemeroids of the human absurd either way it made no great sense and she uttered but one word with great emphasis portishead gerry made a quiet comment to himself probably just a fuck or shit i had no precons and stood there as this throbbing and pulsing sound began to animate the room the walls expanded and contracted to the beat of the music and the floor and the furniture swirled and twirled around me then a lovely high voice began to rise and it came from pattie who was like a silky technicolour animation of herself and i toppled back into a seat and gazed at her as she filled the room with her silver notes and i began to shrink into the sofa until i felt as small as a mouse and pattie was tall as an obelisk everything was blending and blurring into everything else until darkness overwhelmed me when i came back to the world i had moved or somehow been moved into a bed a grey halflight penetrated the gloom all around in the corners of the room it was still night i could hear someone weeping close by and it sounded too close and loud like the sound was trying to unsettle me and irritate me to tell it to put a cork in it before i strangled it but maybe whoever it was would get a jump on me and come screaming into my face you think you got problems your problems i see and theyre fucking petty little nothings you want to know what pain is ill bite your nose off and then youll know all about pain i pushed myself up by my elbows into a semblance of a sitting position and for a moment or two the room swung this way and that i might as well have been on a ship on the ocean in a rough sea but it settled soon enough and i saw then that pattie had her back to me she was sitting on the edge of the bed and she was the one providing the tears and the crying it wasnt dramatic or anything it wasnt the wailing wall or nothing all the same shed plucked me from oblivion and filled my head with questions so many i didnt quite know where to start and i knew some of them were trivial and of no real importance in the grand scheme of things my mouth felt like it was coated with a greasy moss and the back of the throat was cracked and dry and still she kept crying softly almost noiselessly now and i wouldnt have known too much about her predicament but for her upper back and shoulders heaving gently from time to time everything alright i said and knew it was a stupid thing to say as soon as the words were out of my mouth she didnt reply which was probably better than her lighting into me over nothing but maybe she was operating from a principle of conservation of energy or maybe she just couldnt be arsed to talk to me or anyone at all at that grey halflight time of the morning thats the problem with language with talking and communication you think of it as a twoway street you say something and i respond or vice versa but maybe you just want to be left the fuck alone with your quiet or sometimes tumultuous thoughts and a question is not simply annoying it might be prodigiously provoking cos you thought you were alone on a heath or in a private culdesac and the last thing you wanted or anticipated was an interruption from a grinning baboon with no consideration for your state of mind intention thats the nub of the matter its like wearing a bright scarf or tie to a funeral what were you thinking about eh you fucking dimwit you should have been straitjacketed that very morning so you couldnt fuck things up for yourself and everybody else o no you say i was simply trying to look on the bright side to lift the spirts of friends and family alike that death is not an end its only a transition i mean weve all gotta go weve all got to pay the ferryman but why not approach him with a dash of sky blue or amethyst hell still take you over the dark waters of the styx to those who have passed beyond i was pulling on my trousers thinking it was best to beat a retreat and get the hell out of dodge when a tiny voice said dont leave me it was my turn to say nothing i zipped up my flies and came round to her side of the bed just in time to see her inject herself fuck her arm was a mess pockmarked with needle holes and sores she gave me a deadeyed look and there was a sadness there id never seen in another being dont judge me she took the needle out and placed it on a small dish on top of a rickety bedside table she was breathing in a shallow way quick little breaths and her pupils were sort of bouncing around the top of her eyeballs so she showed a lot of the white of her eyes then suddenly she swooned back onto the bed and lay with her mouth open some drool spilling out the sides this will tell against me somewhat especially if youre a stickler for correct behaviour but i could almost have bonked her there and then i mean it would almost have been like humping a piece of dead meat but the evil little thought was there for a moment but then i thought about the practicalities of the matter all the things id have to do to warm myself to the job in hand and i couldnt even raise a semi in anticipation instead i got up off the bed and went out into the corridor to take a look around the sitting room was a catastrophe designed once more by tracey emin and handed over to some terrorist org from north africa gerry was nowhere to be seen which was fine by me cos i knew i wasnt in the mood for small talk with him right then i found a teatowel in the kitchen and ran it under water and brought it back to sleeping beauty in the bedroom well truthfully she was more like the beast but i wanted to help why i couldnt have explained to myself or anyone else her forehead was beaded with sweat and i dabbed the beads away and blew gently on her skin are we on a boat she said were floating on the sea and a lighthouse is sending its beams out to us i want to be a lighthouse she said why cant i be a lighthouse cos youre not mrs dalloway it was a punt into the dark all this allegorical crap about lighthouses fuck knew what was in her mind she opened her eyes and stared at me her pupils were oscillating so fast is she your mother who i said mrs what did you call her dollways i couldnt help laffing she said i was funny then and closed her eyes you can fuck me if you want this made me laff even more youre such a fucking loser you know that these were her last words before she conked out i hung around for some time after that making sure she was alright i didnt take her up on the offer of a free fuck i sort of felt responsible for her it was a new and a strange disturbing feeling would she remember anything when the drugs wore off i decided not to hang around to find out i thought about tidying up a bit but dismissed the thought as i was too mentally and physically shattered to make the effort suddenly i just wanted to get back to basecamp and regroup she was getting under my skin and i knew it was kind of nutso to think about seeing her again but i felt like i was infected with some delirium some disorder of the blood that would have me crawling back to her sooner or later its a funny thing about hackney its both dreary and lively at the same time theres little of beauty in its buildings and it definitely has a depressed air about it and yet there is colour here and there if you look for it youll see some black dude showing off to his mates and he might be one of the jackson five or some reggae prince strutting it and showing off with a cockerels pride i looked in on the paki brothers to buy some milk and a box of cereal they didnt exactly jump up and down or high five each other when i walked into their store it was the same blank look i always got from them still they did exchange a look which probably meant i was giving off the vibe of one of the walking undead my head was kinda numb and i caught glimpses of a ghost in reflections off glass and metal any blood that was sloshing around inside me was nowhere near my face and when i left them they kicked off a jabbering session all about me no doubt thing is what dyou expect a weirdo kid comes in and mooches around buys a few things to eat from time to time doesnt take care of himself looks like pasty shit and gives off an aura of decay moral and physical why shouldnt they talk about me in their place i would there was a oneman reception committee waiting for me at the flat simon and he didnt look particularly pleased to see me i wondered how hed got in he showed me a spare key and saw my fuck this is shit expression this is a violation of my human rights though thats more difficult to get across without saying the words you just look constipated or like an imbecile with a sudoku puzzle anyway i was too jaded and wasted to argue with him and he offered his explanation which ran as follows we keep keys for all our flats in case our tenants get into difficulties and do something drastic like self harming or hanging themselves i must have given him a sort of demented sergeant major look during the zulu uprising cos he became a bit vigorous then and told me dont think it doesnt happen cos it does cut one down just last week not much older than you you see all this freedom can be too much for some youre more fragile than you think you are and right now you are at a crossroads you could be taken back into the mainstream system for your own protection mainstream my eyebrow said and he interpreted it correctly oh yes you could be put back in a ward and given a padded cell and have a couple of gorillas chain and unchain you and wipe your arse for you i was screwing my face up at the very thought of this particular avenue off the crossroads and he took this as his cue to ram home his homily thats right not a very pretty picture cos you know what im talking about youve been there before and you dont want to go back there but there is yet another route and you might think it more appealing cos you simply disappear off the radar were so understaffed and pressured that we havent the time or resources to come looking for you if you take it upon yourself to fuck off into the night he drew breath and looked at me not unkindly you have a great opportunity here to make something of your life but if you abuse this opportunity theres a long line of people waiting to take your place and make this flat their home i dont know what you get up to or where you go but ive been round here a few times and each time no martin to be seen and if i may pass a comment on your appearance you look like death warmed up is this what youre living on he indicated the milk and cereal which i was still clutching to myself youre young martin and have a lot to learn but heres the thing you dont have to pack all of life into one day or one month its a long game so slow down and let life come to you instead of chasing it like a dog running after its own tail simon started towards the door well ive said my piece but really your fate is in your own hands you are the creator of your destiny if you only knew it as he opened the door he fired a warning shot past me youre running a little high with your spending which seems odd cos your food bill cant exactly be a huge drain but if you carry on with your present rate of expenditure your funds will be stopped and your card cancelled live within your means young man if that doesnt sound too dickensian he left me with a smile and closed the door the rage that had been building slowly and secretly within me at his very presence in the flat now erupted and i threw the cereal box at the door and let out a guttural cry that shook my whole body how dare he how fucking dare he lecture me the ballless cunt i writhed and spat invective and verbal vomit and turds until my face was flushed as a boiled lobster and my mouth flecked with foam my ticker was going as fast as a bullet train through a mile long tunnel when i come out the other end i was knackered and heavy with the desire to sleep i felt the milk carton slip from my fingers and land on the floor with a dull thud i dont remember going to the bed and lying down but i do remember this the most terrible weird dream i had ever had i was in a church and the priest was adolf hitler and he was ranting from the pulpit like a rabid dog the congregation were all agog all with their arms raised in salute they were his faithful flock of sheep some even had ovine faces and hard marbly baas but that wasnt weird really i mean people will swallow the stupidest ideas and give themselves to crazed individuals cos they cant stand to be alone it frightens them and they lose purpose better to have a warped purpose than no purpose at all but then i looked at the christ figure on the cross i was walking slowly in the central aisle the congregation were no longer saluting they were pointing at me and shouting death death death and hitler was pointing at me and snarling as only a rabid austrian loony dictator can do and thats when i saw that christ had morphed into pattie she wore a crown of thorns and blood was running down from under her hairline and she was nailed to the cross with syringes the chant all around had changed to judas judas judas take your blood money and begone i woke up then totally at sea disoriented and staring at a block like a rectangle on the floor it was the milk i rasied myself like a giant slug or a sloth feeling weak and nauseous it didnt help much to get a bowl of cereal into me and i paced back and forth from kitchen to living room to bedroom and back again for hours until i found myself staring down at the dogshit park with only one thought in my head i wasnt gonna stay in that flat in hackney for the rest of my natural what was life without a risk it was an avoidance of all that was genuine and true to the deeper self i wasnt gonna rob banks or kill the queen that was for the extreme lunatics the psychos and the deranged i wasnt even gonna sneak into buck palace like a cat burglar dont be alarmed your maj im not here to steal your crown jewels or nothing and i dont want no bauble to pin on my chest i just wanna chat i can see youre a bit discombobulated my being here how did one gain entrance to the palace and avoid ones equerries and footmen never mind that your maj i wanna talk about the state of the nation and the knobhead who is running this great nation of ours into the ground i mean doesnt it make you sick the lies they come out with couching it in olde worldie language the honourable gentleman from the north has made a valid point thats a con right there when what he really means is that twat that scumbag from the unwashed hordes of northern scum has scored one against me but ill get him in the longgrass if it's the last thing i do order ordeeeeerrrr please young man do try to modify your voice philip is a very light sleeper and once awake he wanders in here and his flatulence is something terrible at night but on the question of the pm and the state of the nation yes one would tend to agree with one in ones assessment of the pm for he is indeed as you so vividly put it a knobhead of the very first order and one confesses one pines for the old days when sir winston was pm and one was a youngthing full of hope and aspirations thank you your maj youve always played a blinder youve done alright considering the nonces you has to deal with on a daily basis and all them corgis getting fat and asthmatic and under your feet i should think youd sooner lose one of your family members than one of them corgis after all they havent done anyone any harm or stuck their big neb or knob in where it wasnt wanted ta ta for now got to be going it was some days later i turned up at patties door i didnt know what to expect when i rung the doorbell i could hear movement in the flat and someone padding down the stairs i half expected and feared that she would look like a ghoul all ashen and grey with dark shadows under her eyes but no she was quite the opposite she was alright dont get me wrong she wouldnt have made the cover of country life or vogue but there was colour in her cheeks and a bright look to her eye she gave me a little kiss on the cheek and took me by the hand to lead me up the stairs and it was only then that i realised there was something different about her cos i realised i was staring at the nape of her neck and it was delicate and shaped like a swans when she leant forward she had had her hair chopped that was the thing i was on the point of kissing that neck of hers it was like the beginning of a fetish all the little fine hairs delicate and following a v pattern as they spread outwards from the top of her backbone it was weird cos i could have been in a helicopter looking down from a great height on an area of sparse growth in a forest each tree one of her tiny hairs and a small pimple was a huge rock and there might have been a bear lying under it and having forty winks and dreaming of catching a fuckoff fat salmon as it jumped out at the falls id heard of fetishes before like people sucking toes or fingers or biting calf muscles or a tight arse and all this shit and nonsense was rattling round inside my skull in the time it took to walk from the top of the stairs into the living room i dont really know what i expected or who i expected to see there gerry wouldnt have been a surprise but to see a girl in a caftan surrounded by a ring of stones and crystals and with chains of small bells hung around her neck was a bit strange she had a shaved head and was chanting in a low murmur so i couldnt make out a single word i couldnt even have said what language her head was wobbling a bit and there was an overpowering stink of incense from sticks that were placed at the four corners of the mat she was sitting on pattie sat me down beside her on the sofa and we faced the girl she said was a shaman who started making a low humming sound pattie held out both of her hands and opposed index fingers to thumbs she smiled at me and gave the tiniest of nods by which i understood i was to play my part in this nonsense so when in rome and all that i followed her example and then shaman and pattie were both making this low rumbling vibrating sound which seemed to resolve itself into the one syllable om there seemed no necessity for me to follow them in this particular piece of folly but i couldnt help myself i just had to join in and at first i was just playing along you know sort of going through the motions and i had to suppress a fit of laffter at one point cos i could see myself somewhere down the road in a pub with blokes talking about it and them ragging me and calling me a nonce or all sitting round looking at their beers and chanting om all together and trying to get a rise out of me in the cloud of unknowing of my possible future self course i knew i wouldnt want to share any scrap of myself with dickheads but you never know what company youll end up with just to be with company shaman girl interrupted my meandering river of thoughts and said concentrate on pure breath push all thoughts away still the mind close your eyes and as you breathe in you are breathing pure white light and as you breathe out you purge the mind and the body of all the little thoughts that weigh upon your heart and mind you are breathing out a thick black smoke breathing in and breathing out light in dark out it was strange cos at first i was still in that future pub somewhere time unspecified but it faded to nothing and then i lost all track of time and place i became light and smoke filthy london dickensian fog chundering out of me like i was a tunnel of impurity and the light was battling with the dark until it all resolved itself and i felt clear and calm and so peaceful it was unreal when i opened my eyes the two girls were grinning at me enjoy your sleep pattie said i must have looked surprised cos they laffed then and i could feel my face was hot you were snoring pattie continued no i wasnt i protested the two girls shared a look then and i felt awkward and uncomfortable like id forgotten how to feel since i was a kid and my sisters used to rag me its alright martin said shaman girl its good to relax and let your cares dissolve they left me sitting there in a funk as they waltzed off arm in arm to the kitchen giggling to themselves and whispering things in each others ear i felt i was being made to look like a fool i felt like a fool a twat of the first order a nonce a ponce and a fucking child what man can withstand the withering scorn of a womans laff someone i mean some bloke must have written that somewhere some time just before he topped himself he was probably french and put in a ton of zoots and alores and polished off a couple of bottles of red wine before being carted off to the guillotine to have his neck shaved and to think id been working myself up to kiss patties neck before i came into the seance or whatever it was one thing it was it was a fucking poor show being rumbled like that i mean was it fucking possible that i could have nodded off while thinking i was awake ill admit i wasnt wide awake but i thought i was in the room listening to the oms and all that shit about light and smoke it was being picked on that was most annoying being picked on and rounded on for the tiniest lapse of concentration fucking crime of the century a head appeared in the doorway and looked at me curiously it was the shaman herself are you coming or what were having tea in the kitchen we thought you must have fallen asleep again then the head disappeared and i parked my resentment and followed the witchy woman to the kitchen where an aroma of lemon and herbs reached me before i saw pattie smiling with a look of devotion on her face as cristal took her seat at the table cristals helping me to release myself from the bonds of sufferance pull up a chair and have some tea its a blend of lemongrass verbena and chamomile its pretty awful stuff pattie couldnt stop herself from laffing but i have been told on the highest authority she almost bowed to cristal and put her hands together palm to palm that its good for a lot of ailments emotional and mental its an acquired taste put in cristal i sat down at the table and a bowl without a handle was half filled with a liquid which looked like pee and gave off a mild whiff of a stagnant pond under the lemon and herbs they watched me as i took a sip it really wasnt that bad definitely not the most revolting shit id ever tasted but it did push my face this way and that for a moment you dont like it neither said pattie i managed to connect with the french dude who was being carted off to execution as for enjoyment im not persuaded it sits in a bowl of piss there was a silence from both girls and then cristal burst out laffing i found out then that she worked in local government she was a clerk of sorts and she only did this shaman lark in her spare time she didnt even call herself a shaman that was pattie coming up with that coat hanger but she was very chilled out shed been dealing with patties housing benefit case and had got to know her a bit and theyd hit it off and the rest was nobody elses business certainly not the idiots she worked with they were worse than the people she had to visit to assess their claims why dyou do it then pattie didnt like me asking that question but cristal was cool as cool about it life is an accommodation you know you have a high flier of a job you get really good money you think youve got it made but all youve done is buy into the corporate world its belief system and the money gets you things you dont really need its a drug and you have to free yourself from the drug before you can see where you really are in the world and who you have the potential to be when she had left patties flat she left something of her aura behind the living room for instance seemed to vibrate at some miniscule level with the throaty om of her chanting pattie was charged up and plugged in for hours after her guru shaman priestess bosom friend had gone and when we made love it was weirdly both quieter and more intense we didnt shout and carry on with a verbal commentary like before and the nape of her neck nearly made me delirious with a feeling that careened down my spine and tingled my toes it was only after making love in the replete and sated afterrut when id taken my antlers off and was so deeply at peace and at one with everything in the universe that i thought of asking about gerry hes off in amsterdam he does this every once in a while just to get his head cleared and have a major chill out you ever been to amsterdam i shook my head i was afraid to tell her id never been out of england in case she thought me a half educated untravelled ignorant twat which i was i knew that i just didnt like people pointing it out to me i know what we need she became almost childlike and her face was all alert and not drugged with sex like i felt mine was candles we need lots and lots of candles cristal says they spread an aura of peace and calm which is good isnt it cos theres way too much violence in the world right now she was out of bed like a shot and gathering every little melted down stump of candle and all the while keeping up a running commentary about violence to women children old people animals she stuck in a good dig at the norwegians and japanese for hunting whales as she flitted here and there like a puck or ariel gathering up candle wax and receptacles like dirty cups and ash trays and chipped plates to stand the candles on i heard her rummaging about in the other rooms it was faint and seemed distant and i was dozing off to a sleepy corner of my soul when she came back into the bedroom laden with all the necessary for a relaxing softly lit time of deep meditation and peace matches you got any matches cant find one anywhere look in my jacket theres a lighter there somewhere she dumped what she had on her side of the bed and went out to find my jacket i was pretty sure it was in the living room and the flat was tiny so i thought shed come bouncing back to me toot suite but she didnt and when she did come back it was clear as day that she had swallowed an unhappy pill you find the lighter she gave me a filthy fucking look and i should have taken it for a warning cos the next thing the lighter came whizzing by my head and bounced off the wall behind me who the fuck is she pattie screamed at me you bastard you twotiming shit it wasnt an unhappy pill shed took it was an insanity root or too much wacky weed in the teapot i sat up a bit i dont know what youre on about i aint doing a number with no one else what put that idea in your head i thought we was gonna chill out with candles and peace and love but even as i said these sugared words her face was transforming into a devils mask and she held out a scrap of paper in a hand that trembled and shook with rage i couldnt think what this note held but the old gut was telling me it probably wasnt good news to judge by the state she was getting herself in who is nora the voice was small but it wasnt weak and for a moment my mind was blank who the fucking hell is nora answer me fuck it slammed back into me like a tank reversing at full speed nora shit id totally forgotten about her answer me you shitty fuck i can see youre angry but its really quite simple those words popped out as a kind of stopgap cos my mind was stopping and starting i was a rat in a maze and there was no easy way out pattie suddenly ran to the bed and jumped on it pushing some of the cups and plates and candles on to the floor she stood over me and for the first time i felt a tremendous rush inside me of fear and anger at what might happen she dropped to her knees and they pinned me to the bed she held the note nora had given me with her address very close to my face and screamed at me what does she mean to you nothing she dont mean nothing to me o she doesnt then why the fuck are you carrying her name and address around in your jacket do you collect names and addresses like other boys collect stamps i didnt like the way this talk was going but i didnt know what to say to pattie to make her feel better answer me you lying fuck i only met her once or twice id forgotten i even had the note i mean dyou think id ask you to look for a lighter in my jacket knowing the note was there yes she screamed cos youre a stupid ignorant uncaring idiot arent you yes i heard myself reply cos this was way scarier than being in a fight with a bloke with a bloke i could have broken his nose by now and stamped on his bollocks but this kind of fighting was nasty i felt my soul was being scraped raw with a cheese grater this was bunny boiler territory and i was the bunny well which was it i must have looked very stupid right then cos id no idea what she was talking about all this sudden switch from peace and calm to out and out crucifixion was very trying on the nerves did you meet this prostitute once or twice i pondered this a nanosecond this wasnt fair not fair at all nora wasnt a prostitute and i wanted to lodge a formal complaint with the united nations but i couldnt see pattie buying into that twice i said in a voice that was weak and guilty as hell suddenly id turned into the town idiot and everyone was shunning me turning their backs on me as i limped along main street with my leg in a brace i wanted to protest that yes id met her twice so what crime of the fucking century hang me from a tree by my balls cover them with honey and set wasps on me but the thing was pattie had that look in her eye that said she wouldnt need any persuading none at all to proceed with the most unreasonable torture and punishment she wore an expression of such contempt and disappointment that i was having the greatest difficulty keeping eye contact suddenly she got off me fucking men she muttered under her breath then exploded with words that came out of her like rocks ejected from a volcano youre all the same but you are one pathetic specimen i should have checked more thoroughly under the rock you crawled out from then she flicked my lighter into life and torched the note with noras name and address get out were her next words delivered with a curt finality that brooked no opposition i slid into my breeks like footage of a snake shedding its skin played in reverse and left pattie looking like a mad woman from the ward id left in charge of the gorillas i heard something smash against a wall and a scream like a furious banshee as i walked to the head of the stairs the scream lingered in the silence like a fart in underpants and i should have been down them stairs and scooting out the door faster than jumping jack flash as my old dad used to say but something held me it was like a force like something out of star trek an invisible force from outside and i couldnt even mumble beam me up scottie i felt so bad like i was the one at fault i felt like a little boy and id done something bad and mummy was angry with me and how could i say sorry o christ id wet the bed or worse and i wanted to cry me a river so terribly that i couldnt put a foot on the first step and the front door seemed a long way away you still here came patties voice it didnt sound so angry this time i turned to look at her and our faces would have done well in the national gallery for sados of the 21st century someone fired a silent starting gun and we were running and embracing like it was brexit and world poverty and the mystery of black holes all sorted for all time end of ww2 and the final of im a celebrity get me out of here all rolled into one it was cannons roaring and fireworks going off i was in her and up her before we even got in the bedroom again and id shot my bolt of sticky joy before we hit the bed and we must have said sorry so many times that its a pity there wasnt an official from the guinness book of world records to verify the idiocy of it all but im using 20/20 hindsight here cos i had no idea whatsoever of the rubicon i was crossing julius caesar was 100% aware of the risks he was taking and went across with both eyes fully open i was blindfolded though i didnt know it and had my ears stopped with the music of love or sex anyway cos the next thing i knew i was lying next to pattie and telling her i should move in with her and she was lapping it up the cat had got her cream and she was loving it it seemed so right which later seemed so wrong but im getting ahead of myself i mean you couldnt blame a japanese gent for taking a stroll along the river in hiroshima on a monday in august he couldnt know what was coming his way out of a clear blue sky and it wasnt like everything didnt go great at first all that shit with nora was forgotten about and we settled into a groove we was both damaged and pattie did go on a bit at times about her mum and the time she had of it at home and her stepfather hitting on her and she having to get out from under nearly literally once or twice but she had a fragile soul that made me want to protect her and hold her in my arms i even tried to write some lyrics about her and me but i didnt commit none of them to paper in case it led to another torching session your tattoos are so you so you your world inked into your skin i could read you like a living work of art you tart see what i mean i just kept that one alive in a little corner of my mind and dusted it off if she was in a mood with me cos she could be moody and always it was with me never the shameless shaman cristal who paid us frequent visits at some awkward moments like once or twice i was hanging out of pattie and working towards a regular juddering chinese new year firework display of an orgasm when a tiny knock came at the bedroom door and cristals voice squeaked through from the landing you there pattie my vote was for continuing the pleasure cruise but pattie almost pushed me off her in an effort to communicate with her soul sister cristal stuck her head in round the door and smiled hope im not disturbing you or anything course you are you fucking bint by my throbbing cock and still tingling balls i could wring your scrawny chicken neck but of course i said nothing of the sort i just smiled weakly as pattie got out of bed and embraced cristal with her still moist cunny after all i was just the prick in the bed what did i matter this minor gnat in the ointment was one thing i just had to force the penal colony into submission for the sake of good relations knowing thered always be another time to fuck patties brains out and die a small death but the bigger problem came from a quarter i should have known would prove an obstacle but i had allowed myself to be blindsided its one thing crossing the rubicon then burning the bridge but to turn round after the flames have reached the sky and to meet with a substantial obstacle lets just say i didnt feel exactly clever and it came about so simply that it fogged me at first i went out to the local offie to get us some booze and my card was refused i asked the bloke serving me to try it again but the same thing happened off i trotted back to pattie which brought about an uncomfortable q & a session with me mostly replying i dunno i dunno like a recording of a shitty mafia dialogue what you do with the body i dunno what you mean you dunno i dunno i dunno well what we gonna do now i dunno pattie coughed up the cash for the booze and i went down and got it but that wasnt the end of the matter cos now she started griping about me living off her and her footing the bill and then it struck me that simon had carried through his threat of cutting off my funds when id explained the background to pattie she was less than chuffed in fact she was so unchuffed she made chuffed look like the impossible dream i knew then thered be no rumpy pumpy no in and out rather the opposite cos she was on the verge of kicking me out i knew she was on a tight budget and she didnt work on account of being in rehab but the way things were spiralling out of control was pushing me well out of my comfort zone i couldnt explain it even to myself but i didnt want the false freedom of hackney no more i didnt wanna be staring down at the dogshit park with simon the shit paying me visits when i least expected it and i loved being with pattie joined to her as flesh made one with my hands holding her arse while we shagged she loved that squeeze me squeeze me hard our bodies drenched in sweat unlike a certain member of the royal family must be a german thing passed down the royal hanoverian dna no svets und no hanking panking mit unterage girlies but only going out to kauf pizzas on incriminating dates anyway in the middle of patties rant about money and space i said id get a job she shut up and drank herself into a stupor i didnt carry on drinking i sat thinking about what that meant cos to tell the gospel id never held a job for more than a week and the last time was when i was 14 and mum was dying i worked in a petrol station and sometimes the stink of oil and petrol would mingle with the odour of decay in her bedroom youre born you die and in between theres this godawful creeping towards the grave with a bit of shagging and now the fear of work the search for which got me out of the flat and away from pattie who was more than surprised when i come back one day and told her id landed the position of gravedigger at a cemetery a few miles from islington she wasnt exactly impressed more stupefied and disbelieving but i told her it was the best of the bunch cos id looked into a job at a pleating factory whats that she asked well they have these big rolls of cloth bolts and theyre put through these machines that create pleats in the material she found all this faintly funny and weird and she didnt get what i was telling her cos she asked why at first i didnt know what to say cos i didnt know what she meant why do they pleat the material for dresses and skirts i think her face showed the least interest i have ever seen on any persons face talking about the weather generates more life and movement in facial muscles anyway i didnt take that job which caused her once again to employ the three letter interrogative cos i didnt fancy it and before she could leap in again with another wherefore i told her about the stink of chemicals in the airless factory the heat and the noise of shuttles going back and forth and then this old jewboy who must have been close to ninety but got around the place better than most and turned up to ball anyone out he thought was slacking or doing a bad job like fucking up the pleats and i just calculated it was only a matter of time before this foulmouthed old hebrew spat out his gutter eastend demented argot on me and i fancied id just flip and poke him in the eye so i shoved a bolt in the wrong way and just waltzed out before anyone could notice and as i walked off down the road past other sweat shops and shitty satanic mills it did cross my mind to go back to hackney and try to persuade simon to give me my privileges back but burning bridges and crossing rubicons and all that twaddle i just couldnt see myself begging before that cunt if this was the price of my true independence it was a price worth paying there were two old boys who had been at the cemetery for ever and a day and a manager with a young family who lived in a cottage on site the old boys were called jimmy and percy the manager was in his mid forties he was called graham and he had a young kid only about 3 or 4 and i would see this kid running along the paths that intersected the graves and id lie in wait for him behind a gravestone and spring up and act like a ghoul or a zombie and even though it was daytime it never ceased to scare the little fella and id crack up as he ran off in tears but he wasnt the only one who got a bit of a ribbing among the stones jimmy and percy were a funny old double act i didnt tell them a thing about my private life cos they were always angling for a bit of personal info on me and theyd talk about me in front of me trying to get a rise jimmy would ask me if i was a married man and id just smile then percy would butt in course he isnt married look at that face theres not a line or wrinkle on it this is a boy who hasnt been touched by the whips and thorns of time o lucky boy said jimmy you enjoy this time you play the field and gather roses while ye may you see said percy when you get to our age the old todger has turned a kind of light tan colour through all the rogering weve done and percy winked at jimmy well youve done enough percy to add a few dark patches onto the lad havent you to which percy just nodded they both looked at me and shook their heads and i cant say now which one it was who then said youll be like a tomcat down there wont you martin a thin pink pole but youll not be able to lick it like a tom then they both wandered off together towards the job in hand muttering that i wouldnt be able to do that no not possible hed have to be double jointed and a sort of houdini of the bedroom a contortionist an olympic acrobat i listened to this gentle ridicule as i followed them to the job what we did every day rain or shine was a variation on a theme sweeping the paths tidying the graves cutting the grass and of course digging an old plot or a new one and filling in after a funeral i was the one who always had to go down in the hole to dig they were very handy at giving out the orders were jimmy and percy but i didnt mind it was good exercise and i could lose myself in the zenlike rhythm of the spadework it was just percy and me one time and i was in a grave at least 7 feet deep throwing the sticky clay up over my shoulder onto the mound of earth i had made to the side of the grave percy looked down at me and warned me not to overdo it you dont want to give yourself an injury my face was flushed and covered in a sheen of sweat o this work suits you young man your eyes are all bright and full of energy o yes youre glowing down there i told him he was welcome to take over for a bit but he pointed out that id nearly finished anyhow and i was a keen one when i got out of that grave he handed me a chilled beer and we drank in an easy silence and for the first time i felt i had a place that i had made my own in the world of work mind it had its strange effects too like waiting at the side of a funeral service graveside in the rain and wishing the priest would hurry up and be done so we could do our job and fill the grave in and go have a cup of tea round the heater in the workshed and then there was the services for dead children and that was hard as anything cos you didnt want to be there not for that kind of funeral it was quite different from lowering a casket with an old man or woman whod seen a lot of life and sucked at the marrow of existence but there was something unnatural and deeply at odds with the order of things to see a tiny casket go into the earth like the last hope and despairing farewell of a lost dream i returned from work one evening i had begun to think of patties place as mine as ours it was home and i was happy there but as i trudged up the stairs i could hear more noise than usual and when i opened the living room door who was there with pattie but gerry in a fog of mary jane they greeted me with hoots and cheers but the cheers were close to jeers they were thick as thieves again as if gerry had never been away i quizzed him a bit about amsterdam and he tried to paint a picture for me of the vibe but i dunno why but i wasnt pleased to see him i couldnt even have told you why it might have been the way he just carried himself as if it was his right to be there and i told myself not to let my feelings show through cos it was patties place and she could invite who she wanted i knew i would get that argument both barrels full in the face if i said a peep about that gerry shit turning up like a bad penny he was her friend before i ever come on the scene so i choked back a rising resentment and took a few tokes of the weed to chill out and try to rise above the moment fucking hard when you have the kind of spirit i have i really wanted to throw him down the stairs and kick him along the street but there was no way i could show my real self cos i hadnt even shown that to pattie in point of fact i wondered sometimes who the real martin was i felt so often like a reed in the wind and id be blown this way and that sometimes feeling miserable and weak and shot through with the pain of thoughts about my mother and father and twats like my sisters and the gorillas who kept me prisoner in the institutions id been left to rot in but i hadnt rotted and i hadnt let life beat me and i wouldnt let a nonce like gerry get the better of me the smile i had put on my face was hurting me like anything suddenly pattie flung an arm around me and kissed me with a weedy mary jane kiss and sucked my bottom lip till i thought she was going to pull it right off my face then released me and turned to gerry and cried hes my man gerry hes the one who brings me happiness and joy from the land of the dead gerrys face went through many tiny almost imperceptible but definitely not insignificant changes and i had the distinct impression he was not a happy bunny about me being called her man maybe he thought i was just a kind of itinerant sex worker and should have been blown away long ago maybe he thought pattie couldnt go for the likes of me i dunno but whatever he was truly thinking he kept to himself for his smile had to be hurting him as much as mine was paining me he asked me about working in the cemetery he told me he could smell death off me which surprised me cos the stink of weed was overpowering in the room but maybe my nose had become clogged with the stench of graves and the odour of decay gerry became an almost permanent fixture then and i found myself spending more and more time at the cemetery i longed for the days of cristal and her mildy lunatic ways but she and gerry were fighting over the same turf and she just stopped calling round give her her due cristal was a well meaning idiot and her harmless chanting had done pattie some good which gerry had quickly eroded with his drugs they didnt come free for gratis and nothing and nearly all our money went on them a month after he turned up at the flat pattie was back to looking like shit i was beginning to look like shit and the old boys jimmy and percy were making comments about me smoking i was becoming one of the walking dead in the cemetery and my skin had an ashen hue my cheeks were hollow and sunken they started to call me frankenstein and i began not to care then the drugs became harder id come back to find pattie with a needle in her arm and fuck all to eat in any cupboards the fridge had half a pint of milk that had gone sour and i found three custard cream biscuits in the bottom of a packet in a drawer in the living room and theyd gone soft so even though i was starving i just couldnt force them down gerry wasnt around which was a good thing cos id probably have had a real go at him and though it didnt seem the best time to talk to pattie i couldnt take it no more this wasnt the dream this was a living nightmare a hell that i was gonna have to walk away from even if it meant being locked up somewhere again i just hadnt signed up for this kind of madness i went back into the bedroom and there she was sleeping beauty with her mouth open and her eyes fluttering under their lids she was a mess christ knows what bosch vision of a hell she was wandering in then but i wasnt hanging around to find out there was no point trying to talk to her now to tell her i was leaving i would leave a note shed probably think me a shitty bastard for walking out but i knew there was no debating with a junkie you couldnt reason with them and you couldnt win them over with any kind of rational thought i knew from experience cos my old man had taken his life on an overdose of drugs and alcohol his body bloated as a whale when he croaked it i was so mixed up feeling so lonely and at a loss looking at pattie it was like looking at a shell of a woman and i didnt know if her soul was still in there i went to her dresser covered in little bottles and halfused lipsticks and jars of creams some of them had stubs of cigarettes in them and i had one of those moments you will recall how i started all this dribbling palaver i remember where i was stalking along by the river in chelsea well i will remember till my dying day where i was when i saw this plastic stick i thought it was a thermometer at first and then i picked it up and had a proper look at it there was a window in the stick showing two vertical lines what did this mean did pattie have some disease she hadnt told me about something in my gut told me i had to find out i couldnt walk away from her until i knew the meaning of that display window i thought of bruce lee i hadnt thought of him in an age what would his onscreen character have done he wouldnt have walked out on a friend in need and as i acknowledged this to myself a strange calm came over me and i sat on the edge of the bed and watched pattie sleep and did not judge her for my feelings were flooding back to her stronger than before an age later she came round i hadnt sat with her all the time id moved about the flat like a caged animal like a panther on the prowl fuck id even tidied up a bit when i looked in on her in the evening she was awake but clearly not in much of a mood to move i sat down near her and held one of her hands eventually i showed her the stick with the two lines and she said fuck but so softly it was no more than a whisper on a breath whats up i said you ill is that what this is about she didnt answer she closed her eyes and before she drifted off i was gonna have my say its been shit since gerry come back from amsterdam you know that dont you i thought cristal was a fucking dipstick but shes harmless id take her any day of the week look at us all the money going on drugs i dont want this no more were not eating well and its like im working to pay gerry to fuck your mind and soul up dont you see that you can thank him for making you ill i stopped talking it had all come out like a tumbling rock from above but at least id told her what was in me and how i felt she opened her eyes and searched deep inside me to locate the someone who wasnt angry or confused or full of the need to justify himself im pregnant martin and im scared even as i sat there still and quiet there was a kind of terror rooting me to the spot my soul however was running through a bombed out urban landscape without another human being in sight stumbling over rubble and broken nmasonry and bleeding all over the place and wanting to scream but no sound would come out of my throat are you sure yes she answered with feeling thats what the test shows and she moved a finger feebly towards the stick i was holding in a whiteknuckle grip fuck fuck fuck fuck fuck i said but without much force or attack what we gonna do i said we were there in the room not 3 feet apart but it was more like we were two wounded souls struggling to reach each other across that bombed out landscape do you want me to have the baby what you asking me for what for cos youre the father dont you want to have it i asked you first i cant even begin to tell you my true state of mind right then confuseddotcom wasnt even close i was in a maze blindfolded and with my ears stuffed and my hands cuffed behind me and there were rabid vicious dogs growling and getting closer by the second o for fuck sake is it always like this every time those fateful words are uttered to an unsuspecting bloke who was only looking for a bit of fun god in his infinite wisdom must be in an eternal state of paralysisinducing laffter at stupid pricks like me i mean what did i really expect the way i carried on well i wasnt god and i wasnt seeing the funny side neither was pattie there were tears and holding each other as if our very lives depended on it and an unwritten constitution was hammered out for how we were going to live from that time on no more drugs no more drugs and no more drugs and definitely no more gerry the fulfilling of the last item bringing an unholy argument in patties living room some days later he was so fucking angry so livid i thought i was gonna have to go full bruce lee on him and convince him of the error of his ways but there was a force holding me back and it was pattie she didnt have to say anything to me i just knew it was out of bounds to have a go at him cos even though she knew deep down that he was peddling death she couldnt help having feelings for him they were two grifters who had got along fine before i came on the scene gerry had a good go at me i was the one who had changed pattie and from his point of view it had been for the worse pattie told him about the pregnancy and without as much as a faint ghost of a deviation in his thinking he accused pattie of being blinded by me dont you see what hes done to you the finger was pointing straight at me hes fucking up your lifestyle youre no longer free girl to make your own choices ive always brought you the substances that lead to the opening of the doors of perception and now you want to share a nothing existence with him hes just closing you down youll see seven months from now youll be at each others throat and youll be cursing your child and each other i must have made some sort of movement towards gerry quite far below the radar cos i wasnt aware of doing a thing pattie put a hand up to check me and spoke very firmly to gerry telling him to get out and never come back they were both upset but he did leave and when he slammed the front door i felt a wave of relief pass over me it wasnt the same for pattie she was well worked up on the verge of tears she buried her face in my shoulder and gripped me fiercely i said nothing i just held her i would never understand how she could be friends with that type let alone have deep feelings for him i suppose gerry must have had more than a touch of the svengalis about him when youre immune to fateful charms its like watching a nuremburg rally and shaking your head at the utter nonces who were zieg heiling and carrying on like fruit loaves before their adored fuhrer mit bomben droppen on the stinken kopfen ve winnen zieg heil zieg heil zieg heil i think my right hand must have twitched in a secret desire to give a salute and then goosestep round the living room like john cleese shouting about not mentioning the war you alright she asked me and i said yeah id live we were one right then it was our body heat and our breathing and our touching our flesh and we were alright we began to live as two separate beings but joined in our universal soul i went off to the cemetery with a deep contentment and the old boys jimmy and percy noticed the change in me they fished about the sly old dogs until they got it out of me about being a father and then the lectures came so that id be prepared for the caca in the nappies the consistency of thick soup and with the smell of a blocked drain in the summer and then the nights of being woken at 2 or 3 in the morning and the crying which wouldnt stop and for which an explanation would not be found this would be me crying i managed to put in old percy liked that jimmy shook his head and muttered something about me having a lot to learn the governers little boy came running past the shed while we were having a tea break id stopped teasing him the game had lost its appeal he was a good boy and percy pointed to him and said that might be your boy in a few years just a bundle of energy without limit you ready for that jimmy chimed in with his no ones ever really ready but at least youre young be a bloody disaster if you was our age isnt that a fact perse the pair had a decent chuckle at that and i never minded what they said at that time even when i was in six inches of water inside a grave and the clay was clogged and saturated i didnt mind it was all one to me as long as i got home to pattie and she was alright cristal had come back into her life and there was a lot of mediatation and chanting and herbal teas and purification visits to the antenatal clinic too of course and i had to participate in classes how to be a good dad fuck i smiled and played dumb and went along with it all cos i thought back to my mum and dad and couldnt see them going through the same malarkey but they must have though i doubt it had much effect on the way i was raised the bigger patties belly got the more i wanted to make love to her course she wasnt up for it all the time but when she was it was a mad delirium of flesh blown up and wobbly yet tight as a drum across the belly it was like making love to a numpho covered in a michelan man suit im not gonna pretend it was wall to wall morning to night bliss cos pattie had mood swings that would have made hitler look like a saint but i just ducked and weaved and kept the head down till the storm had passed but it wasnt just her being pregnant that msde pattie lurch sometimes like a demented hurricane swinging a door off its hinges there was the drug thing too she didnt say nothing but i knew her body must have been weeping like an angel on high for just one more hit me and cristal ill give her her due she might have looked like a nutjob sometimes in her pink leggings and baggy lavender sweat shirt but she was a trooper shc kept pattie on the straight and narrow while i was out at work and there was a little part of me i kept locked up in a soundproofed room who was terrified that what was gonna come out of pattie wasnt going to be like a normal baby but some kind of monstrosity with horns and eyes that glowed in the dark i know its straight out of rosemarys baby but i couldnt help thinking about this and there wasnt a soul i could turn to to tell my fears it would have been good to have had one true friend to spill it all out to who could have said youre just worrying about nothing youre letting your imagination run away with itself and it wasnt like there were any scans that indicated anything but a normal laying in period but all the same i had this dark premonition that something was going to go wrong even on the day pattie gave birth i just expected someone to turn round to me and say im terribly sorry but your child is stillborn in the event i was proved wrong i was at work when patties waters broke and i got to the hospital as fast as i could though i neednt have rushed it wasnt like he popped out all at once fuck me the torture pattie went through it was beyond anything i thought was endurable and i felt as useless and redundant as a third nipple every time i stuck my head into the delivery room she was gritting her teeth and practically growling at me i couldnt bear to watch but when the miracle happened and my babys head come out into the world all covered in goo and wet it was like seeing creation from a godseye all the time i was spending at the cemetery surrounded by death seemed a puzzle to me great christ in the morning here was the antidote and the answer to death and when i held this little man in my arms i was floating in a bubble of love and oneness it was me and him and pattie and beyond us some voices of the kindest strangers on earth they were angels in uniform and i couldnt thank them enough my heart was overflowing with a feeling of warmth and love for each and every one of them i probably babbled such nonsense at them i know they was smiling at me and indulging me cos they must have heard it all before but i didnt care cos i was a dada and the world was reborn in my image i got a couple of weeks off work to be at home with timmy timothy john thats what we decided on pattie and me and it was very strange and very lovely each morning i woke up and wanted to pinch myself very hard to see if what i was experiencing was real or just in my head pattie was the same too we werent getting the best of sleeps but it didnt matter it was all good we would make it good for the boy id be the pork pie hat dad id be anything he wanted me to be and id never seen such a glow in pattie shed left the shell of the druggie behind her and she was loving every minute of being a mother we began to talk about getting married even that notion would have made me run a mile just a bare 6 months before but now it seemed the right thing to do when i got back to work jimmy and percy were full of it giving me all the benefit of their combined age of 130 and they laid it on thick about the various stages of a childs development and the different illnesses that could come at different ages they were a bit like laurel and hardy theyd always struck me like that cos jimmy was on the portly side like he was concealing a football under his shirt and percy was short and thin but i could see from the twinkle in their eyes that they meant well for me and i took it all in good stead jimmy even got a bit excited telling me about his own youth and how his dad woke him up at 2 in the morning to watch mohammed ali fight someone and the whole fight was over in 2 minutes we were laffing about that one when mr jameson the manager stuck his head in at the shed door he was a dapper man with a pencil mostache quite old fashioned sort of like the spiv character from dads army and we avoided him as much as possible but he didnt tick us off or dish out any orders no he smiled which id never seen before and now made him look like the actor terry thomas on account of a gap between his two front teeth here it comes i said to myself i say you chaps any chance one of you might do a lick of work today but again no he suddenly produced a bottle of sparkling wine and we had a drink and he congratulated me on the first of many that set the old boys wobbling with laffter and a few comments flew about the shed which escaped into the cemetery with no harm done cos nothing could have spoiled my mood i wasnt much of anything in the wide world and digging holes in the ground and filling them in again wasnt the greatest job or much to write home about but it was fine by me i was earning money i was keepin my nose clean and i was looking after a little boy who was the centre of my world and pattie and me were looking after each other i found it utterly amazing and bewildering confusing and confounding what my life had become and what it was before its like id been a caterpillar all my days warding off trouble with poisonous spines but now id become a butterfly and i was dancing and tripping on the air my spirit was light and lifted me effortlessly on wings of gossamer my soul had taken flight and i looked back in dumbfounded incredulous amazement at who i once was caught in the dance of the illusion that was my life that had fallen away and brought me to my bliss

Chapter V
Into the Fire

i am walking through a deserted house at night the sounds i hear are the distant hooting of an owl and the cry of a fox from the woods outside most of the furniture has been removed what remains is broken and covered in dust and rubble the bare wooden boards of the floor creak beneath my footsteps the moon breaks free from behind its curtain of clouds and then a scream shatters the silence of the house it is a scream that turns my blood to ice i cant understand where its coming from but it wont stop the house itself is beginning to shake with sobs and cracks appear in the walls i will fall through the floorboards any moment now and the scream is so loud i can feel its powerful embrace i awoke to find pattie at the end of the bed shaking and sobbing and screaming all at the same time she was like a mad woman a woman out of her wits i tried asking her what was the matter but she didnt answer it only seemed to make matters worse when i tried to put my arms around her she became almost furious fighting me off like a wildcat with a fury born of some fierce and terrible demonic energy and thats when i knew with a certainty that came not from my mind but from the very core of my being that something was so wrong it couldnt be put right by anything i could say or do not by holding or saying comforting words not by willing or giving all of my heart and strength to pattie it was of no use whatsoever like trying to hold fast and save yourself in a hurricane i knew before i went into timmys room that our little joy our wonder boy had been taken from us i cant even describe to you the pain that went through me seeing his little body gone pale and blue at his tiny hands and feet he looked so terribly quiet and still and pattie was screaming and screaming that it wasnt long befoe police and ambulance were round with their flashing blue lights and their uniforms and their blankets and their calm and control it was a blur of a nightmare scenario people were talking at me and pattie and i could hear myself answering but i have no idea to this day what i said they gave pattie sedatives cos she couldnt have answered anyone no how she must have been as numb as a corpse cos i was having out of body experiences looking at myself going through these motions in front of strangers who kept coming and going before me saying things that made little sense to me and repeating themselves so that one part of me wanted to snap my fingers and magic them away or magic me to some special place where there was no pain where timmy was alive and well and it was all a horrible nightmare that id invented to torture myself so that when i finally woke up from it i could tell him how much i loved him i could hold him in my arms and kiss his little face over and over and over till he was laughing and giggling with joy and the sheer happiness of being alive in the world and loved beyond the measure of all that is reasonable and good loved till my heart ached for respite but i wouldnt stop cos i would show him a love without bounds without limits beyond sense and all care for my own self and dignity i would show the world what a doting father was and i would not care if the world laffed up its sleeve at me and thought me a great fool an idiot who drew comments like who let that nonce become a father id smile at them and wouldnt feel a twinge of anger cos my heart would be bursting with love and overflowing with mercy for all mankind but the days passed an endless stream of deadness and numbness turning into weeks i stayed in patties flat like i was the mayor of the necropolis i had paid charon his dues and ferried my beautiful boy to the land of the dead but i had not yet returned across the styx they kept pattie in a secure residence for her own good i couldnt begin to imagine what she was thinking i visited her not every day but when i did we sat like two strangers with nothing to say to one another it was as if timmy was there in the room with us but his presence was painful beyond words and neither of us dared speak of this pain lest we broke the silence and started screaming and screaming to try to tear apart the fabric of reality where was the bliss now where was the calm and holy centre of the world it was elsewhere it was not with us cristal turned up from time to time she tried in her own way to pour her love and calming balm on patties pain and anguish i didnt mind her droning on in the silence and sometimes i would just get up and leave wanting to restore my own silence upon the torn and rent fabric of reality they must have got in touch with work cos i got a note of condolence from the old boys and the manager telling me to take as long as i liked off work and expressing their sympathy for my loss it was funny but i broke down and wept till i was sore and empty curled up on patties bed and then i slept for i dont know how long but it could have been close to two days what did time matter when youre dead time washes over you like the waves of the sea and drowns you till your body floats down to where the fishes consume you to the bone there was another letter arrived one day from social services and it detonated like a bomb they were taking a case against me and pattie for neglect of our child it felt like the cruellest unkindest act of an uncaring state i wont bore you with all the ins and outs of meetings i had with solicitors and how i tried my best to keep pattie away from the circus but it nearly broke me in two i went back to work while the whole process was going on for one thing i just needed to talk to someone about what was happening and jimmy and percy were solid rocks for me to lean on they couldnt believe what was happening and they tried to assure me it wouldnt even get to court but it did and towards the end of the whole thing pattie was there in attendance sitting with cristal i did wonder about the wisdom of her being there but she had insisted to the authorities and i didnt even try to dissuade her the prosecutor was a prime cunt a needling ponce in pinstripes and id have loved to slice his stomach open with the old noboguchi and feed him his guts but he didnt get his unjust rewards cos in a strange twist of fate the judge dismissed the case for lack of evidence neither me nor pattie jumped for joy cristal was doing that for both of us timmy had died a cot death that simple and that tragic the beak said it should never have come to trial and old and wrinkled and ugly as he was i could have kissed him it wasnt that much longer that pattie came back home and we resumed an existence together that had a weird unreality about it we didnt speak much except in short simple sentences that required little or no response we slept in the same bed but apart as if there was an invisible partition down the middle neither wanted to feel the touch of the other i was grateful for work i wondered often as i went about my chores what pattie was doing with herself while i was gone i wanted to be stronger for her for both of us but i felt hollow inside as if the old me had been stolen away that night timmy had died and been replaced by a double who went through the motions of being a human being and then one day i come back from work and as soon as i opened the front door i knew something was up it wasnt like they was making a riot or nothing it was probably the smell of weed wafting on the stale air of the flat i went into the living room and guess who was there the prodigal drug mule had returned i cant say as my heart leaped up to behold gerry and he barely mustered a smile for me it was no more than a curl of his lip there was a dense fug of weedy mary jane smoke and pattie stated the obvious for no sensible reason gerrys back i felt like i could have exploded i can see that ive got fucking eyes in my head of course i didnt say a dickey bird what would have been the point why he was here and how he had got in was all down to pattie so i couldnt see how any vesuvian eruption from me would help the situation hows work in the cemetery said gerry as i stood looking at him and pattie its a grave business i said this with no hint of a smile on my lips gerry didnt find it funny in the least but pattie burst into laffter so dramatically that i really feared she would laff herself into tears but she calmed down quick time and asked me to join them in a celebratory spliff what we celebrating i heard a small voice ask the voice belonged to me but it sounded as if it had come from outside the room the return of gerry pattie said with an enthusiasm that smacked of desperation i tried to smile cos i felt like weeping woo hoo i said just like old times though it wasnt just like old times the blue body of the dead boy was hovering in the room invisible and intangible but not forgotten and not locked away in a vault in the mind his cremation had been unreal i couldnt even watch as his tiny coffin not much bigger than a shoe box descended to the flames below the room where me and pattie and cristal had sat why it had come back to me there and then i couldnt say but the mind has doors that open and shut beyond our will i was struck dumb by the memory anything i might have said to pattie or gerry would have turned into a howl of black despair and i could feel my face getting tighter and tighter and the pressure building behind my eyes gerry got up and brought me a half smoked reefer go on mate this is really good shit you take a strong hit on that and youll feel much better i gave in and joined the party im being fucking ironic as hell cos it was a party in the dead zone but that was ok by me and pattie seemed a little more alive and there it was gerry had insinuated his way back into patties life and i didnt have the strength to fight against him i was fighting my own battles every day with myself as i mooched about the cemetery cutting grass or filling in a grave or just staring off into the distance across the tops of the gravestones i wondered where it all would end but perhaps i always knew there was only going to be one conclusion pattie got more and more hooked on the drugs gerry was bringing her i shut myself off from both of them and avoided the truth but i still couldnt believe the way the end came she had stopped eating more or less she was thin and wasted and i had started to go a little that way myself i wasnt giving over all my money like before but that didnt seem to matter to gerry he was cleaning up elsewhere and just fed pattie her fix like it was his pet pleasure to push her towards oblivion i didnt know what to do or feel i could see traces of coke about the flat and stubbies of reefers but then the needles came back i couldnt follow pattie down this dark road but i couldnt stop her either i knew she was in torment i knew she needed help but a part of me also knew she wanted release from this hell on earth and i wasnt capable of pulling her back from the edge i was nothing i was just a poor excuse for a man a boy who hadnt grown up who had lost his chance of happiness in this life i wasnt the rock she needed i wasnt the shelter against her hurt and pain and this one day i came back from work and there was a foreboding a terrible feeling inside me and all around me that something was wrong you think of the love and hope that a mother has for a child and you think it will carry that child through the rest of its life but it doesnt it cant its just the faint lingering aroma of a perfume dispersed on the winds of change anyway all her mothers love and hope and all mine too for pattie came to naught that day as i opened the door of the flat it was quiet eerily quiet and as i crept up the stairs i thought about announcing myself but the thought was choked back somehow it just didnt seem right to call out to her i went straight to the bedroom cos pattie had taken to lying in more and more sometimes for the whole day i lissened at the bedroom door but couldnt hear a sound then i pushed the door with the gentlest touch and it opened just a crack but enough for me to see that the curtains hadnt been opened and everything was gloomy and in shadow im not afraid to admit my heart was beating loud in my ears i could hardly breathe but i had to go on i pushed the door open all the way i could make out the shape of pattie on the bed i called to her gently and as i got closer to the bed she stirred babe she said is that you yeah its me im sorry babe i couldnt wait there was something so soft and weak and pathetic in her voice i knew with a dread certainty that something was badly wrong and then i saw the needle sticking out of her arm o pattie what you why my words were lost in tears but she seemed not to notice or be affected i couldnt go on its better this way im just so tired of fighting this life i think things were always stacked against me and i tried babe i tried i so wanted things to work out for us and timmy but when he went i went with him too dont think bad of me i love you babe i loved you from the very start youll always be a part of me and live in my soul suddenly she convulsed and a shudder went through her whole body and i knew i knew she had gone i lay down beside her and wept hard and long i didnt know i had so many tears and it was hours later i pulled myself away from her i didnt know what to do but i couldnt stay no more in the flat i was choking i needed air and i wanted to be away from this scene of death pattie was gone the dream of bliss and hope and love was destroyed there was a letter for me on her dressing table and a needle ready and waiting with my name on it and certain mortality in its delivery but i was not for dying at least not yet and not there the ferryman would have to wait a while so i took the letter though i did not open it and i ran faltering and stumbling with madness raging in my heart and a wild fury in my mind and when i was some distance from the flat i gave a quick call to emergency services and gave the bare bones of what had happened they tried to detain me on the phone and winkle out more about me but i shut down and turned off the phone and wandered the streets like a warrior who had struggled off a battlefield dazed and disoriented with gaping wounds everything terrified me and i hadnt a clue where to go i walked along a canal and the water invited me at every turn to throw myself in and drown i saw leaves floating under the surface twisting and turning and sinking and it looked so easy death just surrender no great dramatics just slip into the water from the edge of the path it would be a heavy cold winding sheet and all i had to do was give up the struggle just not fight it i looked down at my reflection in the water i knew i looked a mess i looked like the bogey man come to frighten small children with his crazy staring eyes and grimly turned down mouth i found myself back in hackney it wasnt exactly a plan or if it was it was a fucking stupid one and i knew i wasnt thinking straight i wasnt thinking at all or i was trying not to think fighting my thoughts and memories at every turn so it happened almost by chance the part of me that was a carrier pigeon had found my way back to where my freedom had kicked off a freedom that felt like a disease that had taken over my body and there was the dogshit park once more larger than life and full of mutts shitting and people jinking between the piles of shit i didnt feel anything about the place no nausea or feeling of desperation i had stared desperation in the face when i looked at my reflection in the waters of the canal now i just wanted to get into my old kip and put the head down and sleep but when i tried to put the key in the lock it wouldnt go in and thats when i noticed that the lock was a new one and while i was standing there like a useless dildo i could hear feet padding towards the door from the inside of the flat awright awright hol on your high horses now im coming and the door opened and there was this black guy who towered over me and was looking at me like there was something strange and out of place me thought you was simon what you want i was so confused and empty inside i couldnt think of a thing to say you got a tongue in your head i was the only word that came out of me you what used to came next and with a final spurt of effort live here crossed the line about three hours after the marathon was over well you dont live here no more and he shut the door in my face i could here him giving off muttering to himself as he padded back into the living room i stood there breathing staring at the door and then i moved position to the wall that ran up to the door and leaned my back on it pretty soon i was sliding all the way down to the floor there wasnt any effort involved it was more like the floor slid up to meet me and i sat with my legs spread open and stared into space some time later the door opened i couldnt tell you how long i had sat there cos time was not important and the black guy came out into the corridor and looked down at me from what seemed a very great height you still here he asked but i didnt reply then he bent down and picked me up if he was going to hurt me i wasnt gonna put up a fight i had no fight in me but though he was strong as a bull he was gentle and he brought me into the flat it was very changed i hadnt done a thing to it for me it had been a place to doss id never given it any personality cos i knew i didnt see myself living there too long but jermaine the black dude had posters of bob marley and usain the lightning bolt and all kinds of weird bobble hats and knickknacks id never seen before it was a cave of rasta kultja and i couldnt even believe id ever lived in the place yet the same old dogshit park was outside and all the rest of the wonder that is hackney he told me i looked like shit in one breath and in another he said he could see i was in trouble and he wanted to help i guess he must have got tired of me not really commenting or responding cos he was on his feet and making coffee and putting on bob marley the coffee had a kick it had this strong undertow of rum and it went down my chest with a beautiful afterburn the light was fading from the room but he didnt put on a light and soon all i could see of him was the white of his teeth and the glow of the tip of a joint a tiny little homunculus inside me squeaked about no drugs but the rummy coffee had already destroyed any resolve of the moment and i wanted to forget myself for a while forget the world of pain that i lived in forget just forget for that time and that place with a black angel called jermaine at one point he suddenly started laffing and told me he had got the wind up when i first come to the door that simon fuck hes a ball breaker you know he said ball to rhyme with gal and for the first time i smiled he must have had pretty acute eyesight cos he laffed and said you think so too hes the biggest ball breaker in hackney and i said ball like gal jermaine flicked two fingers up in the air youre awright there martin i dunno whats going down wit you but you take it easy and you get some sleep tonight cos youre safe here he was as good as his word it wasnt too easy to get off to sleep at first but then i must have drifted off and lost all consciousness of where i was i remember nothing of falling asleep or anything of what i dreamed if indeed i did dream and when i awoke i looked about me for some moments as if i had no idea who i was or how i had got to be in this flat with all the rasta trimmings jermaine didnt press me in the morning for more information i was a bit more communicative but still tight lipped and unresponsive i knew i couldnt stay for one thing i had no desire to meet the ball breaker of hackney in person and so i took my leave of my black angel and told him he had helped me at a very bad time sorry for you friend sorry for your trouble wished i coulda done more you done loads jermaine you done more then you think i really didnt know how to thank him and so i threw my arms around him and hugged him for dear life i dunno who was more surprised of the two of us as i walked out the door he told me to take care and one love was playing in the background back out on the streets i didnt have a notion what to do with myself and somehow i found myself ringing the cemetery mr jameson was funny with me not entirely but i could tell i wasnt fully fitting into his world plan but at the same time there was a concern for me it wasnt like i gave a stuff about the job it wasnt being head of the united nations or anything with real clout or kudos it was just a filler but all the same it was a small boat on a great ocean for me and the crew were about the only people i knew who cared even a little for me i let terry thomas talk me into coming to work my mind was all over the place anyway and i felt i might as well be there as anywhere else what good was i to anyone wandering the streets like a bad smell of course the wisdom of this decision to go to the cemetery was to be tested almost as soon as i entered through the gates and cast a dull eye over the ranks and rows of headstones it darkened my mood i felt it almost as a physical experience like putting on an extra layer of clothing jimmy and percy were quiet with me maybe they read me too well they couldnt have known what had happened or did they had there been some item of local news but if so they gave nothing away they gave me some light duties and went off to smarten up some borders and clip some hedges i tried to get into sweeping the paths but there seemed no point this hour or the next something would be blown onto the paths and the dead wouldnt know or care after a time i just stopped and stood stock still and leant on my brush it seemed as if i was alone among the dead i could have stripped to the buff and gone running and screaming through the gravestones but instead i lay down with my back against a headstone and looked out at the sombre crosses and stone angels and wreaths and dried up dessicated flowers where was she now pattie she was across the river in the land of the dead and i hadnt been there for her i hadnt paid the ferryman i had failed her some hero me why was i among the living when she and my mother before her had gone into eternity like smoke that leaves not a trace on the air i was tearing up when a small voice said boo close to my ear i didnt jump i didnt react at all it was terry thomas little boy tommy he seemed a bit bigger than the last time id teased him but i wasnt in a teasing mood that day perhaps he was trying to get his own back on me he came and stood in front of me and he was a bleary blob in a bleary teary cemetery where all edges had lost their sharpness you crying martin i tried to smile but it felt so painful i got the wind in my eye thats all my dad gets that sometimes does he i said unable to imagine jameson sr crying over anything though what did i know his little boy seemed happy enough so he couldnt be all wrong are you sad said tommy i wiped my eyes and nodded what you sad about where did i start well i couldnt tell a little boy about pattie and her drug habit or my failure to save her or my mum or the amazon rain forest or the planet im sad for the ghosts who wander this cemetery theyre lost and lonely and they want to get home they want to go back to the people who love them ghosts said tommy and his expression was changing from happy to neutral to sad all in a nanosecond where are the ghosts can you see them theyre all about us tommy all about us but we choose not to see them well that did it like a cloudburst on a summers day little tommy ran off screaming which brought his dad thundering down on me and giving off with jameson jr balling his eyes out in the background jimmy and percy were brought into the scene by the carry on and i was mostly to blame for that raving as i was shouting and writhing on the ground the sky had fallen in on me and i was sinking into the ground hours later i came to in a shed i thought it was the workshed but it was percys shed at his home he was giving out tea and sympathy and i was lissening to him as if from behind a thick screen youll be alright here martin you dont need to do anything my wifes a good cook and you just need to relax and get on your feet again shes gone perse shes gone i said these words so matter of fact and old perse just nodded i know this wont mean much to you at this time martin but i lost a daughter a long time ago she was all the world to me and it broke my heart it took me years well i nearly said to get over it but thats not true ill probably never get over it itll be with me till the day i die and ill tell you straight son ill never understand why god took her she was ten years old at the time swimming accident we was on holiday in cornwall and i didnt think nothing of her going in for a dip but i should have been there you know i shoulda been by her side all the time thats what a father does anyway it may not seem right to you here and now but life goes on its a lottery thats what it is no doubt about it and all you can do is grit your teeth and bear with it but look ive rabbitted on enough here you just take your time ill have a word with mr jameson but i dont think hell be looking for you around the cemetery in the next days or weeks he left me then and i slept and woke and slept again and in between i ate what food was left down for me and used a bathroom and shower at the back of the house it was a strange twilight existence i was so numb i could sit and stare into space for hours i was in a fog all the time it didnt matter to me if it was night or day jimmy called round the odd time and he and percy got their double act going but very gently they gave it to terry thomas but only in a grumbling niggling kind of way there was always a wink and a grin mixed in with the complaints i was staggered to learn one day that id been a whole month in that shed at the bottom of percys garden it was his hideaway you see and hed kitted it out for his own comfort with a sofa and a heater and a radio and some books one day i came out into the garden and i could smell change in the air spring had arrived and the buds were opening the birds chirping more loudly id been thinking about what old perse had said to me what seemed an age ago about gritting and bearing with the shit that life threw at you i wasnt convinced but i was still in the world and i knew i couldnt stay on at his place indefinitely i wanted a place of my own and i wanted to get away from the cemetery i couldnt see myself prospering there to walk among the dead and not be touched by them you had to be close attached to the living and my grip on life was highly tenuous and this i knew perse got me a room in a house with other men i didnt want to know them and they didnt want to know me so we kept ourselves to ourselves and lived our separate pointless existences mr jameson to give him some credit didnt harbour any ill feelings for me he helped me get a job as a cleaner it was all i required i didnt want to have to think and pushing a mop back and forth across a floor fitted the bill to perfection slop wipe wipe wipe slop wipe wipe wipe a mindless synchronisation then back to the room which held everything i owned in the world which was nothing it seemed everything like a fair recompense for what i had put into the world of course i thought about pattie often i tried not to think of her as i had left her but the body growing cold and blue and the eyes staring out blankly into her dark bedroom these images haunted my dreams and my waking hours one night i couldnt stop the swirl and slew of emotions and thoughts i was sure my head was gonna burst open and give me a fit that would bring the house down and bring the men out from their rooms above and below me in their housecoats or ragged pjs with the smell of stale cheese and flat beer on their breath they all me included had the stink of putrescence hanging over us it was a rank decaying odour it came from the mushrooms that flourished in the showers and under the sinks dont get me wrong i like mushrooms in the right place you know in an omelette or on a pizza but im not keen on staring at them while im soaping dangle berries out of my butt hole so i had to get out and wander the streets to let the storm in my head abate i wandered for miles paying no attention to where i was going it didnt matter nothing mattered just the putting of one foot in front of the other and letting the world present itself like a 3d 360 degree imax cinemascope extravaganza even if it wasnt the grand canyon i was looking at and there wasnt no hollywood siren to pass the time with and i didnt even mean to end up where i ended up across the road from patties place maybe i did mean to go there in some way i wasnt conscious of one last look at a place i had once called home before time and the devil stole it away and as i looked i thought i saw net curtains move at one of the living room windows that put the wind up me alright i couldnt move and my heart was having a mild attack then the front door opened not wide just so much as to let me know it wasnt shut no one appeared or anything it wasnt like it was an invitation as such to go in i was having a right old party in my head with all sorts of nonsense flying back and forth the craziest notion being that pattie was alive somehow shed survived i mean how did i know she was dead im not a doctor and maybe when they got her to hospital they was able to revive her stranger things have happened but then a voice at the party was bellowing and carrying on that i knew she was dead id been there i was a witness the only witness and was i gonna deny the evidence of my own eyes i had to go in no two ways about it i had to find out what was going on in the flat otherwise it would drive me totally round the bend and id be wailing and shouting all through the night i pushed the door open and closed it very gently very quietly behind me there was no one waiting to greet me even so i crept up the stairs like i was afraid to breathe the silence was hissing in my ears when i got to the top of the stairs i could see light from the living room doorway a thin stretched bar of soft light and there was low music so low i couldnt make out who was playing well id got that far there was no hesitating now and i pushed the door open gerry was sitting in a highbacked chair looking at me he said hello he called me by name and invited me in i sat down at the end of the sofa as far as i could sit from him we didnt talk for a few minutes we just sat staring at each other sizing the situation up at last gerry told me hed expected id return one day he thought it must be hard for me to stay away cos the flat would hold such memories for me his expression was nothing not a flicker of emotion showed anywhere he could have been wearing a mask what are you doing here gerry what am i doing here he passed back to me in a distorted echo i own the flat i must have looked more than a little disturbed and confused cos gerry quickly filled me in on details id never known or heard of i lived here with pattie long before you come on the scene like a ray of sunshine bringing light and joy into patties life cut it gerry cut it out why said gerry isnt that the way it was i could feel a terrible anger growing inside but gerry was cold like a winters night when the frost sets in it was over between us before you showed up but still she was my girl first and i didnt let him finish you killed her i shouted you killed her with your supply of drugs cos you dont care about a thing in this life except you turn a profit gerry was shaking his head slowly and his face looked sour and grim now you killed her martin and you know how i waited i wanted to hear his distorting lie you killed her with hope you killed her with big dreams that were never gonna to happen you filled her with a fantasy of a life she could never have and when that dream that fantasy crashed and burned thats when she came back to me looking for release you came into her life and you turned it upside down you stood pattie on her head so she couldnt tell up from down or the ceiling from the floor and when she stood up again everything was spinning round her so fast she couldnt stand on her own two feet so it was you martin you sent her spinning to her death i couldnt lissen no more to his lies and deceit i was on my feet and over to him hoisting him up from his chair as he laffed at me i put my hands around his throat when i heard a click and barely saw the flash of a blade but i felt the slash as the blade ripped into my face with a burning tearing cut i grabbed the wrist holding the blade and got gerry to release it the fight was mad and wild and the last thing i recall was banging his head again and again and again over and over on a low table there was blood everywhere on me on him on the table on the floor when i stopped he had lost consciousness he was a limp stuffed mannekin with dead eyes that had rolled back into his head i went to the bathroom and looked at my face in the mirror fuck i was a fright the gash in my cheek was throbbing and aching so much i could barely think i filled the basin with water and plunged my head in fuck i wish i hadnt done that dont recommend it on any level in the kind of scenario i was in i knew i had to get out of there and pronto i reeled off a wad of toilet paper and dampened it under a tap and pressed the wad against the gash and then i practically fell down the stairs there was no one about when i come back out onto the street i thought id better get to a hospital but id no idea where the nearest one was the wad helped a bit but it filled up with blood too soon and i threw it away i was stumbling all over the shop like a drunk when i went off balance and was nearly hit by a taxi lucky for me the cabbie wasnt a cunt like most cabbies he was a decent human being just told me not to bleed over his seats and got me to a hospital double quick i dont even recall his name now mustafa or some such and i cant remember much of what he said i suppose he was just talking at me to stop me from conking out and spilling blood all over his precious seats anyway im not gonna knock the guy cos he probably saved my life or any rate my face and when he got me to the hospital it was all e r and full on being wheeled here and there in a chair with the overhead corridor lights flashing by and a drip in my arm and nurses crowding round me and this one and that turning my head one way or another and the drugs flying through my veins i felt so weak i just wanted to sleep but they wouldnt let me kept asking me questions my name my address where had i been was i with anyone there was enough of a spark of life upstairs that i think i just told them i was out for a walk when this fucker came up behind me and i spun round to see who it was but didnt see the knife and he slashed me before i could do anything to stop him a doctor cautioned me about my language funny thing is i hardly remember the stitches going in and when i was in recovery still doped up a bit the police arrived and after theyd spoken to hospital staff they come over to me and started pumping me with more questions i was so tired i kept answering keeping it simple and when they finally left i must have dozed off like rip van winkle and slept my way through the rest of the night even though there were interruptions of nurses coming and going scribbling on a chart and adjusting my drip these comings and goings were only dreamlike flashes in the dark and it was fully light when i come to in a bed surrounded by screens the left side of my face was swollen and tight and aching there was a covering bandage that i could see when i looked down i touched the bandage very softly and again very softly touched the inside of my cheek with my tongue fuck i was in a bad way heres me the great swordsmith the great stalker of the streets of chelsea who was once upon a time going to carve up every cunt that moved well the big joke was on me i was the one god was laffing at now what was it that was written in the bible they who live by the sword shall die by the sword well i wasnt dead i was still in the world but i had been taught a lesson and could i learn from it i would have laffed out loud at the irony of it but i couldnt do that now with my face like a hard mask anyway my laffter would have been laced with bitterness the events at the flat were coming and going in my head i had come a long way from the roisterdoister catchmeifyoucan larking messer with his perfect symmetry of noboguchi power and precision i was just a walking disaster area a twat in a hospital bed with a bakers dozen of stitches in his face feeling fucked and dead inside and utterly utterly clueless how to go on how are we feeling this morning came almost at the same moment the screens were pulled away the light hurt my eyes and i must have winced cos it hurt my face feeling any better o tip top your regal whitecoatedness never better must go out and get the other cheek slashed so i can get some balance and proportion in the old phiz anyway i tried to smile but even the twitch i made was a source of pain a couple of nurses joined the doctor who didnt seem much older then them it was like 3 members of a club talking a secret language always referring to me in the 3rd person like my opinion was not really required and it wasnt i knew that i couldnt say that i minded cos i was waiting for the final sayso and when it came all the rigmarole receded all the dance of white coat strutting his stuff mattered not a jot youll be going home later today well give you painkillers to take with you and my advice is just to rest up for a number of days and take it very very easy with that it was handing my chart curtly to a nurse and dr house was off down the ward at a clip at another clip i was up and out of the bed and in a wheelchair and parked in a waiting area in one of those charming gowns so thin they barely hold in a scrap of body heat and show your arse if you dare to walk about in one well i wasnt doing any walking and by late morning i was feeling much stronger and wondering quietly to myself when i might actually be allowed out of the hospital it was early afternoon when a nurse came breezy as could be and wheeled me to a changing room where i got dressed in the clothes i had come in bloodstained shirt and all i was given a placcy bag with a good supply of pills and stood up to walk out of the hospital i was quite unsteady on the pins to begin with but i took it slow breathing deep as i went i was waiting at a lift to go down to the ground floor and exit there was a group of nurses coming along the corridor at some distance from me i must have half turned to them before the lift doors opened and as i got into the lift and the lift doors were closing it was odd but i heard a shout it wasnt clear what was said and anyway the doors had closed and the lift went down there were two porters in the lift and they seemed entirely blank and unconcerned about anything except a checklist on a clipboard when i got back to the boarding house i got a good examination from the one resident i passed on the stairs a man in his late fifties with a sour face and a bald pate o he looked me up and down like i was a walking experiment in plastic surgery gone wrong but he made no remarks and i was too shattered to say anything to him it would have gone against the grain anyhow no one talked in that house you kept yourself to yourself christ someone could be dead in one of the rooms and how would you find out the smell would blend in with the pong of the mushrooms in the showers and the musty stink of carpets that hadnt been cleaned since being laid down more than 20 years before i closed my door and all i could think of was sleep id taken a taxi back from the hospital but all the same i was just a heavy bag of walking bones i wasnt pleased to be back in the room but whatever i was going to do would have to be done after i had recovered and to recover i had to sleep and blot the world out if only for a night i would need to take stock cos right then standing alone in that room i couldnt think of one good reason why i should be on the face of the earth sleep helped a bit not much it was like a sort of suspended animation i was in i slept at different times of the day or night and when i was up and moving about it was mostly in a grey halflight the only window to my room looked out at a blank brick wall and the sun never shone in at it the sun was somwewhere behind the wall i took plenty of painkillers the first few days and they helped it also helped that the house was a morgue in some ways there wasnt a peep out of the other residents night or day that was probably due to the fact that they were all in their 50s and 60s and clapped out just waiting for the end i came to the conclusion that i was destined to join them i had no appetite no energy a lethargy had taken hold of me body and soul it was an effort to push out a stool and when i did it was thin and watery the part of me that felt most alive was my scar as the days passed i could feel a tingling and pricking sensation around the stitches they were going to come out by themselves and i could feel the strain in the threads at last i couldnt bear it no more and i had to take a look i went to the narrow full length mirror near the door and peeled off the bandage i was naked and id lost a fair bit of weight what had happened to me that was the thought that went through my brain of course i knew the answer but all the same i felt so low cos i looked like frankensteins monster or the monsters underweight nephew theyd told me at the hospital that the scar would fade considerably through time it didnt matter i shouldnt have gone back to patties flat i began to think a lot about her and what had happened timmy was in my head so much sometimes i fancied i saw him curled up in the shadows in a corner of the room the stitches pinged apart and left me with this thin pinkish line down my cheek i thought about the job i hadnt even told them yet and for the first time in a week or more i smiled so what the world turns and we busy ourselves with petty tasks that mean absolutely nothing even the high and mighty dont put a thing on their gravestones about what they worked at not unless it was unbelievably important first man on the moon would be good that might make you stop and ponder a bit over a grave but opened a wellie boot factory or cleaned a building for 30 years well youd only laff wouldnt you were all just drops in the ocean none of us matter at all to most others and thats when it come to me i made the decision to pull he plug this farce that was my existence had gone on long enough i couldnt protect and love those who needed my love and protection what use was i to man or beast id sucked up enough air and wasted enough time the clarity of it brought a great calm and peace to me it wasnt that i couldnt live with a pathetic scar cos the facial scar was as nothing to the scar deep inside me no it was more like if a bomb fell on the building and took out me and all the other numbnuts below and above me it wouldnt raise a single tweet or a two inch column in a local rag i could even write a headline for it bunch of totally forgettable wasters blown to kingdom come what a waste of munitions i waited until i was entirely out of food id been surviving on water and the last of the painkillers and i pepared everything quite carefully i didnt write a long farewell note what was the point theyd burn me in a long cardboard box anyway with no one to bear witness who had known me when i was fully alive id lost contact with the sisters and for all i knew they were dust themselves now it all points in the one direction thats what i set down on a sheet of paper and then i opened patties letter id been putting this off cos i knew it would tear me apart but i had to be a man maybe the one time in my pointless futile life i had to be big enough to read her last words i had the syringe shed prepared for me id taken that too on the day id watched her die and i thought about using it first but then i rejected that notion and ripped the letter open

martin you have been the best thing that came into my life i bless the day you found me and i have loved every minute of being with you you turned my life around when i got pregnant and felt a new life living within me it was a true miracle i began to hope and it was a feeling id never felt before it was like we were standing on the shore of a great lake or sea and the world seemed brighter the wind was fresher and just to have you at my side was everything and then when timmy came along that hope was mixed with fear i thought i was being irrational why should something happen to our beautiful boy can god be so cruel and unfair i used to watch you as you slept after work and i said a silent prayer that you and i and our little magical child would be together always and maybe one day we would leave london and its miles and miles of bricks and streets and its cars and noise and find a peace together in the countryside a humble home filled with love and care and the joy of being together and then when timmy died that awful night it was as if my heart stopped and began to shrivel up im not strong i know that i am but a weak and foolish woman all my demons came back to me all my mistakes and the bad times with my father in a life i had run from i thought id escaped i thought you and me and timmy had all escaped but i was only fooling myself forgive me my love i will hold you in my heart till the earth grows old and dies the dream is over our magical boy is gone im so sorry i couldnt face life without him but i will meet you and him one day i love you more than life itself your pattie

the letter fell from my grasp it fluttered down to the floor there was a pain in my chest i wanted to howl out loud enough to reach the stars but only a thin hoarse whimper came from my throat even my sobs were muted cos i was struggling not to give in completely to my emotions one swift action and all this pain would soon be over i owed it to pattie not to wimp out of my unspoken pact she was gone and timmy was gone and it was my turn to man up and be counted wiping the tears from my eyes i steadied my breathing and took hold of the syringe and as i did so i could hear the sound of feet coming up the stairs and it stopped somewhere on the landing outside my door why i listened so closely and intently i couldnt even tell myself but i was waiting for the sound of the feet to go back down the stairs when there was a knock on my door i sat there frozen in indecision maybe whoever it was would simply go away but maybe it was the police and they would break the door down and find me with the syringe stuck in me and put me through hell to make sure i lived and me injecting myself would be for nothing a second knock came at the door a little more insistent than the first and then there were voices one female the other male i couldnt make out clearly what was being said but i knew they were talking about me then the conversation stopped and there was silence for some moments i imagined i heard a soft padding of feet receding on the stairs followed by my name being called it was a woman i couldnt think who it could be i mean no one i knew would have known that i was living where i was living it made no sense whatsoever it couldnt be pattie i didnt believe in ghosts especially not ones knocking on doors in the middle of the day i approached the door as quietly as i could wiping the tears from my eyes who is it i said and i know my voice must have sounded a bit strange cos it sounded strange to me and the answer wasnt at all what i expected its nora nora i repeated softly to myself but she heard me so she must have had her ear right up to the door nora grayson the name was careening round my room bouncing off the walls and reverberating in my skull open the door please she said and for a long moment that seemed paralysed in the spacetime continuum i regarded the handle on the door as a foreign object quite unfamiliar to me just a moment i said i had to hide the syringe so i dropped it into a box of tissues and opened the door we looked at one another nora and me like i think robinson crusoe must have looked at friday we stood just staring and saying nothing until one of the other residents opened his door and started coming down the stairs i pulled nora into my room and shut the door there was so much to talk about yet we were oddly tonguetied and hesitant it was like a weird game of chess we played and every move every word and phrase seemed loaded with possibilities and avenues to be explored i was more than curious to know how she had found me since i didnt go broadcasting to the world and his uncle where i lived but it was easy enough explained she had seen me get into the lift at the hospital she was the one who had shouted after me but i hadnt realised at the time then shed

117

made enquiries at a&e and of course they had my address so she wasnt the greatest female detective in the world after all it was an odd visit from nora coming as it did right when i was ready to top myself at first i was anxious she should go but another part of me wanted her to stay and she didnt seem in a hurry to leave me she told me later that having found me she wasnt going to let me slip away again we talked and talked until the light grew dim in my room and i wont bore you with all the stuff we talked about it wouldnt make much sense cos i dont think for a second it mattered what we said it was just being there being in the same space together i didnt have any inclination to get physically close to her and she seemed totally ok with that after all we had only met a couple of times before but at the same time there was a connection she had sought me out and wasnt gonna let me go into the dark lands to join pattie and my lovely dead boy i dont know how it happened but i must have grown tired of the sound of my own voice i had curled into the foetal and nora i couldnt even make her out no more not even the shape of her solid and real as she was she took my head and put it on her lap and ran her fingers through my hair i didnt feel like crying no more i didnt feel anything really just a terrible heavy tiredness and i dont remember the moment i dropped off but i remember entering a basement and creeping down a rickety flight of stairs i thought i was going to fall through one of the steps or i would stumble and trip and go flying off the steps into the darkness below but i kept going putting one foot down on a step then the other and when i got to the bottom there were two coffins open and inside one coffin was my little boy asleep but so cold looking and in the other was pattie she was asleep too but her eyelids opened and she saw me she got up out of the coffin then and moved towards me with outstretched arms they were covered in pock marks and holes and her face was eaten away there were worms wriggling on it i backed away from her and fell against the bottom of the steps and woke up with a start i sat up a bit in the half light nora was sitting in a chair close by watching me you were making little noises in your sleep were you dreaming yeah thats right only it was more like a nightmare what time is it something after 5 you been here all night yes she said then she got up and made me a cup of coffee and we sat not talking overmuch as the room brightened i dunno how i done it but nora persuaded me to go to her place she had to go to work later back at the hospital and she wanted me to be in a safe place and somewhere she could find me again she had done the hard work of tracking me down and she wasnt gonna let me out of her sight again at least not soon and not for the next good while will that make me your prisoner then i asked her on the top deck of a double decker bus as we headed to balham so much of london is a carbon copy of other parts but i didnt get the sinking feeling like i got when i went back to hackney nora smiled enigmatically a sort of cheshire cat smile and told me to relax it was all going to work out and be good for her and me i was getting that feeling again the same as the time after she had pulled me back to her dads caff what seemed an impossibly long time ago but couldnt really have been more than 8 months or so weird effects of time distortion and weirder still was me going along with it all sitting on a bus with a girl i still hardly knew and feeling it was alright to put myself in her hands i knew i was feeling not quite in the world not quite with it and i saw a few passengers giving me a troubled look on account of my scar but what was i gonna do shout at them and carry on like a bazooka making a lot of noise and trouble cos i was feeling nervous and upset its not a convincing argument to run amok and rave at the moon so as to insist upon your sanity anyway at last the ordeal was over and we went into this red brick house at the edge of a common it had a spacious hall and there was a rack of letter boxes and then a flight of carpeted stairs and noras place was on the first floor when she opened the door i was hit by a blaze of light stunned actually and she must have seen me blink and put a hand up to shield my eyes cos she laffed its a bit yellow no it wasnt it was totally yellow a sort of canary shade and it made the light dazzle nora quickly followed up with a strong assertion that she hadnt chosen the colour scheme never mind that cos it was roomy you could have fitted my place in nearly three times over nora busied herself and got ready for work when she came out of her bedroom in her nurses uniform she looked transformed her hair was done up in a bun she had to leave soon and i suddenly felt at a loss what to do with myself she told me it was up to me i could do whatever i wanted go for a walk on the common or take a look at the market and then it come to me the question i should have asked before we left my place why are you doing this you dont know me hardly at all and yet you invite me into your flat and i lost the track of what i was trying to say cos i just didnt get it i must have looked a proper twat cos i felt awkward and out of place but nora wasnt to be put off by my feeling of discomfort i want to get to know you better its as simple as that youve just come through a trauma and i want to be your friend i really have to go now but i hope youll stick around and not feel that you arent at home then she gave me a hug which took me a little by surprise and whispered in my ear dont go back to your place martin at least not yet you need to be with a friend right now i spoke to someone at your place before you opened your door to me he was strange i mean really strange you dont need that type of person in your life then as suddenly as she had embraced me she let me go have to rush theres a key on the table and she was gone out the door and down the stairs shutting the front door with a bang i took a look around the joint there were no mushrooms in the shower in fact the shower the kitchen and the whole flat smelt so much better than my place that i could only admit that nora was right about me not going back too quickly i felt so much better just being there and it suddenly hit me that i was alive and not dead with a needle sticking out of me fuck the needle where had i put it i couldnt remember i knew i had it as i stood at my door talking to nora suddenly i felt like having a shower i felt scuzzy and grimy and my skin gave off the odour of sour potatoes she must have noticed that nora thats why she bolted out the door couldnt wait to get a breath of fresh air i thought about her as the water from the shower head ran down my body i didnt have a sexual feeling at all i just wondered why she was having anything to do with me it didnt make much sense but then what did make sense about nearly anybody you could think of my mum and dad they made sense about the only two who did at least from my standpoint they knew where it was at and they had the thing between them so well taped down and what did i know but mum had kept him alive longer than he would have survived if she had been the first to go suddenly i saw the syringe in the box of tissues id left on the table fuck what was i thinking i was in a dark dark place last night and no mistake i turned off the shower and dried myself i got dressed in the rags id come over to balham in wasnt ideal by any stretch but i had no choice then i sat in the living room and just lissened it was a quiet house maybe it will be noisier in the evening when people get back from work but there wasnt much sign of life except for faint noises from the top of the house i looked out the windows of the wall opposite the door into the flat there was a street lined with cars and i watched as one or two passed below the windows completely unaware of my existence this area i told myself straight off is different to hackney it wasnt like the people i saw were dripping with jewellery or dressed to the nines like in chelsea they just didnt look like complete twats and ponces they looked sort of ordinary but not weighed down with the woes of the world or looking as if ready to mug you and stick you with a blade the common i could see from the front windows it was a proper park fringed with plane trees and horse chesnuts it was very wide and even though there was a main road running the length of one side it looked a sweet place to take a stroll the people at the far end were just dots i could tell it wasnt no mangy dogcrap pen where youd have to watch your step and keep an eye out that hoodies werent sneaking up on ya fuck i had the feeling id arrived well maybe that was going too far but i did feel a weight lifting off me just a little and enough for me to think i would stay on for a few days and chill out i think id already made my mind up i wasnt going to pursue a career in sanitation i hardly thought my mopping was of an olympic standard and i might be reported mia already but the clocks hadnt stopped the buses were still running and the world was still turning so much for my utter and complete insignificance and general irrelevance in the grand scheme of things in the great ant heap of life i was never gonna get to the top so what very few do and they kill themselves in the attempt so for the moment i could honestly say i was content being without a menial job and without much of a safety net i didnt know if things would work out between me and nora but she wasnt coming down heavy on me and if she did id up anchor and disappear like jack the ripper though without murdering a string of prostitutes and slicing open their guts i sat down in an armchair and gazed out at the park trying to get my head round the night before i was in a very dark place i knew that and i needed to dig deep into this at some point but now didnt feel like a good time to open the wounds so i just sat there feeling drained and lethargic not quite knowing what to do with myself i heard the front door of the house open and slow footsteps come up the stairs when the doorbell rang i was in half a mind to try and hide myself but i hadnt even got to the point of getting up out of my chair when a key was turned in the lock and a dumpy old baggage with her hair in a bun and thick ankles entered and stood looking at me wheres nora and who are you i really didnt feel like talking to this faded remnant from the 60s she might have danced on totp to the stones and looked good in a mini skirt but time had flowed by and all had gone south leaving her like a beached whale of a carcass all saggy and breathless and ill admit my attitude wasnt the best right then fuck i just wanted to be alone and have a chance to take it easy so i probably wore a sour expression whats the matter with you you got a tongue in your head she had very jowly cheeks and they wobbled as she spoke i rose from the armchair like i was a puppet pulled up by my spine and walked towards her she drew back from me and i could tell she was apprehensive at the very least i can only assume my scar didnt present me in the best light as calling cards go its a strong card to lead with so i smiled at the old dear and tried to feel all gooey and bunny rabbits frolicking in a summer meadow on the inside in the hope that i might generate warmth and a lack of threat i couldnt be sure it was working and i pondered quietly to myself as the rabbits disappeared down rabbit holes one by one that the old baggage if she had ever possessed a drop of empathy it had found its way out of her bones and been flushed down a toilet when maggie thatcher had the queen in a headlock during a weekly tiffin at buck palace anyway i found my voice at last noras gone to work im a friend of hers who are you and what dyou mean by coming in here when shes not at home i had her on the back foot for a moment but what i was to learn about mrs dobson that was her name as i found out when nora got back from work what i learnt was she was indestructible she was a survivor like the building i was in that she owned and nora was her tenant cos i did take a walk later and i could see a whole row or nearly a whole row of big houses all built some time around 1910 three storeys and plenty of rooms that had become flats and bedsits over time as the upkeep of these mansions just became too much for one family one couldnt get servants any more to have nooky with while wifey was distracted and then kick out of service for being wayward and sinful strayers from the path of righteousness and other such bollocks and devious use of double standards ah the good old days fuck a long time ago but dont you just wait for some scandal to break on the box where a whole town is hiding some dreadful secret and then you wag your finger cos you think youre better human nature and all this shitty crap was rattling round in my head as i strolled on to the common and looked back at the houses i could see perfectly what the dobson baggage was on about cos thered be this new build smack in the midst of the models of 1910 and this was because of someone called gerry whod decided to unofficially do some town planning and drop bombs on the houses of the area old dobbers said her mums nerves were shattered and only recovered in time to be shattered again by the introduction of the mini skirt i couldnt imagine dobbie dedob in a mini skirt it was sort of disgusting to think of her as a girl a man could have got a boner looking at but shed had children and had a grandson jeremy who was a bit older than me and knew nora cos by coincidence theyd both gone to the same private school in surrey look i found all this out over time im just giving you the lowdown in a big infodump cos i wanna get on to other more important stuff about me you think youre the hero or heroine of your life dont you well same for me im the hero of my life although you should see my face twisted into a bitter mask when i say that to myself cos if youve been following this disjointed mess of a tale youll know i aint no hero and i was never cut out to be one the funny thing was that later that evening after nora got back i discovered she had a soft spot for the dobson creature said she was always dropping in and nosing around and you like that i said she doesnt mean anything by it not really i think my look said otherwise but nora insisted it was just her way she liked to know what was going in in her property what about privacy i objected you have a right to privacy nora smiled youre making too much of the whole thing am i cos i dont think she likes the idea of me being around here ill have a word dont get excited over nothing i didnt push it after all i didnt even know if i was going to hang around as a permanent fixture in souf london i told nora why dobbers had landed in it was to tell her that men would be coming in to do some rewiring in the late morning i said id get offside and head into the centre or maybe check out the sights of balham suit yourself said nora and seemed almost peeved about what i couldnt think but i wasnt going to let it get to me if we were going to have any kind of a relationship it wasnt going to be one moody storm of a fucked up tragifuckingcomedy with her digging at me and me digging at her at least that was what i was thinking as i settled down for the night on ther sofa gazing out at the common with the flash of car lights coming and going on the main road off to the side i did get off to sleep alright and something woke me up in the wee hours nora was standing in her pjs looking down into the street that ran along the side of the building it sounded like piccadilly circus i got up from the sofa and joined her at the window there was a stream of cars almost bumper to bumper and there were girls walking by the cars there was some chitchat between the prossies on the street and the drivers which explained why the cars were moving so slowly i checked the time it was 2:30 in the am what the fuck is going on i asked nora and she was quietly fuming explaining that it was a recurring nightmare the police cracked down for a while and then the tarts came back out onto the street and the circus would start anytime after midnight right on cue a window opened across the street from noras flat and a womans voice shouted out that she had rung the police and that they were on their way this provoked a cacophony of horns being tooted it was like a warm up for the last night of the proms but no one was in festive mood certainly not nora who stomped off back to her room with an angry outburst im on early tomorrow these bastards i stayed at the window and watched the police arrive and the cars quickly disperse it was all very surreal and if id had a job to go to id have felt as pissed off as nora i didnt even hear her go out in the morning there was a note asking me to stay on but i didnt fancy bumping into mrs dobson again cos i knew shed be back to oversee the workies who would be doing the rewiring you ask me she was the one needed the rewiring but i didnt want to upset anybody or tread on anybodys toes and maybe id overstayed my welcome i didnt know what i was thinking really nor what was in noras heart and mind you put yourself out for someone else a fellow traveller on lifes journey but you expect them to conform to your habits and fit into your world and when they dont its gunfight at the ok corrall i wasnt strong enough for that so i had a shower cobbled together a decent breakfast of toast and tea and cereal and landed myself in the street heading towards balham underground it wasnt early by the time i got going well not early to start the day i mean it was nearly midday but looked at another way it was ridiculously early cos id got about 500 metres from the corner where all the commotion had been the night before when this cliche of a scotsman came swaggering down the street towards me yes he was a ginger and yes he was wearing a fucking kilt and when he spoke to me his accent was thick as overheated porridge eh where wid the ladies of the nicht be found like i looked like a pimp or what maybe i did to him anyway i thought to myself hes fucking keen this early in the day i pointed back to the corner and mumbled something about good hunting and watched him saunter off with that swaggering gait as he fired up his bagpipes and woke the neighbourhood with a keen swirl of scotland the brave okay okay im laying it on a bit thick there cos he had no bagpipes but he might as well have had i mean what on earth possessed that looper to go looking for cunt and ass at that hour of the day well i just shook the head and strode on to the tube i had the rest of my day to sort while the mighty jock was walking up and down streets looking for ladies of the night at the wrong time of day maybe its the orange effect red hair and testosterone being a bad combination while i was still in the land of nod he was scrubbing his arsehole and lathering up his wee lad exhorting it to action later in the day like a sergeant major giving his troops one last rousing speech to fire them up for the battle ahead dont fire off your shot until you see the whites of their eyes and make sure your bayonet is sharp so it can go into your enemy like a knife into butter gawd i could see that looper jock up to his hilt inside a woman and screaming freedom like mel gibson as he had a ferocious rough celtic orgasm and rolled off his rentaparamour with a glassyeyed look of utter exhaustion mental and physical hed need a transfusion of whiskey and irnbru just to revive him and even then he wouldnt be such a cock of the walk for the rest of the day it took me most of the tube ride into london to shake this scot off my back and out of my mind and when i came up for air in leicester sq i kinda knew i didnt want to drift about soho or mooch around a museum i was going back to my room to get that syringe and when i got back to the house it was the same morguelike atmosphere with only dull and distant sounds being made by the walking dead occupants in the other rooms thank god i didnt see a one of them on the stairs cos i was comparing this renters purgatory very unfavourably with noras place in balham even despite the nighttime kerb crawling as i opened the door id almost come to a decision that i didnt want to stay there among the half alive i didnt know if there were any legs in the relationship with nora i couldnt even say why she took an interest in me but my room and all the other rooms were like alcoves in a mausoleum no id get the syringe and lose it somewhere and go back to noras and just see where the flow took me but the odd thing was when i picked up the tissue box it felt light i gave it a good shake but nothing rattled in it i turfed out the tissues and peered into the box as if just by the act of looking the syringe might magically appear i am not a methodical nerdy type youve no doubt worked that out by now i never collected stamps as a boy or filed things away for future reference like a weedy librarian or office clerk but all the same when i am certain something must be in one place and one place only it near drives me round the bend to not find it in the place it should be and its not even as though i wanted to top myself i didnt if anything i wanted to catch up on my zeds what with all the fun and games in the middle of the night outside noras flat but how could i think about sleep when something was not in its place the universal order had been disturbed nudged off kilter and i was gonna do not a thing just go and lie down and fall asleep as if nothing had happened i flew into a whirlwind of activity emptying drawers and shoving furniture this way and that to cast an eye over regions of carpet that hadnt seen the light of day in quite a while and when the batteries had run down and i couldnt think of another item to lift shake rattle or roll i sat on the end of my bed and stared bugeyed at the disaster area around me and then i knew i had to get out of there so i shoved dirty washing into a bag and grabbed my copy of chaucer and headed back to balham which led of course to my first fight with nora she didnt play dumb or anything she gave as good as she got in fact i think she got a kick out of it this is what she told me that night in my room she had watched over me as i slept and then shed needed to use the lavvie only there wasnt a shred of toilet paper anywhere in the bathroom this was a common failing of mine not keeping the toilet roll holder stocked and so shed come back into the room and she saw the tissue box well once shed found the syringe she suspected the worst and smuggled it out when she left she emptied the contents down a sink in her flat and chucked the syringe away did i really mean to end it all over what i was so angry i was shaking but i wouldnt share with her my memories of pattie or timmy nora had cooked a meal for her and me but i told her i wasnt feeling hungry and if she didnt mind id spend one last night on her sofa and in the morning id be gone so she could have her precious peace and quiet and her fat and frumpy landlady wouldnt have to strain her bloodvessels worrying over my presence in the flat that was a humdinger of a first argument nora stormed off into her room and slammed the door of course i couldnt get off to sleep easily but eventually i did drop off and i had a scrambled mess of uneasy dreams which brought me awake in the middle of the night i knew someone was in the room even before i turned round it was nora of course i couldnt sleep she said her voice was full of sadness and melancholy im sorry martin i didnt mean to hurt you i just wanted to save you i knew that syringe was probably lethal and i couldnt leave it there for you to use i dont know what happened to you and if you dont want to tell me thats alright its none of my business i lissened to her and it was as if all the anger had gone from me i didnt say anything for a long time and she sat on in the half light from the street lamps why i said at last why do you want to know me now it was her turn to be silent and she sighed a few times i dont know thats the honest answer i want to get to know you remember that day in my dads cafe it seems an age ago like a different world almost thats when i saw you were different from others i wanted to help you i cant explain it better than that i thought about you often and then i saw you again in the hospital and there must be a reason for that or else its just a stupid accident and it means nothing she stood up then you do what you want martin i cant hold you but id like you to stay then she went back to her room i lay on staring at the ceiling and lights moving across it as a car passed by outside after a while i got up and went to her room i opened the door quietly and stood there looking at her asleep well i thought she was asleep until she spoke what do you want she said and i answered i dont want no trouble but i just wanna lie down and hold you and so i did and i felt more peaceful than i had felt for a very long time maybe for as long ss i could remember when i woke up nora had gone but she left me a note and some money told me to explore beautiful balham and that shed be back in the early afternoon if i wanted to stick around i thought she had to be joking about beautiful balham but she wasnt far wrong there were plenty of streetcafes and i didnt feel the need to be looking over my shoulder all the time for freaks and druggies and knife gangs i dont know why but i felt a weight lifting off me maybe i was fooling myself and i was entering some kind of bubble some fantasy i was building in my head but if it wasnt chelsea it certainly wasnt hackney either or my squalid shithole of a room at the back end of islington who knows her house noras place mrs jowly porkfat dobsons house might hold a few characters worth getting to know it just looked the sort of place that would hold a hoarder or two someone who devoted his life to stamp collecting or buying first editions even though he lived on bread and water as a result and when i got back to the house around 1pm id just come through the front door when this man appeared at the top of the stairs in a dressing gown with a tartan design and a pair of slippers from which a pair of porcelain white legs stuck out he was anything between 40 or 50 with a big dome of a forehead and a scar barely concealed by a receding hairline i thought you were mrs dobson he said i am i thought to myself just popped out for a quick sex change and rejuvenation whaddya think the man at the top of the stairs swayed a bit on his very pale very white pins are you the plumber he asked and i thought o dear o fuck this isnt the beginning of a bad british sex comedy the kind that my dad said he watched as a teenager no i said cos i thought id best enlighten the poor bastard in case he was getting his hopes up im staying in the flat 1st floor right front thats noras place he said quite matter of factly like he was informing me of something i didnt know as i climbed the stairs towards him he moved back and when i reached him i saw he was only about a smidgen over 5ft short which made him something more than a midget but something less than a fully grown man it also made his head look abnormally big and cos i was staring at it i couldnt help but see how lined his forehead was and how big his eyes nor that he was merry as a newt in the mud of a riverbank as we walked together up towards noras flat he was telling me all about his waterworks not functioning i wasnt really lissening so i dont know if he was talking about himself or his flat i told him more than once that i wasnt the plumber or the plumbers mate nor did i know any plumbers in the area or in london generally or in the whole wide world for that matter but it made not a bit of difference to bernards dribbling old monologue he had a bedsit across a landing on the same level as noras flat as he opened his door to go back inside his realm of wonders i could see it was stuffed ceiling to floor with books and objects i could also hear the constant drip drip drip of a tap somewhere out of sight you a keen stamp collector bernard i quizzed him as i slyly gazed past him into the bricabrac jumbled world he inhabited howd you know that he answered and his eyes widened as he blinked and steadied himself against the door jamb i tapped my nose with a finger and told him i could always tell a philanthropist just by looking at him that tickled old bernard and i left him swaying and chuckling to himself though if im honest id not meant to say what i said i just couldnt remember the right word for a collector of stamps weirdo waste of space would have been nearer the mark or anorak nora came back soon after that and changed out of her uniform i couldnt wait to tell her about old bernard she smiled and said she had a soft spot for him he was harmless and lonely yeah but a housecoat and slippers in the middle of the day its not a winning combo i insisted nothing broke noras calm demeanour she held herself not exactly aloof or apart from me but i got the feeling she was reading me and that there was an unspoken response to my judgment of bernard as i was to learn through time there were depths to nora that were not visible except after a great deal of association and a lot of time spent lissening and bearing with maybe if shed told me straight off not to be too hasty in my assessment of people i wouldnt have stuck around her but youve sussed by now that i did if i was being judged that day that time i was only dimly aware of it i could see a deal of activity below the surface of the stream and was intrigued but what i didnt know then and was completely innocent of was the fact that the hook i was dangling in the stream was going into me little by little sutily silently imperceptibly and almost painlessly i dont know exactly when but some weeks after id started living with nora she said she wanted to go down to see her mum in guildford why dont i come along not particularly honeyed words in fact it was more like nora had thrown off the suggestion as an afterthought and i heard myself assent to the invitation even while a part of my brain was asking me what i was getting into nora had a little run around peuge and off we tootled out of london in a general southwesterly direction and it wasnt until we were well on the way that i thought to ask what she was like the mother o shes a dreadful dragon said nora and practically roared with laffter what do i call her mum that made nora go all serious again no that wouldnt be a good idea well whats she called then morag morag i said the name a couple of times softly to myself as if getting used to a strange word cos id never met a morag before shes scottish said nora o hoots mon will she ken what i say nora looked at me with a rebuke in her eyes she doesnt sound scottish in the least whyever not dr finlay but nora wasnt smiling and warned me not to pull any crap with her mother i should have heeded the warning but probably nothing could have prepared me for meeting morag grayson even the description of her mothers house was a false steer she lives in a terrace gave me to conjure a row of small dwellings squeezed together under slate roofs and while those no doubt exist on the fringe of guildford i knew i had been sold a lame dog when nora led me towards an l shaped private enclave of houses with a communal garden which was more like a small green when we got inside the house itself we were met by this little bird of a creature surrounded by bookshelves stuffed with tomes of poetry and lit crit and she might have been small but morag gave me a look that pierced me to my spine i can only describe that first meeting with her as an inquisition nora intervened at moments to try and steer the talk to something less personal and intimidating but without much success of course i slept alone in a guest room but it wasnt as if it mattered cos nora and i hadnt got round to shagging at that stage i lay awake most of the surrey night fuming i kept thinking what she the great mother figure was thinking of me and i guessed she was displeased at what her daughter had dragged in shed probably have been happier if guildford had a stockade around it and armed guards were given strict instructions to keep riffraff out of the city particularly lowlifes with scarred faces jesus she most likely saw in me a developing magwitch who was corrupting her little girl when i made my way downstairs the next morning i felt so shitty and angry in a vague and restless way the whole order of the world seemed wrong and there they were mother and daughter smiling and laffing together out in the late morning sunshine at a table in a narrow suntrap at the back of the house i had to steel myself as i went out to join them i put on a mask of comedy even though underneath i was experiencing a seething resentment and urge to do violence all round me how did i sleep last night like a top i lied we were going to rouse you earlier said morag but nora said let sleeping dogs lie more laffter and exchanges of smiling glances between mother and daughter i was on some horrendous reality tv show and about to be booted off but then i found myself rising above it all youve got a lovely place here morag and this is a bonus sitting here being kissed by the warmth of the sun both nora and her mother looked at me i suddenly couldnt have cared less what either of them thought of me cos inside my head i had really said youre a horrible hag from beyond the far north and i dont care what you say or think about me and with that i smiled and closed my eyes feeling the suns rays on my face and a warm reddish glow on my eyelids morags voice admonished me to eat and drink something as she wanted to clear up the earth was turning and the day growing old by the minute i opened my eyes and still continued to smile as i bit viciously into a slice of toast as if it was her tongue and i was dr hannibal the cannibal lecter while mother and daughter did the dishes after theyd waited for me to finish my breakfast and wed come back indoors i leafed through some of the poetry books on her shelves this was the heavy artillery mostly modern stuff but all the greats and more what did she do with all this reading nora answered that unasked question as she strolled in from the kitchen she taught some classes at a university they actually pay your mother to waffle on about poetry okay i didnt actually use the word waffle but nora was getting defensive about her old ma and i dropped the subject i could tell she was narked with me cos after i replaced the books id lifted off the shelves nora made a point of rearranging them in the order she knew that her mother had put them in fuck it was like being in a minefield in that house careful what i say and do and gawd forbid i should touch any of her precious poetry books we had a tense and brooding drive back to london and almost the instant we were back in the flat in balham we had a blazing row you know on a hot dry summers day that a thunderstorm is on its way and when it comes it bursts dramatically and the heavens open and down pours the rain so it was with the argument nora and i had that night yeah it all poured out nonstop me accusing her mother of being a snob and nora having a go at me for having a chip on my shoulder i was very very hot under the collar i love books i shouted at the top of my lungs my dad used to read to me when i was little i began to quote some chaucer and as i did so i could see the face of the old woman gracie in chelsea she had criticised me alright but i had felt a love or a warmth beneath her words morag was a cold fish she was divorced from her husband and when nora had first talked about the divorce i had felt sorry for her mother cos i could see the damage and hurt it had done nora but now having met the mother my feelings had done a lightning switchback and if id been the husband id have scarpered and left morag to her poetry and her bitterness and got as far from guildford and surrey as i could get we were staring at one another in a sullen obstinate stand off in noras living room when there was a dull slamming of a door at the top of the house then came a girls voice and she must have had a decent pair of lungs cos her words reached us clear and unambiguous im wasting my life with you nora and i stared at each other and im sure the same thought went through her head as went through mine that those very words were exactly what we were thinking as the rancour and frustration of the situation hung in the air neither of us seemed to want to move in case the spell was broken and we said something so terrible that there would be no way back i guess we both knew there was something in our being together otherwise why did we have such strong feelings for or perhaps against each other and even while these thoughts idled round inside our heads a knock came at the door fuck i really prayed it wasnt the old baggage of a landlady mrs dobson cos another naysayer and i would go doolally right then and there and strangle the old bint at the first sign of a sarcy comment or a curl of her top lip but when the door was opened there was a bloke standing there with a grin on his face and a sweater tied around his neck he had a squarish build and black wavy hair a something on his top lip which was halfway between bumfluff and a moustache and his skin was a sort of olive complexion nora immediately put on a smile and gave him a hug this was jeremy and he was in the neighbourhood on account of visiting his gran who was none other than old dobberbody herself i couldnt quite figure it but then a clue was dropped in that jeremy was half indian though he talked nothing like a citizen of the subcontinent and his head didnt wobble as he spoke i said as much after he had left the flat and the embers of our argument earlier that evening burst into flames all at once nora was seething with anger and called me all sorts of names racist and narrow minded and pig headed and a troglodyte and she shut me up good and proper cos i couldnt get a word in edgeways when her fire subsided i asked her in all innocence why she had called me racist you are martin and you dont even know it youre a casual unknowing racist you drop into your talk all these little remarks about people you dont know as if its okay to say lets get a chinkie when you could as easily say what about a chinese meal tonight and yes some indian people do nod their heads as they speak but why do you feel the need to mimic that action its not funny its not clever and i find it offensive that you feel its okay to allow yourself to behave like this in one of the most cosmopolitan cities in the world at this time when the world is getting smaller and the excuses for your behaviour are getting thinner and thinner actually there are no excuses its as simple as that she stood looking at me defiantly and with such strength of will that i should have known better than to answer her back but the words flew out of my mouth before i had really had a chance to formulate them properly youre very like your mother right now if ever a sullen reproach was put into a look that time was now she turned on her heels and i heard the word fuck said under her breath as she stomped off to the bedroom i didnt feel too clever after that and i also didnt feel like i should go into her room she definitely didnt want me near her and we both needed space so it was back to the couch and the view of the common in the dark for me i fell into an uneasy sleep dont ask me how cos when i lay down to try to get some rest and closed my eyes it was as if there was a racetrack in my brain little mad cars were zooming from side to side of my skull and i felt shudders going through the length of my body that made my legs and arms go into spasms that i could only control with difficulty it was a riot from top to toe and i thought i couldnt possibly get any shuteye under such circumstances but the weird thing was i couldnt open my eyes there could have been a madman with an axe staring down at me and just dripping with saliva at the thought of chopping me into pieces and i couldnt defend myself i could see him even though my eyes were shut then i realised it was gerry o fuck hed found out where i lived and hed come for his revenge the cars were going totally nuts inside my head burning rubber and scorching the track dont gerry dont do it i tried to get these words out but nothing could be heard above the roar of the cars then i saw pattie floating over me where i lay o christ she was in a state her flesh was hanging off her in places she was all mottled and blue and green o fuck there were worms dark worms slithering out of her nostrils and eye sockets and she was offering a bundle to me something wrapped in a blanket dont dont i tried to say but no sound came out cos i knew it was timmy and he was all dark and bruised and cold and my arms and legs were thrashing like the snakes of the medusa and lights were flashing all around as the blare of horns crashed through to me it seemed i was in a room somewhere and there was someone wrapped in a blanket looking down at me and there were lights cold and blue flashing across the ceiling i lay staring and breathing loud and fast as my mind tried to take in where i was martin martin are you awake i didnt answer i dont know how you could sleep through this what i said at last another night of fun and games in balham it was nora and i realised i was on her couch and the pimps and punters and prossies were having a fine time of it with the boys in blue down on the street i sat up and blinked nora was at a window taking the spectacle in and after some moments i got up and went over to her she was angry i could see that but at least it wasnt with me she turned her face to me and our eyes met i knew i had to kiss her those eyes they regarded me so clamly so warmly all the activity on the street the noise the lights the police pulling men out of cars none of it mattered and the kiss was not the kiss of two animals in heat it was gentler so much gentler than that and when we went off to her bedroom and made love it was quieter and full of respect it sounds stupid putting it like that but i wanted no harm to come to her i wanted to protect her even as i was rogering her arse and the end result was the same as ever cos every man has to feel a bit like samson after making love his force spent his load shot his body like a spring uncoiled and i lay in noras arms all the bickering and resentment flushed out of my body wondering like an astronomer gazing through the infinite void of space at an object light years off whats all the fuss about why do we squabble and fret ourselves into an early grave this time when i went off to sleep it was undisturbed and calm as a millpond when i woke up it was already bright nora wasnt on an early i could smell eggs and coffee and i anticipated she would be wearing a gingham dress and talking to blue birds at the kitchen window with perhaps a squirrel chittering on her shoulder of course it wasnt that dopey when i hauled myself all the thirty feet from bedroom to kitchen but all the same the change in the world was marked it was the change in us we exchanged a few words i cant even recall what they were now but that doesnt matter what i do remember is i was looking at her her profile and those green eyes when she moved a hand across the table and took one of my hands i didnt want the moment to end no words no thoughts just that moment to live and relive and to be in with her for a moment that would endure but the moments of love and togetherness are just that moments that vanish in the hustle and bustle of days that gather the harvest of time and thresh all memories away the doorbell rang it was jeremy he was so bouncy and full of chipper energy i could have stoved his head in with a mallet and a pocketful of glee he seemed totally and blithely unaware that he had interrupted a moment between nora and me but i dont suppose most people expect moments of intimacy over the cornflakes at the breakfast table and before noon has struck on balham high street he came bearing news old grandma dobson wanted a flat repainted after the couple moved out from the floor at the top of the house it was the couple who had had the shouting match while nora and yours truly were fighting the bit out anyway the job was mine if i wanted it there was a fair few bob in it was i any good with a paint brush it was way too early in the morning for me to dissemble so i gave a shrug and jeremy seemed satisfied well thats settled then and he helped himself to coffee and toast i imagined this wasnt his first breakfast he just had the sort of constitution that burns up food always on the go always in a hyper mood and never upset by anything i think it was the indian side of him which came from his mother she was anglo indian so it was watered down a fair bit but all the same there was a touch of gandhi or nehru about jeremy an unperturbability an unflappable quality that allowed him to take everything on the chin and not be thrown down into the dumps or was it just having a family behind him and around him and a family with money at that ive got to fess up right now that the job wasnt the panacea for my finances that i hoped it would be in fact from the high point of us holding hands at that breakfast things began to disappoint on so many levels not just me but nora as well i mean for one thing i was nearly always at home when she got back from the hospital and i came to loathe the sound of her key turning in the lock i cant imagine it was much of a picnic for nora but for me a resentment began to grow like a tumour inside me but let me tell you about this pain in the rectum of a painting job i was given all the required brushes and rollers and trays and paint and at first i was left alone with a radio to get on with it no problemo everything was hunky dory and i knuckled down to it easing myself into the zen of the to and fro the backwards and forwards rhythmic swish of the brush up and down or from side to side of a portion of wall but then the evil landlady started showing her ugly mug and things started to unravel not fast cos i needed the money and she didnt overstay her welcome or come on too heavy with advice on how to go about the decorating but then the day arrived when it was titanic meeting ice berg out in the north atlantic i was quietly getting on with it i was even enjoying myself there was a good programme on the radio which was looking back at the relationship between morecambe and wise my dad loved them the nation loved them they were a national treasure and i was quietly having a bit of a chuckle to myself when the old cow walked in and started throwing her weight about i didnt even lissen to her at first i just kept slapping on the paint and trying my level best to attend to the radio programme but at last she fired an arrow straight at me have you been lissening to a thing ive said to which i replied im trying to lissen to the radio programme which you interrupted by coming in here well that was a declaration of war and id set a bomb off under dobbers enormous backside she was like a bloated mastiff with a bone she wasnt going to let go and give up so i dropped my paint brush in a tray and walked out of the flat with her frumpy fatness giving off fit to burst a blood vessel nora was unpleased by my behaviour and jeremy was round like a shot in the evening once the family tom toms had broken the news of my egregious scandalous indecent and disrespectful behaviour those werent his words of course he couldnt stop smiling and gently berating me for letting his granny get to me if he said once you know what shes like you know what shes like you just have to ignore her he said this at least a dozen times it was a fucking mantra with him and it didnt make me feel a jot better or more disposed towards him or the world i was feeling murderous to both of them to nora and jeremy but especially to the bumfluff kid i seriously began to question what the fuck i was doing living with nora and it hardly helped escaping to the wilds of surrey it was alright for nora going back to see her mother but for me it was akin to lying down on an operating table and having my liver removed sans anaesthetic i was prometheus and her old bird of a harpie of a mother had very sharp talons and a beak that could slice me open of course i didnt go every time i cried off when i felt i couldnt face it which led nora to give me a sour look and some cutting remarks of her own it was one of these weekends when nora took herself off to the humble terrace in guildford that i felt at such a low ebb that i couldnt even bear to be by myself in the flat in case that extra from the curse of frankenstein turned up playing eyegors fat mother or jeremy sprang round to needle me with more of his boring mantra so i took myself off into the centre of town and found myself almost without thinking about it drifting around the streets of soho nora had given me some money to tide me over and if id had any sense i would have stuck around balham with a takeaway pizza and a few beers but i didnt feel very sensible no not sensible at all i felt bloody minded and mixed up and full of all kinds of emotions i couldnt properly put a name to there was a lid on my pressure cooker and if i wasnt careful i would explode id mooched in off oxford st and found myself in carnaby st fuck it was a living museum it had been old hat and past its sell by date when my dad ponced up and down here as a 12 year old in the late 70s he fancied himself as another mick jagger until my mum got hold of him and sorted him out all the same them officers tunics were a good look at one time and i would fit one alright but people would look at you like you werent alright in the head if you ponced off down oxford st like a great grandchild of jagger or richards or any of the strolling bones i was just imagining the mayhem and havoc i could conjure up dressed like an edwardian cavalry officer and with a fuckoff great sabre at the end of my right arm slashing and thrusting the blade all around me carve up on carnaby st that would be the headline in the sun when a voice in my ear made me turn to this large barrel chested bloke in a loose fitting shirt he was sweating profusely it was a warmish day but he was sweating buckets he had a large moon face very hairy eyebrows and thick curly hair he looked foreign and his accent was east european or somewhere like that pleeze where ladies im sure i looked a bit thick and gormless at that precise moment cos id no idea what he meant the fucking street was full of ladies well young women so lets just say i was weighing the situation up waiting for the next clue in this game of interpretation painted ladiies it was a slomo double take for me i could see the coin going into the slot as the seasons turned and the wind blew over a vast plain on which bison roamed and then the penny dropped he was asking me about prozzies for fuck sake did i look like a pimp first balham and now here was it the scar were my eyes too close together he took out a handkerchief and mopped his brow he wasnt half a sweaty pig of a bastard youre in the wrong place mate he looked confused and uncertain i asked him his name it was stavros and he was off a container ship that had come from australia via the suez canal then piraeus port then marseilles and finally tilbury hed come a helluva long way for a poke and i took pity on him well i took some interest in him at least and led him away from the museum of pop to the gritty end of things in soho proper i didnt think hed appreciate the climax and its raffish clientele so i took him to greek st the irony wasnt lost on me via wardour st and planted him fair and square at a narrow dingy doorway where a flight of stairs led up to who knew what pneumatic bliss there was suzy on the ist floor for french lessons babs on the 2nd for spanish and lulu at the top for dictation you come with me said stavros i must have looked more than a trifle discombobulated not to say mildly concerned and put out i shook my head and told him he was on his own what did he want me to do fold his trousers while he performed or suck his dick till he was ready to enter my eenglish not good you dont need english i told him you need money how much o fuck me i was beginning to get tired of babysitting this huge baby and i began to back off him where you going he said and there was a concern in his voice not unlike a threat never mind that i said im not going in there i pointed at the doorway pick a number i said dont let them charge you too much how much is too much i wasnt staying for no more of this nonsense and retreated further and faster the last thing i heard from the big lummox was i dont speak french or spanish i sloped off down a passageway lined with porn shops and slid into the doorway of a pub called the crown i half expected stavros to come bursting in all redfaced and aggrieved that he had been ripped off and hadnt learned a word of french or spanish and i was still smiling and having a quiet laff to myself at the counter of the bar over a pint of guinness when i remembered this girl id seen the other night on the street that ran past noras flat she was very attractive and id lost myself in a bit of a fantasy about taking her into the flat and giving her one i didnt do it of course but it was just the thought of getting away with it while nora was at the hospital i knew the girl was on the game it was the way she walked more than the way dhe dressed it was a slow ambling gait as if she was trying her level best to go nowhere fast i finished my pint and left the pub of course stavros was nowhere to be seen what was gnawing away at me now was no longer him and his weird questions nor the girl on the street in balham the fucking shitty truth was i fancied learning a new language then and there i wasnt going back to balham cos you dont shit on your own doorstep and i wasnt going back to where i had left stavros cos there were plenty other doorways in soho offering the same linguistic services it was like id been taken over by a disease i couldnt shake it off and i couldnt find the calm centre of my being to relax and let the desire go no the centre had been invaded by an unruly mob and i had to go and knock on one of those doors as if i was a contestant on opportunity knocks i just had to know the contents of the box mavis was her name and she was on the 2nd floor of another dingy old narrow building and she was black and tall and skinny dressed in a teddy garters and stockings and red high heels i was giving her the once over while she talked business said she was going to give me a discount on account of me being a good looking young man i was looking at her tight bum cheeks as she paced around the room which was pretty basic it had a bed of course and i hadnt actually said i was gonna get down to it when there was a knock on the door she sort of raised her eyebrows as if to say i wonder who that could be and then she smiled and opened the door there was a well tailored old gentleman he must have been 80 years old he had a camel hair coat which must have set him back a bit fuck i thought to myself he cant be serious he must have swallowed a whole bucket of viagra just to get himself up the stairs and he would have been poncing about carnaby st when london was swinging and jagger had the moves he pulled the most sour face id ever seen and muttered the word no about 3 or 4 times and then turned on his heels and took wobbly steps back towards the stairs the girl closed the door and shrugged it was no odds to her she must have had that reaction from punters any number of times and she for sure never let on that she didnt want a particular client cos it would take too long for him to get it up and keep it stiff till he had entered her warm and moist slit but i did i cant say exactly why except i couldnt think of a good reason not to i wasnt exactly panting for it and i did take a little fine tuning to get in the mood but she had a good mouth and knew how to use it cupping my balls and giving them a gentle tug and a squeeze as she went back and forth along my pipe it was my first time with a black girl her skin had a sheen it reflected back some of the light from the red bulb hanging from the ceiling she rode me reverse cowgirl and the way her ass cheeks bounced up and down brought me off though to be honest my mind wandered a bit in the middle of the whole exerrcise she only charged me £30 and she told me i was a lovely fella an then i was pulling on my pants and getting the hell out of dodge i went back to that pub id been in the crown and had a couple of pints of guinness just slowly taking in what id just done it didnt seem real it was as if someone else had used my body or else a part of me was on holiday and id gone through the motions to keep up appearances that someone was at home i didnt feel bad no it wasnt that i just didnt feel anything except a kind of hollowness a nothingness in my centre the guinnesss going down was giving me more pleasure than the bedroom exercise and it wasnt the girls fault shed done her bit well it was me now that it was over and i was back in the ordinary indifferent world of sports on tv and wet newspapers clogging drains i wondered about myself and what the whole stupid edifice of existence was really about we all went along with some grand deception all fooled all living a lie all blinkered and scared to look to the right or the left as we went about our petty tasks those were the thoughts rattling round my cage when who should walk in but the camel coated old geezer who had turned down my carnal delight i looked down at the counter of the bar as he ordered a double brandy i didnt want to risk eye contact with him the embarrassment of both us recognising the other would have been too funny for words so i just lissened to him chat to the barman about the horses and the chances of this or that football team winning the premiership and he didnt once allude to having climbed the stairs in a dingy old building for french lessons no he kept well stumm on that subject but then i was no better i finished my pint and ducked out the door i headed back to balham and the quiet life i didnt need no more stimulation for the weekend now i could sit and stare into space all the tumult the up and down and general bouncing around of my emotions had left me why couldnt i be this way all the time but a tiny voice inside played devils advocate in a mocking way but then youd be dead wouldnt you or as good as fuck but what if i ended up like camel hair seeking his camel toe aged 85 o christ another 60+ years of traipsing after whore pussy and some young ponce looking me up and down and laffing at me on the inside or maybe even to my face then a line come to me it was something my old man quoted to me once from some french philosopher and it was to the effect that all the problems of the world are due to the fact that a man is unable to stay in a room and be at peace well i did my level best to do just that until nora returned on sunday evening i dunno if it showed in my face but i felt strange and awkward with nora now that she was standing in front of me she asked me how my weekend had gone i tried to shrug the question off like i hadnt done very much and it had passed in a blur of general lassitude and indolence that was the name my dad gave himself when he fantasised about being a bigwig in ww2 general lassitude course it was his fathers war and grandad was a sergeant in the army so all that was a great irrelevance as i stood before nora trying to look like i hadnt been a bad boy and messing about in soho studying french and watching old fruitloaves like camel hair i tried to switch the focus from me and asked her how she had got on with the old dragon you know i didnt refer to her mother in those exact words but nora gave me a look and then made it explicit by asking me if i really wanted to know suddenly i felt like the floor was giving way beneath me it was turning into quicksand and i was sinking fast alright alright i was only asking and with that i moved towards the door just before i went out of the flat she fired a question at me where you off to now im going for a walk is that ok i knew my tone was edged with sarcasm but it was only a front cos i knew how guilty i felt and that right then i couldnt face nora a second longer i had to get away and put a little distance between us until i had pulled myself together i just hadnt seen how easy it was to be caught out in a lie so i had manufactured an offence on her part i could always apologise when i got back in i would apologise and i would work it out as i walked how to make it as natural as possible fuck id never felt like i was a fly caught in a web of lies why was i doing this to her and me it had been straightforward enough with pattie id always felt that she and i we were a fit course in the end i was majorally off target there but what was it about nora that kept me from running a mile from her and keep going did she have some power over me was she slipping something in my tea that was fucking me up conflicting with my will or suppressing it was this little foray into the dark side simply an aberration a one off never to be repeated or had i stepped over the line and was gonna end up like the double brandy camel hair merchant of filth 80 odd and still sniffing around the gutter for a bit of hows your father and the last hurrah of a morning glory fuck i had to stop this swishing washing machine swirl of ideas round my noodle before i went back to the flat id wandered into the common even though it was near dark and the people still walking about had become indistinct shadowy shapes it was early summer and when i took a breath i could smell a whole symphony of earthy smells of leaves and grass and trees and buds it was like the city smells amd noises receded even though the sight and sound of cars was just beyond the line of plane trees and in daylight seemed so much closer and louder the common was an oasis of life in a concrete and asphalt world i marvelled that id not explored it before maybe it was the encroaching dark it added allure and magic to the space of course then i heard a motorbike charging down the road on the periphery no it wasnt a motorbike it couldnt be it was smack in the middle of the common and it was coming in my direction but i couldnt see it the noise got louder and suddenly something shot past my head i spun round to try and see what it was i must have looked a little ridiculous like a wrongfooted out of position goalie cos a voice some feet away disembodied and ethereal said stag beetles i turned towards where i judged the voice had come from they fly about here this time of year i thought it was a motorbike a remark that even i knew sounded foolish and out of place theyre quite large as beetles go and the sound is made by their wings then whoever it was began to move off i could make out a figure not tall but i already knew it was a man and just assumed he was a beetle hunter or some such anorak anyway id had quite enough of the common and its hyperactive insect life and went back to the flat nora was already in bed so i sat up for a bit staring out at the common thinking of the flying beetles and other insects still active while the human population around the common and spreading for mile after mile to hackney and beyond was sleeping and completely unaware of other forms of life it come back to me then that some years ago on the south bank near the national theatre and the tate modern id seen a fox in broad daylight bin hoking and totally indifferent to me or anyone else poncing about round there i admircd his moxy the little fella had balls i know they get a bad press from farmers and theyd kill a chicken as soon as look at it but thats just their nature fucking sooner have a fox as a friend than some shitting loaf of a farmer with mud all over his boots i must have fallen asleep with these muddled up thoughts all in a jumble cos i sort of came to with a stiff neck in the early morning nora was just leaving and she shot me a bruised and hurt look as she went out the door there was a note to the effect that she and i needed to talk well we talked alright more than once none of these little chats went well if we had started out like germany england in 1914 things soon deteriorated into a crude stalemate from entrenched positions the one trying to undermine the other with psychological warfare i was accused of having a huge chip on my shoulder and i told her that she had a snob of a mother and her father was a sane man to get away from the witch of guildford she was upset about that one and it felt like one final push one last charge over the top and it was defeat for one or maybe both of us what i recalled most in all the heated and frustrating to and fro was her telling me that she wasnt her mother she was she sitting in front of me in the here and now couldnt i see that sounds blindingly obvious doesnt it but i couldnt though there was a part of me a little boy locked away in a dark room and gagged who wanted to blurt out i fucked a whore and she rode me ragged but i opened the door to that room and read the riot act to that twat what good would it do to tell her it would be the end for sure but if it was the end so what wouldnt it be better to be out of the whole mess than to continue with a lie but the weird thing was i couldnt do that thing of walking away why was that what was i afraid of was it that i would top myself in some dingy poky hole i didnt think so cos id walked away from that dark place it wasnt as if the shadow wasnt there it was it would probably be there all my life but the compulsion had gone one thing was for sure i needed a break i broached the subject with nora and thought shed throw a wobbly and give off to me about running away but she said it was a good idea and that we both needed a little space and some time to reflect i took the eurostar to brussels and had a look around for a day or two and then took a train to hamburg my old man had mentioned hamburg a few times when hed put on a beatles cd said that theyd cut their teeth there way back even before he was born so of course i had to take a look at the reeperbahn i had a strong suspicion that it was cleaned up a lot from their day i mean you walk past these buildings in london or wherever and you try to think of all the people in the past who have traipsed along the same street past the same buildings but its just not possible to bring that time back or bring those people alive its the most pitiful form of time travel you cant even bring your former self back like me if i went back to chelsea now even though its not that long ago really im not the same i might have a terrible out of body experience seeing myself looking in the window of that anteek shop with bowtie and his assistant mr wilkins but here i was in hamburg and i was drifting by loads of windows with light bulbs all round the edges and sitting in the windows were all the girls from all corners of the wide world and they packed their goodies into tight bras and draped themselves in sheer negligees it was a strange experience cos they didnt exactly engage with you well some did and even gave a slow nod of the head back into the dim area behind them where there was always a bed and a box of tissues and bottles of creams and oils and quite often a dildo or two fuck i could see old camel hair face down on one of those beds with a dildo up the crack of his arse and a big domanitrice with a whip alternately shafting his saggy arse with the dildo and whipping his arse to shreds hed have been munching the pillow then and squealing like a pig i havent had such a good arse buggering since the conservative conferences in the early days of maggie thatcher yes blame her for a lot but she did throw a good conference the longer i drifted the less i felt inclined to go into one of those rooms behind the lit up windows instead i took myself off to a bar which was just as garish and neon lit as the windows with the girls there were bowls on the counter of the bar and i did a double take when i realised they were filled with condoms i pointed at a tap and got a litre of german bier it was better than anything id ever tasted in a pub in london and i was quietly congratulating myself on simply being in a part of the world where id never been before it struck me that i could be whoever i wanted to be whoever i wanted to present myself as maybe if i didnt open my trap people would look at me and think i was a rolf or a dietrich and while these thoughts were idling round my headspace i took it in that the place was for men only cos there they were in their tight leather trousers and leather jackets like they were all going to audition for a camp version of grease and some of them were giving me the eye this was definitely not a watering hole for the likes of camel hair unless the old bastard was a queer steer and swung both ways as well he might probably having gone to a good public school where his buttocks were thrashed on a regular basis theres no surmounting that early education it leads to a tender seat in the house of lords as the spanked posteriors of yesteryear sit in deliberation on bills passed by lesser spanked botties from the lower house i finished my german bier and left the leather boys to their own amusement i hadnt gone very far when a voice said something to me in german i turned to face a small compact man of asian extraction he looked indian to me but what did i know i must have looked puzzled cos he then spoke in english and said dont you speak german i shook my head he was indian and his name was arjun what was i doing in hamburg where had i come from was i staying long fuck the questions were flying out of his mouth like a plague of flies we strolled on out of the reeperbahn him doing most of the talking he told me he was studying engineering and had left india 3 years ago you going back then when you finish your studies he shook his head in a solemn sort of way i dont know exactly where i want to live but i know its not india why i think india must be a great place to live yes india is magnificent my country is a great country but even with an engineering degree from a german university i would have a terrible time i mean a real struggle to make a good living hey your english is pretty good it should be he said with a strong emphasis i spoke so much english before i came to germany now it is getting a little mixed up in my head with german so will you stay on in germany and get work here he shook his head and there wss just a hint of a wobble it is a good place to study they are very serious about academic life in germany but it is not easy to meet people here and then he told me he had an uncle in bradford and maybe he would ask this uncle to look into the possibility of him being allowed to come and work in england it all comes down to paperwork he said with a shrug but im sure the authorities the civil service or what cannot be worse than in india there the civil servants are like little gods and the paperwork is a kind of torture invented by an evil spirit to break a man and reduce him to the lowest of the low you are told to get a document stamped in one department and you do this and they give you another document to get stamped in another building half way across the city there is no end to their hierarchical interference and procrastination and why do they do this for the sheer hell of it i offered no not that well yes there is an element of that to be sure because they are petty little men with a little bit of power that has gone to their heads but also they are making money by stamping pieces of paper and they are in league with each other the one scratching the others back they are like macacques you know the monkeys that infest the banks of the ganges the sacred river for hindus picking fleas off each other he paused and looked out at the wide river elbe we were walking across from the docks and there were container ships huge and imposing i couldnt help smiling thinking of what my dad had said about what grandad had said about germany and the war fuck i couldnt even picture what the place would have looked like after it had been bombed to hell and look at it now a real hub of life and a scurry of activity arjun asked me back to his place for a bite to eat i should have said no it wasnt like i was lonely but i felt his loneliness and id warmed to the little guy i felt kinda sorry for him he was a clever bloke but wherever he was going to end up he couldnt go back yet he was struggling against a kind of magnetic pull from his homeland a huge maternal tug that threatened to draw him back and smother him he made a good curry and we washed it down with red plonk the thought passed through my head that it must be impossible for an indian to make a bad curry at the same time i wanted to tell him that hed fit right in with bradford society cos it was nearly all pakis and indians there now for some reason nora came into my head just then and i remembered what shed said about my racist tendencies maybe she was right i had this knee jerk racism and i needed to watch it all this was going on inside me cos i hadnt said a dickey bird to arjun however the internal debate must have shown in my face in some form or other either i was having a touch of acid reflux or a build up of gas in the bowel region cos arjun looked concerned everything alright martin i hope its not my cooking i made the curry mild i assured him i was fine i was just thinking about my girlfriend you are missing her he asked and the question was strangely unsettling cos it wasnt a simple answer i could give i wasnt entirely sure i was missing her or not there was definite relief at being away at not having to check with her what i was doing or saying but there she was sitting in my head still talking to me and ticking me off for my rough and boorish character it was all i could do to force a smile cos sure as hell i wasnt gonna open any can of worms in front of my little indian who was sitting i realised suddenly a little too close for comfort the problem was mostly down to the lack of space he lived in a bedsit about 12ft by 8ft and it hadnt seemed to bother me until that moment do you know anything about indian philosophy he asked and his face was alert and calm at the same time i shook my head everything is one we are all part of the great breath of life of god at the highest level there is no separation no distinction between man and woman this distinction operates on the lowest level so that the world goes on turning but it is turning in the dance of illusion we are breath and our breath comes from the highest it is the same it is one but we will not be free if we cannot rise above the common everyday and see the world for what it is we are born we die and in between we beget and we kill but all the time we are enslaved to the illusion we were both sitting cross legged on the centre piece rug i was thinking about what had just been said arjun suddenly leaned across and gently tugged the hairs that stuck out between the bottom of my jeans and the top of my socks youre very hairy he said this girlfriend of yours is it a casual thing o dear i had a sudden feeling in my guts that i shouldnt be where i was arjun touched my hairy leg again and an alarm went off at the back of my head a phone call was made to security and the boys were scrambling to the paddy wagons dont do that why said arjun dont you like it i shook my head and thought o fuck im gonna have to smack him in the mouth but instead i looked him in the eye and told him as politely and firmly as i could muster im straight this didnt quite have the effect on him that id hoped for cos he didnt seem discouraged in any shape or fashion sexuality is a moveable feast it is not a fixed entity two bulls in a field if no cow is available one bull will mount the other where had i heard that before o yeah raymond of the tortoiseshell specs i stood up then cos id lissened to quite enough bull for one day are you going arjun looked hurt and offended and i felt a genuine sense of dismay and confusion but i couldnt stay i blamed myself partly cos i should have seen he was a little fruitloaf and even though hed overstepped the mark there was no real harm done he was one lonely little fucker and probably thought all his birthdays had come at once when i agreed to go back with him to his place i wandered back towards the reeperbahn thinking to myself what a strange world it is its the dance of illusion alright but its all we really know i needed a drink another fine german bier just to wash the taste of curry from my mouth i wasnt angry or disgusted just a bit fed up with the world and its infinite ways to frustrate and disappoint us it wouldnt have been so much the dance of illusion if hed had his tongue in my mouth and feeling all my fillings or giving my arsehole some engineering work with his engineers pencil all that would have been real enough i reckon it would have been thin and short unless he was a freak of nature i cant tell you the trouble i had getting this image of him mounting me from the derriere and talking nonstop about the great buildings of the subcontinent the taj mahal and udaipur and nitin patil fuck hed have been like a noisy macaque riding a tiger i had more than one bier and then went out back onto the streets into the hurly burly of punters strolling up and down and leering in at the ladies in their lit up windows after a time i came across this impressive doorway with two fuck off huge bouncers who looked like they could have been pro wrestlers over the doorway was a pink neon sign that read haus fantasy i was looking and not even aware that i was thinking of entering the building when one of the bouncers crooked his finger at me and then swept his hand towards the door i know an invitation when i see one and for some moments i hesitated there on the threshold but i knew i had to go in it was very dim inside the door led straight into this wide room with pillars there were girls just like the ones in the windows and they were standing about or moving languidly from one spot to another there were lots of blokes all milling about no one making much eye contact and from time to time one of the blokes would stop and exchange a few words with one of the girls i drifted about for a while like a ghost we all seemed to be shadowy ghosts and not feeling the need to speak to anyone punter or pro it was like the best worst party id ever been to i supposed i could get my rocks off for the right price but i didnt need to get half cut in order to speak to a girl neither did i have to make stupid inane chit chat with some nonce id never see again or lissen to the most boring monologue in the world about football or politics or why i was overlooked for promotion once again by the saddest slaphhead in all of southern england no one could be under any illusion why they were in that room it was a cattle market plain and simple the men were the buyers and what a strange and listless lot they were i was definitely one of the youngest there were blokes with hairlines that had receded like the wehrmacht on the eastern front during the last stages of ww2 there were short and stumpy guys and ones who were running to fat on too many bratwursts and too many biers i quickly grew tried of this parade of the half dead and walked towards a doorway in the corner of the room farthest away from the entrance where there was a bright light spreading onto the floor when i left the dim room i entered a passageway with a flight of stairs leading to floors above all these floors were full of light and here were rooms with girls standing outside talking to the same kind of men down on the ground floor talk was only about one thing price i kept moving all the way to the top of the house it didnt get any better or more lavish the higher i went but i was a curious cat and i wouldnt have been content not getting all the way to the top when i was coming back down a girl looked at me in a challenging way like was i up for it i scrounged around in my head for the few scraps of german i knew wieviel she took a moment to answer as if assessing the potential of this customer achtzig ohne sechzig mit i gave a knowing nod and moved on achtzig achtzig thats 80 and sechzig is 60 but with and without what and how much moolah did i have on me anyway i was pretty sure i had nearly a hundred euro and then it struck me that the different prices were with or without a condom and it further struck me that i was thinking seriously of having a poke i stopped at the door of a room on the 2nd floor there was a girl inside with her hair in cornrows she had skin with a light olive complexion and looked latino she also had firm ripe tits and a bubble butt i must have been gawping at her cos she said something in german which made me look at her face do you speak any german since she had addressed me in english there seemed no point in pretending to be able to string more than two words of german together at any one time i asked you if you were going to stand there staring at me all day do you want to come in and play i moved into the room which was much the same as the other rooms there was a kind of massage table covered in towels an armchair off to one side and a dresser with a fuck load of dildos and eggs on a string i think there was even a whip she told me to shut the door and i was on automatic pilot so i just did what she said i wasnt feeling entirely comfortable but i wasnt entirely out of my comfort zone either whats on your mind she asked keeping her distance it was all i could do to force a smile are you feeling alright i gave a nod she ran me by the prices she was a bit more expensive than the girl i had spoken to on my way up the stairs but anyway i agreed to the price mit as i didnt fancy getting a dose of the clap or going back to nora and telling her id got a new girlfriend called chlamydia my grandad had got a dose in italy i dont remember him at all but dad said he was a complete original and didnt give a tinkers fart what people thought of him hed gone with this girl who was probably only 16 and he was 19 and then he had this dark green slime come up out of his bell end he was lucky there was penicillin around or hed have probably gone impotent and neither me nor my dad would have been around to tell the tale anyway that was the first and last time he tried to get lucky in the war course he didnt know he was necessarily going to live through it and he didnt meet my grandmother till he got back to blighty with his bandaged up knob all these stupid thoughts were cramming in on me even as latino girl sucked me so well i had to get her to stop or id have shot my load in her mouth i gave it to her doggy on that massage trestle and i was harder than id been in a very long time i was holding her bubble butt for dear life pressing it and squeezing hard as i could when i couldnt hold it in any more and i could feel my eyes rolling back and i squirted my love juice into the condom sheath i was still panting like roger bannister at the end of a sub four minute mile when i withdrew and the strong one had become the limp one the condom nearly slipping off my dick the milky collection pulling it down you fuck very hard you are bruto i couldnt tell if she was angry or paying me a compliment i felt like popeye in need of spinach i felt weak and out of sorts i pulled my pants on and got out of there as fast as i could the bouncers gave me a knowing look as i walked my unsteady walk off down the street i ducked into a dive and bought a bier but after the first mouthful i felt distinctly odd queasy and uneasy what was i playing at what was i doing with my life id seen some of those late 19th century paintings of men and women sitting in dark snugs over some poison like absinthe and the yellowy lime drink gave a tone to the picture of disease and corruption some bloke would be staring off into the middle distance and the artist had captured a sort of quiet despair was it always this way i used to see my dad after a few drinks with the same look of the damned in his eyes fuck imagine hed worn a condom the night i was conceived id just have been a dollop of jism hed have flushed me down the toilet and never thought about the consequences cos there would have been no consequences nothing to think about and worry over no little monster to get up his nose and tweak his nostril hairs no one to shout at no one to dismiss with a sarcy comment no one to hate and blame and put down when he wasnt feeling good about the world which was more and more his default position the more he drank and no one to love or be loved what was i doing i had to stop this i couldnt go on this way was i diseased was i some form of low life id come to germany to escape for just a little while the constant infighting with nora but i couldnt escape from myself did i even know who i was i stared at my bier going flat in the glass and i doubted i knew anything about anything was it love what i found with pattie id thought so at the time but what was that feeling based on i loved her body but she was wilful and i couldnt reach her i couldnt really talk to her not in a completely open and vulnerable way i could talk to nora more yeah for sure we argued about her mother and her background and she was right about me having a chip on my shoulder would time bring a change would we grow together and reach a quiet place out of the hurly burly of the spinning world a still centre where we would know each other and know that what we had was love o fuck i didnt know how to attain that but one thing i knew about love was that it wasnt a bunch of roses and a valentines card and a big red heart and a bucket of champagne at a candlelit dinner a penny for your thoughts these words came from a man in a leather jacket who sat down quite uninvited unless i was giving off some vibe i was unaware of you speak good english i told him and he smiled i practise hard do you then you should understand this no problem go fuck yourself and leave me alone his demeanour altered on the instant and he said something guttural and raw in german i didnt need a translation cos he was just returning the compliment i threw the remainder of my bier in his face and then ww3 kicked off with both of us grabbing lapels and jackets and lurching like a drunken enraged beast all over the shop banging into tables and scattering customers before us the polizei were called two burly uniformed men towered over me and asked me questions in english what was my name my age what was i doing in hamburg of course that one should have been who was i doing in hamburg but i neglected to mention any massage table entertainment they probably knew anyway what were most men over 18 doing in the reeperbahn i was nearly 21 but i felt like a kid a stupid kid who had started a fight for no sensible reason or because i couldnt find the answers to the problems i was creating for myself i was dr frankenstein and his monster all rolled into one it wasnt like the police made me feel bad they didnt need to i was doing that all by myself after some hours of cooling my heels in a cell and being periodically looked at by more germans than i had ever imagined would take an interest in me they let me go with a caution well martin wilson dont get into any more trouble in hamburg have a good trip back to london if you come back again be careful what you do i knew i wouldnt be back id nailed the coffin shut on the hamburg experience and lowered it into the ground the train journeys back were entirely uneventful i had time to think about what i was going to say to nora about our relationship if i was unclear and uncertain about it before i went away i cant say i was any the wiser when i got back to london the flat was in darkness when i opened the door i thought nora must have gone to bed early i didnt put the light on and just stood quite still taking in the fact that i had made it back the room seemed a bit darker than usual and i realised all the blinds were down had a nice time in hamburg i turned in the direction of the voice i could just make out nora she was sitting in a high backed amchair i didnt see you there i said i couldnt hide the surprise in my voice what are you doing in the dark thinking she said then she switched on a standard lamp next to her armchair it cast a cone of light over her come and sit by me she said and there was a quiet firmness in her voice i felt she had something to tell me and i was right i sat at the end of the sofa close to nora we have our differences she said i nodded in agreement cos it couldnt be denied i wanna know what you think of us us i said yes our relationship i thought you might have had a chance to think about that while you were away i did have a chance i said and i did think about it about us i paused she looked at me curiously her head tilted to one side and any conclusions any thoughts lots of thoughts not many conclusions but some she said no not really but did you come to any conclusions i want to know this was getting like before i went away to hamburg but deleivered so much more slowly i need to know what you think about us being together its important i began to feel tired i wanted to lie down and sleep it was like my brain was frozen why did we have to do this right now you dont like my mother admit it well i could hardly deny it i know shes a tough old bird but shes been through a lot theres a side of her youve never seen maybe so i said but she never makes it easy for me when im down at her place no my mother doesnt do easy nora conceded but heres the thing shes outside of us martin dont you see that whats important is whats between us i must have rolled my eyes or something cos nora got suddenly angry am i boring you you too tired to talk about things now i am tired i said cant this wait till tomorrow no she replied and it was such a firm no it felt like shed slammed a fist down on one of the arms of her chair i looked at her face and what i saw in there was that she had something to tell me something that couldnt wait im pregnant martin i didnt say anything i was just aware of a tension in my forehead and a kind of pain in my chest dont you have anything to say christ there was a heavy traffic of thoughts in my head all bumper to bumper and all honking their horns at the same time are you sure i said at last in a faltering voice that sounded like it came from someone elses throat how do you know i missed my period so i took a pregnancy test and its positive but how when i mean boy i was as inarticulate as i was insensitive when she said not more than 4 or 5 weeks ago how and here she gave a special sarcastic emphasis surely you dont need me to draw you a diagram i sat there with my mouth open barely able to take in what she had said you could at least tell me how you feel i could see nora was close to tears i dont know what i feel right now im just trying to take in what youre saying i chewed my bottom lip for a bit how far on are you nora was almost shaking now shed gone very tight lipped and her breathing was coming fast and loud enough for me to hear whats that supposed to mean you think im gonna abort this child my baby our baby and now she was shouting i put my hands up to try to placate her im not saying that i protested what are you saying martin and dont for christ sake try to wriggle out of this by thinking its not your baby cos it is i never said that im not saying that dont be putting words or thoughts in my head that arent there i mean its just early days and i need time to get my head around this nora calmed down a fraction and spoke like a reasonable and rational person it is early days but i want to know that the father of my baby is on board with this and the fact that were having this struggle to talk to each other doesnt bode well in my book ive seen couples at the hospital dozens of them over the past years and they are so happy and together so blissful with their bundle of joy and i dont feel this with you and i wonder if i ever will she stopped and looked at me i was as stunned as a fish hit on the head our baby is probably no bigger than a prawn inside me all curled up and not even aware that its alive but i feel its alive and whether it becomes a little boy or a little girl im gonna love him or her with all my heart youve got some thinking to do mister and i want your answer soon cos i cant go on with the unhappiness between us i want you in my life martin but only you hold the key to your happiness she stood up and looked down at me im on an early tomorrow youre a good man i know that but i need someone to share with me the hard times as well as the good its not going to be easy bringing a life into this world ill do it alone if i have to but id rather you were by my side she walked off and disappeared into the bedroom i sat on too overwhelmed to move even my thoughts had ground to a halt or they circled slowly and very deliberately round the single idea that a new life was coming into being it could have been only half an hour later that i got up from the sofa it felt like an age had passed there was no sound from the bedroom and i hoped that nora was already asleep i knew i couldnt yet go to her i needed to get out and clear my head if that was at all possible i doubted it but all the same i needed to wander in the night and try to get some perspective on the things that nora had said to me as i came down the stairs towards the front door a figure came in and weaved towards me it was bernard the strange singleton across the landing from us he was half torn and stumbled on the first step of the stairs he lay sprawled face down and letting small moans and groans escape from his mouth i was in half a mind to just trundle on but felt he would just lie there all night if i did nothing so i hauled him up and saw that his eyes were all the way up inside their sockets his dome of a forehead seemed even bigger than usual it crossed my mind as i supported him to his door that we all make such a fucking mess of our lives well him and me anyway i had to fumble about in his pockets for his door key but i found it eventually without violating his manhood or in any way compromising our relationship as i placed him inside his bedsit and handed him his key he must have had a moment of lucidity cos he hiccupped and blinked at me youre a good man gunga din i shook my head yes you are and your girl is very nice you make a lovely couple youre very lucky you know that i never found the right girl never had any luck there he almost lost consciousness just then and i had to steady him then he managed to collapse into a chair and i closed the door over and went down the stairs and out onto the street lucky man was i that depends on your point of view i said to myself i headed onto the common and at once all the smells of trees and grass overwhelmed me

Chapter VI
All Things Must Pass

the night wrapped me up in its cocoon the darkness on the common engulfed me and i lost myself in thoughts of what had been and what was to come all my petty concerns the small change of trivial feelings seemed as nothing with the news from nora it was so unexpected it had come like a steamroller or a tank and quite obliterated all my selfish dancing on the reeperbahn the egocentric jiggerypokery of a cocksmith on the streets of hamburg who was i quintessence of dust homunculus a spectre haunting the earth in human form who was martin wilson was he afraid in his soul of failure would he withhold himself now and retreat from life where before he had so keenly and lustily given himself as lover and father i couldnt now see my future clearly as i had once seen it the glass was dark and the vision obscure i was glad the darkness hid me my face was turned away from the stars and the light of the heavens was it always this way had it been thus for my father and his father before him and all the way back to adam it hadnt been much of an upbringing for me they had abandoned me my mum and dad for death is the final abandonment and after they were gone the family was gone i had never been close to my sisters they were a triad a sort of secret society who turned their backs on me and shut me out i know now the violence and pentup fire and fury i felt was a sign of weakness or how i dealt with it was i was lost and alone thinking al the time i never would find my way home but had i by the longest roughest road found my way back did i have a chance now a real chance with nora did i love her did she love me i couldnt answer that which required an answer urgently and persistently maybe i was looking in the wrong place maybe thats what id always been doing who knew what love was im not even sure my dad knew wasnt he as lost and feckless as me finding truth and a little bit of bliss at the bottom of a bottle i think the man i never got to know who died before i was born my grandad who returned from death and destruction and married a local girl and raised a family on little enough seeing out the rest of his natural as a teacher and popping his clogs in his 63rd year i think he had a life worth living nothing to shout about from the rooftops but just embedded among the mulch and ooze of life one of gods creatures in his element who knew the true value of life the things he might have passed on to me if he had lived longer an old man in his late 70s bouncing me on his knee an impossible improbable world me unborn and he already passed on from this life i could hear whirring stag beetles like motorbike scramblers from all directions the common was alive and aloud with nighttime activity suddenly i was struck on the forehead by a stone and staggered backwards some fucking arsewipe of a cunt had thrown a stone at me i looked around wildly trying to make sense of shapes in the dark id fucking open the cunts bunghole and make him bleed for a week then something caught my eye in a patch of light from a streetlamp i gazed at this wriggling writhing little ball of struggling energy and realised it was a stag beetle on his back with all his legs moving at the same time he was trying desperately to right himself he was the stone that had struck me i knelt down and picked him up he struggled all the more violently for some moments his horns were enormous in relation to the rest of his body well gregor samsa i forgive your error in smacking against my forehead no harm done i placed him back down on the ground rightside up he walked a short distance before taking flight i had to admit i marvelled at his utter indifference to me and the impediment to his progress i had for a moment presented he was the rhinoceros of the insect world big or small it was only a question of scale we all of us all beings on the face of the earth insects rhinoceroses bears antelopes elephants whales and apes and marmosets and eagles and wrens and humming birds and kangaroos and wallabies and emus and llamas and rent boys in soho even my 3 ugly sisters were all just trying to keep the spark of life lit keep the flame from blowing out in the storms of life wasnt that what my grandad was doing keeping his head down in italy and my dad in his own mistaken misguided way he just didnt know how to protect that spark within himself its hard to be a human being perhaps the hardest thing of all we know not what we do and our knowledge of who we are and what we could be its only lighning flashes on the darkest of dark nights when we draw back in fear aghast at who we are and what we do we kill the days and murder with bombs and bullets or sometimes just blind stupid neglect i thought then of all the people i had known in my life susan and christine and laura dubbed the 3 ugly sisters and poor mum and dad and old gracie who took no shit from anyone i recalled what she had said to me about not being able to buy a soul in the soul store and i knew what she meant the endless buying of things was deadening it wounded the soul with a hidden secret and mortal wound how i missed her there suddenly on the darkling common she was one of my ghosts one of the phantoms who lived within me and would die with me when one day i would be that ancient relic standing before a mirror regarding myself with a bland indifference my memory shot and my hard body gone to ruin i pictured them quietly to myself as i turned to go back to the flat stumpy bert and caruso the gorilla peter suyvesant and janet with her pinhead on a giant sumo wrestlers body one day i wont remember the half of it all these people ive encountered poor norman id left behind staring from a window as i was driven away from grangemount theyll all fade with time all be squashed together like the movement of a concertina and ill talk to the sun and remember nothing at all of the things i have done and the places and people i have seen everything is corruptible everything decays this was true before i was born and itll be true to the end of the world richard the tramp hed seen the truth but it hadnt made him all twisted and buckled beyond repair hed come out the other end of his despair smiling through his tears i could see him turning to me as he left the caff in hackney all things must pass thats what he said he was something else he was how he found the strength to pick himself up and go on the suits would never get it and the kids who havent lived yet but i was ceratin sure hed been put in my path to help me i would never forget pattie and my little boy timmy and the life i lost with them but here i was with a second chance and was i afraid to grasp it i couldnt even see that i was deserving of a second chance but what did i know what do any of us really know about the deeper life that runs below the surface of the everyday the current of life runs strong too strong if you find yourself struggling against it the current switches this way and that and watch out or youll end up six feet under and your mouth stopped with clay i was approaching the house now thinking of my dad back in the days of my childhood and the stories he told me he loved the story of jason and the argonauts but i dont believe that he saw it was his story and mine too and every sinner under the sun were all in a boat out at sea we leave behind so much in our wake all the sacred memories of loves lost and never to be refound i thought of nora was it love and if it wasnt love i felt for her what was it perhaps too much is made of love we are on a journey she and i sitting next to each other in the boat can we brave the storms ahead and not gaze back at what we have left behind i wasnt a reckless fool any longer possessed by fantasies of knives and beautiful japanese swords i had the spark of life and it was strong in me now and i would join it to noras spark keeping it lit and passing it on to the child coming to life inside her thats all you can do hold and protect the spark and pass it on i was at the door of the house now in a moment i would cross over the threshold and go to the new life that called to me.